# NANCY DREW

## DREW

GIRL DETECTIVE®

### #19 *Cliffhanger*

STEFAN PETRUCHA & SARAH KINNEY • Writers
SHO MURASE • Artist
with 3D CG elements and color by CARLOS JOSE GUZMAN
Based on the series by
CAROLYN KEENE

New York

Cliffhanger
STEFAN PETRUCHA & SARAH KINNEY – Writers
SHO MURASE – Artist
with 3D CG elements and color by CARLOS JOSE GUZMAN
BRYAN SENKA – Letterer
MIKHAELA REID and MASHEKA WOOD – Production
MICHAEL PETRANEK - Editorial Assistant
JIM SALICRUP
Editor-in-Chief

ISBN: 978-1-59707-165-9 paperback edition
ISBN: 978-1-59707-166-6 hardcover edition

Printed in China.
August 2009 by WKT Co. LTD.
3/F Phase I Leader Industrial Centre
188 Texaco Road, Tseun Wan, N.T.
Hong Kong

Distributed by Macmillan.

10   9   8   7   6   5   4   3   2   1

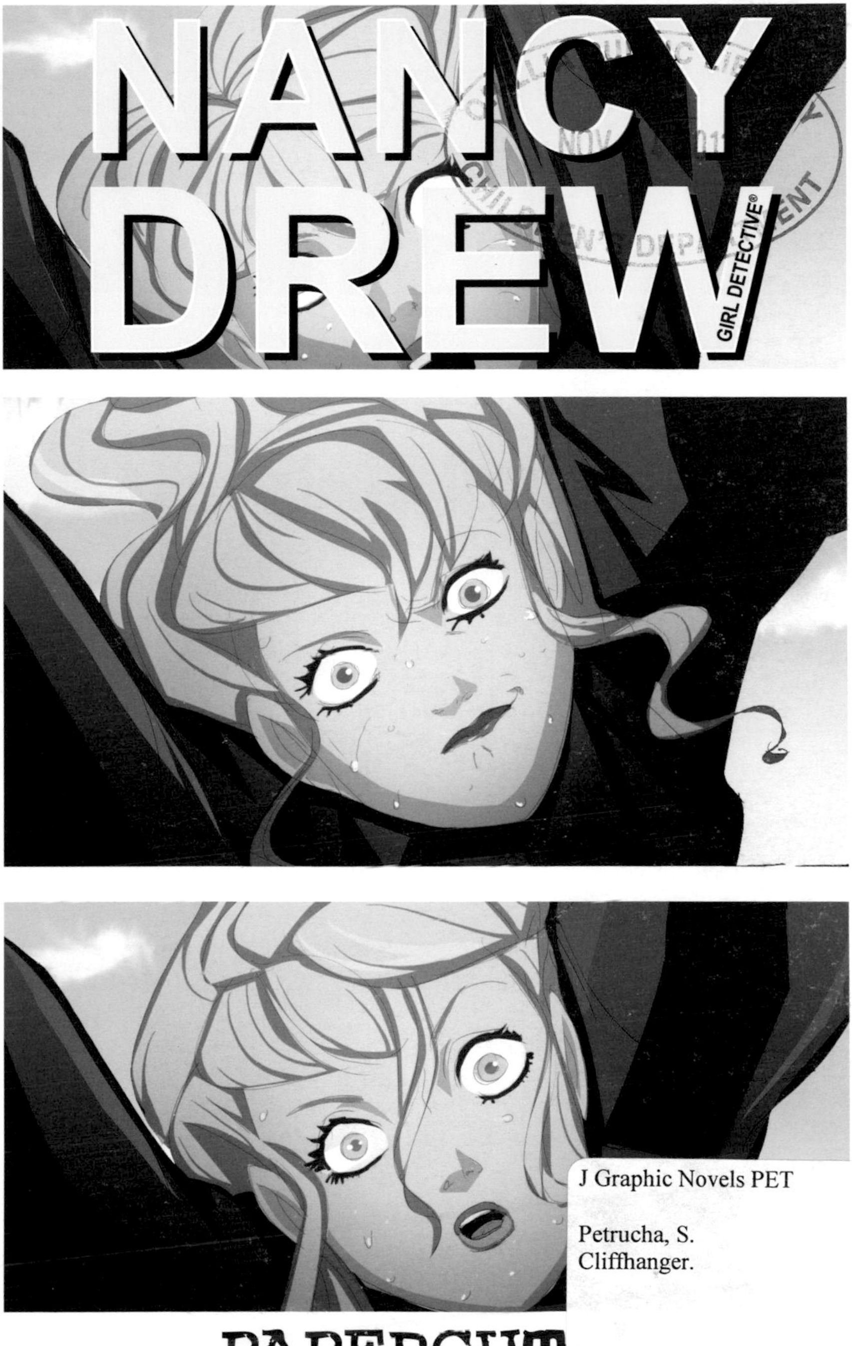
NANCY
DREW
GIRL DETECTIVE®



PAPERCUTZ

# NANCY DREW GRAPHIC NOVELS AVAILABLE FROM PAPERCUTZ

#1 "The Demon of River Heights"

#2 "Writ In Stone"

#3 "The Haunted Dollhouse"

#4 "The Girl Who Wasn't There"

#5 "The Fake Heir"

#6 "Mr. Cheeters Is Missing"

#7 "The Charmed Bracelet"

#8 "Global Warning"

#9 "Ghost In The Machinery"

#10 "The Disoriented Express"

#11 "Monkey Wrench Blues"

#12 "Dress Reversal"

#13 "Doggone Town"

#14 "Sleight of Dan"

#15 "Tiger Counter"

#16 "What Goes Up..."

#17 "Night of the Living Chatchke"

#18 "City Under the Basement"

#19 "Cliffhanger"

Coming February '1 #20 "High School Musical Mystery"

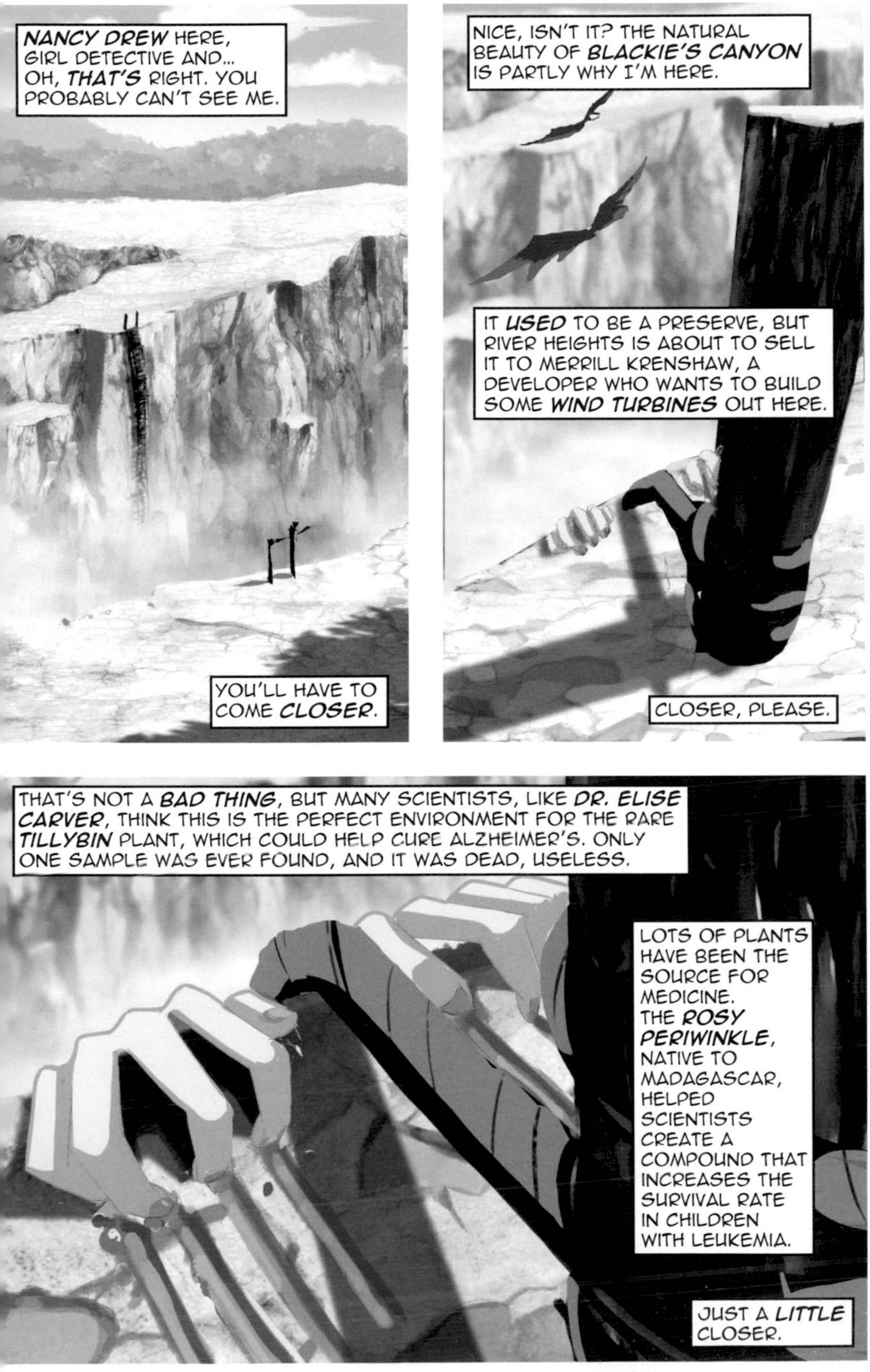

NANCY DREW HERE, GIRL DETECTIVE AND... OH, THAT'S RIGHT. YOU PROBABLY CAN'T SEE ME.
YOU'LL HAVE TO COME CLOSER.
NICE, ISN'T IT? THE NATURAL BEAUTY OF BLACKIE'S CANYON IS PARTLY WHY I'M HERE.
IT USED TO BE A PRESERVE, BUT RIVER HEIGHTS IS ABOUT TO SELL IT TO MERRILL KRENSHAW, A DEVELOPER WHO WANTS TO BUILD SOME WIND TURBINES OUT HERE.
CLOSER, PLEASE.
THAT'S NOT A BAD THING, BUT MANY SCIENTISTS, LIKE DR. ELISE CARVER, THINK THIS IS THE PERFECT ENVIRONMENT FOR THE RARE TILLYBIN PLANT, WHICH COULD HELP CURE ALZHEIMER'S. ONLY ONE SAMPLE WAS EVER FOUND, AND IT WAS DEAD, USELESS.
LOTS OF PLANTS HAVE BEEN THE SOURCE FOR MEDICINE. THE ROSY PERIWINKLE, NATIVE TO MADAGASCAR, HELPED SCIENTISTS CREATE A COMPOUND THAT INCREASES THE SURVIVAL RATE IN CHILDREN WITH LEUKEMIA.
JUST A LITTLE CLOSER.

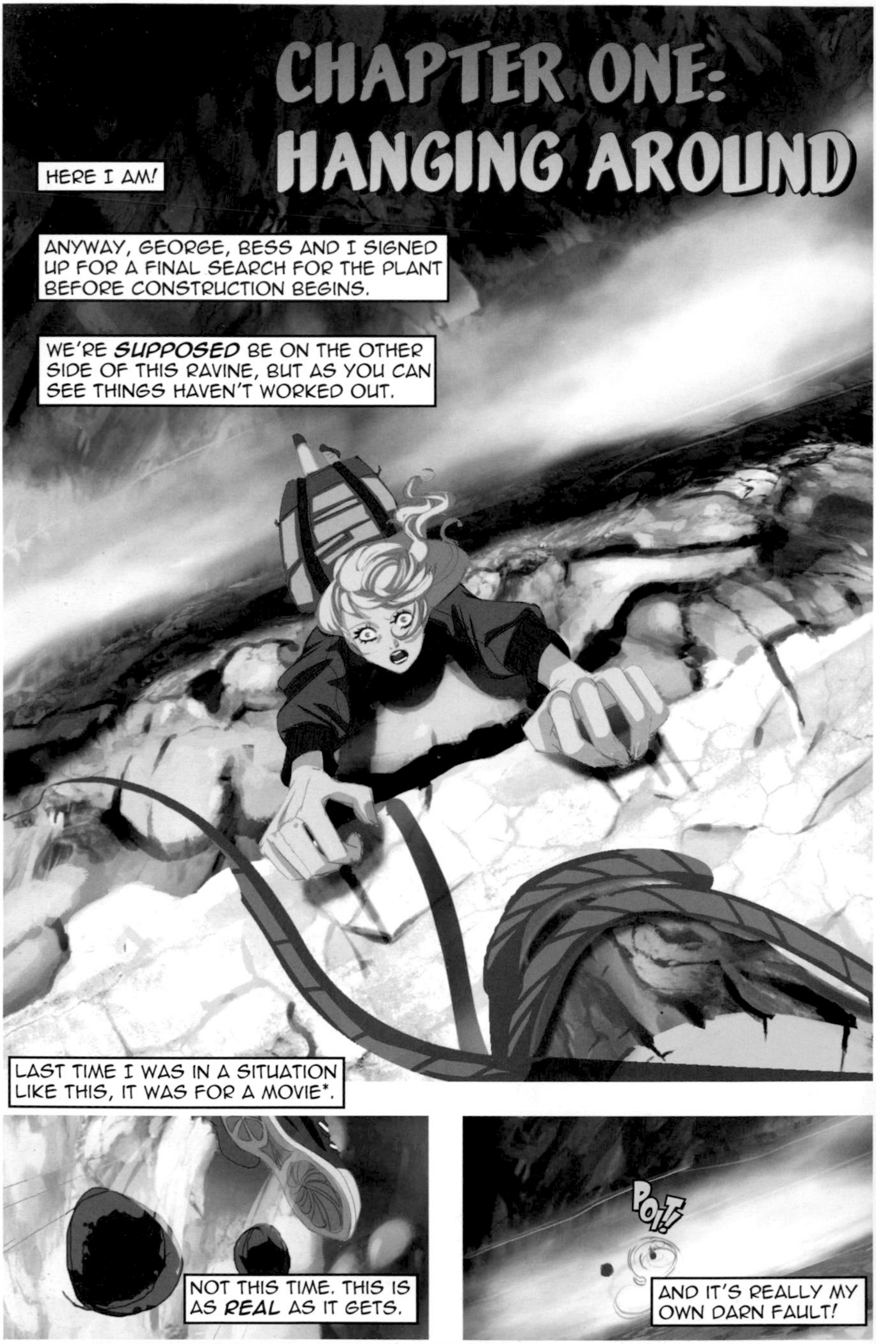
CHAPTER ONE:
HANGING AROUND
HERE I AM!
ANYWAY, GEORGE, BESS AND I SIGNED UP FOR A FINAL SEARCH FOR THE PLANT BEFORE CONSTRUCTION BEGINS.
WE'RE SUPPOSED BE ON THE OTHER SIDE OF THIS RAVINE, BUT AS YOU CAN SEE THINGS HAVEN'T WORKED OUT.
LAST TIME I WAS IN A SITUATION LIKE THIS, IT WAS FOR A MOVIE*.
NOT THIS TIME. THIS IS AS REAL AS IT GETS.
POIT!
AND IT'S REALLY MY OWN DARN FAULT!

*See NANCY DREW Graphic Novel #1 "The Demon of River Heights" or go to www.papercutz.com/nd/fn3

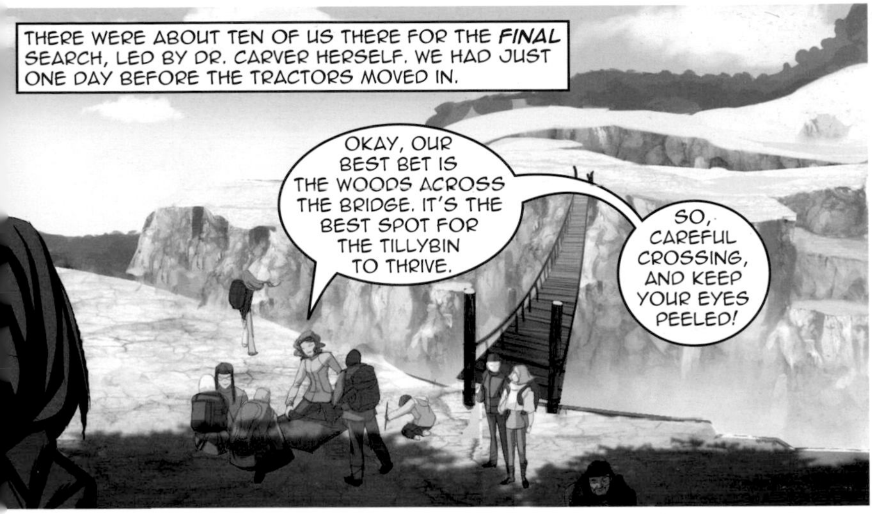
THERE WERE ABOUT TEN OF US THERE FOR THE *FINAL* SEARCH, LED BY DR. CARVER HERSELF. WE HAD JUST ONE DAY BEFORE THE TRACTORS MOVED IN.
OKAY, OUR BEST BET IS THE WOODS ACROSS THE BRIDGE. IT'S THE BEST SPOT FOR THE TILLYBIN TO THRIVE.
SO, CAREFUL CROSSING, AND KEEP YOUR EYES PEELED!

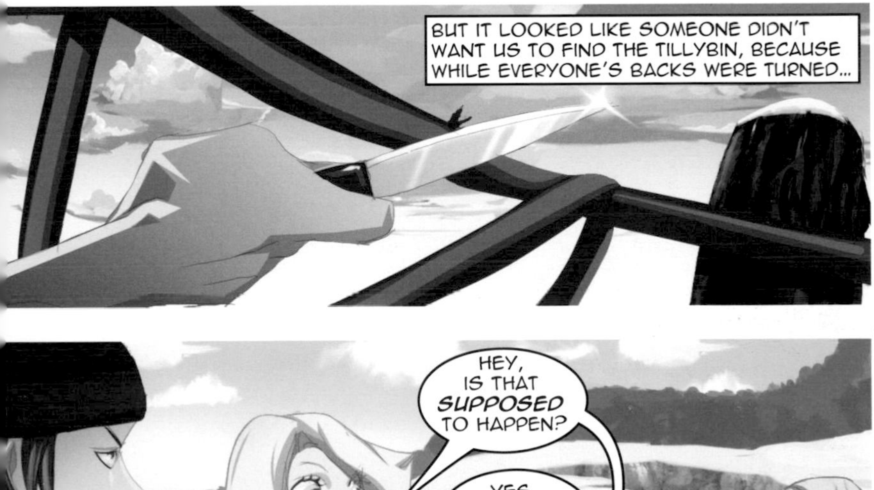
BUT IT LOOKED LIKE SOMEONE DIDN'T WANT US TO FIND THE TILLYBIN, BECAUSE WHILE EVERYONE'S BACKS WERE TURNED...

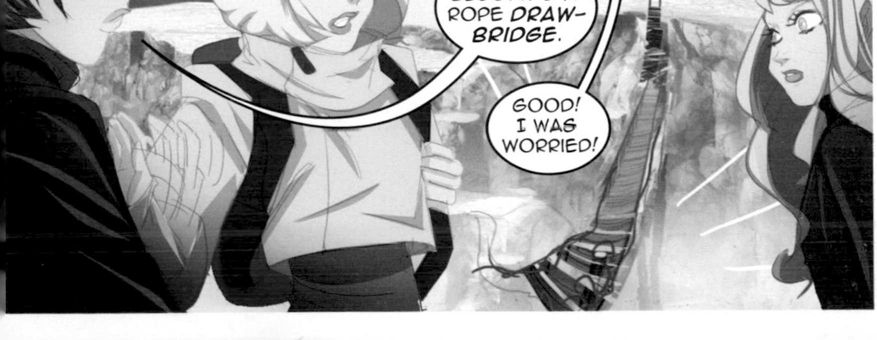
HEY, IS THAT ***SUPPOSED*** TO HAPPEN?
YES, BESS. IT'S A ROPE ***DRAW-BRIDGE***.
GOOD! I WAS WORRIED!

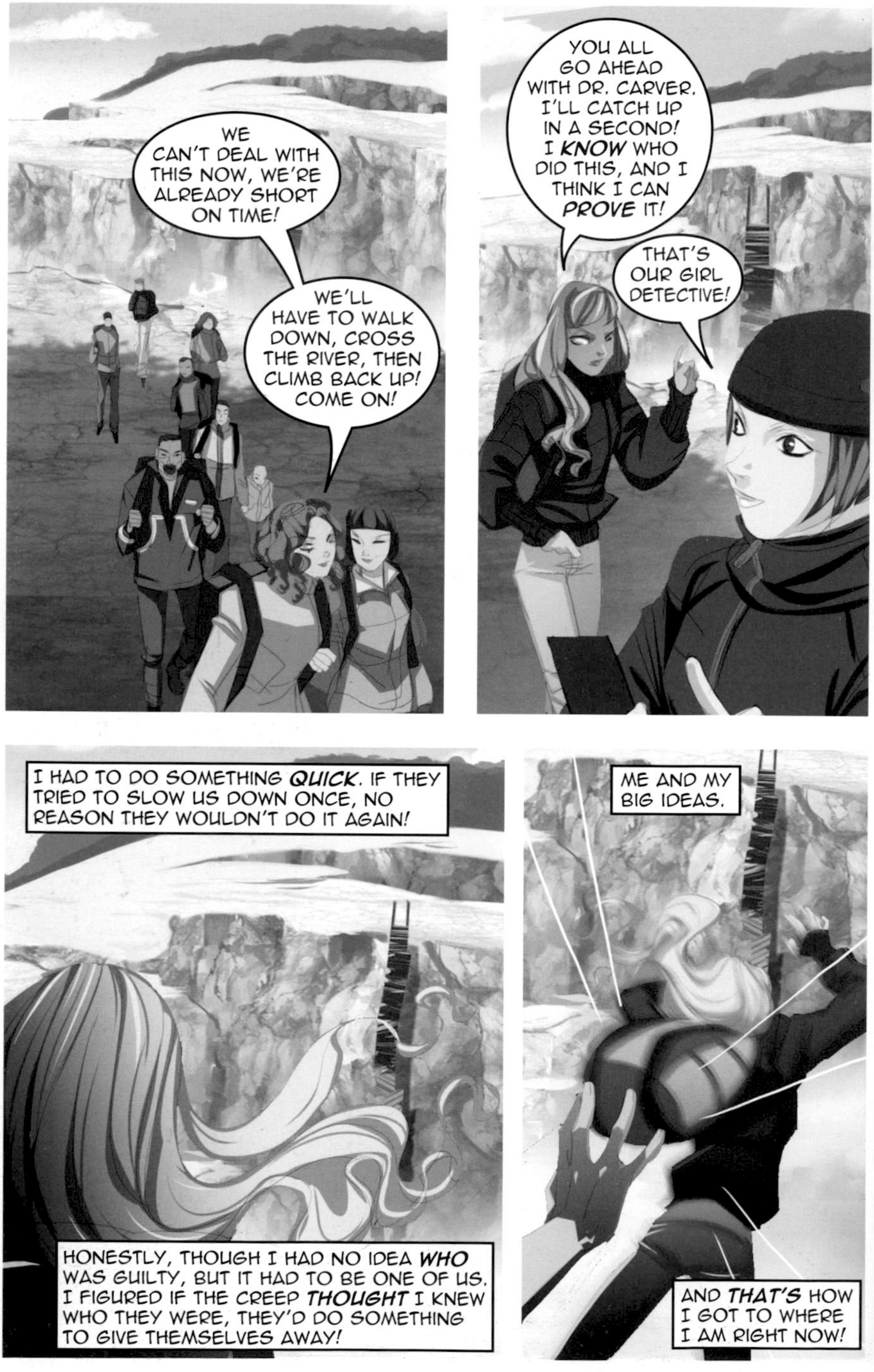
WE CAN'T DEAL WITH THIS NOW, WE'RE ALREADY SHORT ON TIME!
WE'LL HAVE TO WALK DOWN, CROSS THE RIVER, THEN CLIMB BACK UP! COME ON!
YOU ALL GO AHEAD WITH DR. CARVER. I'LL CATCH UP IN A SECOND! I KNOW WHO DID THIS, AND I THINK I CAN PROVE IT!
THAT'S OUR GIRL DETECTIVE!
I HAD TO DO SOMETHING QUICK. IF THEY TRIED TO SLOW US DOWN ONCE, NO REASON THEY WOULDN'T DO IT AGAIN!
HONESTLY, THOUGH I HAD NO IDEA WHO WAS GUILTY, BUT IT HAD TO BE ONE OF US. I FIGURED IF THE CREEP THOUGHT I KNEW WHO THEY WERE, THEY'D DO SOMETHING TO GIVE THEMSELVES AWAY!
ME AND MY BIG IDEAS.
AND THAT'S HOW I GOT TO WHERE I AM RIGHT NOW!

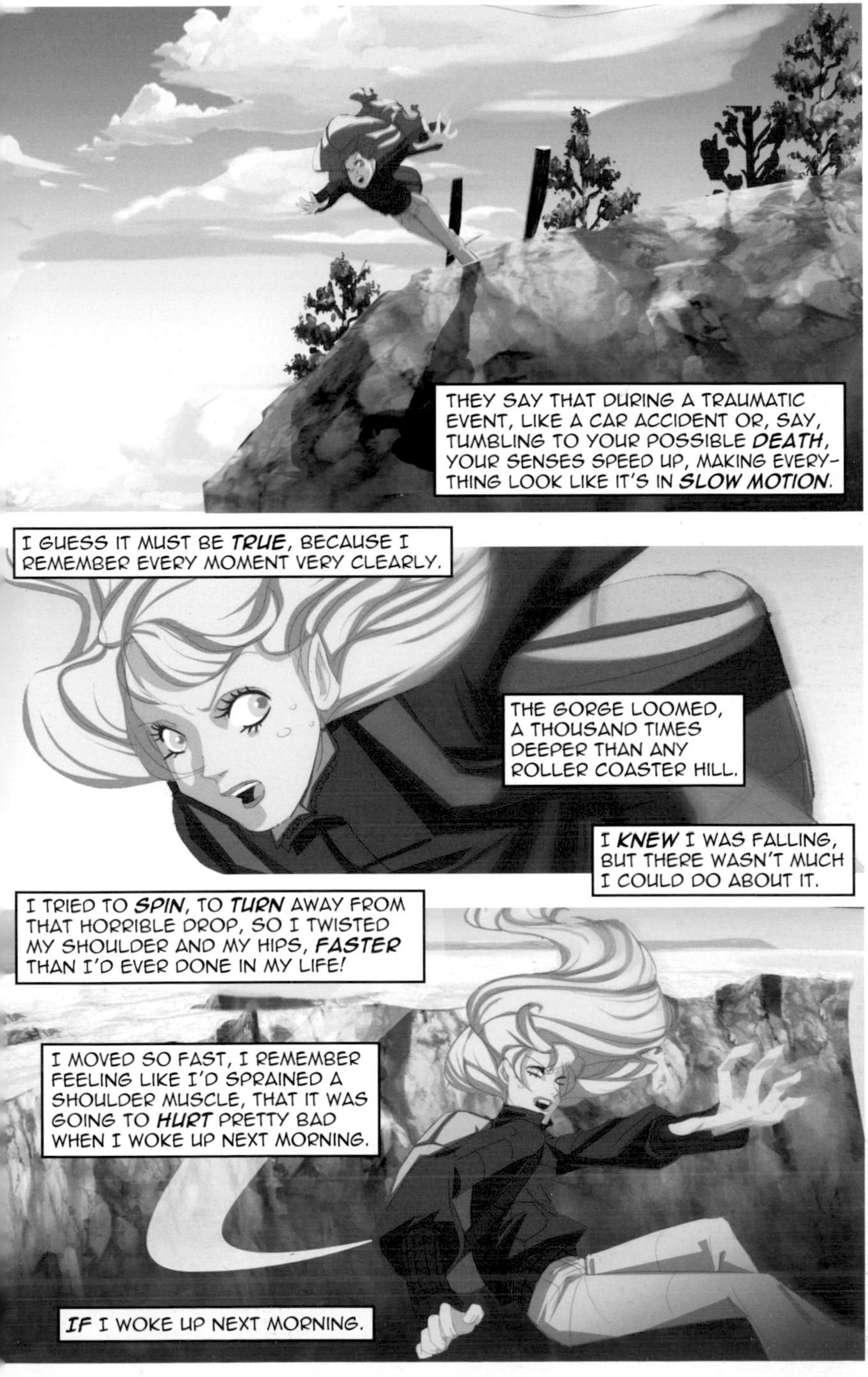
THEY SAY THAT DURING A TRAUMATIC EVENT, LIKE A CAR ACCIDENT OR, SAY, TUMBLING TO YOUR POSSIBLE *DEATH*, YOUR SENSES SPEED UP, MAKING EVERYTHING LOOK LIKE IT'S IN *SLOW MOTION*.
I GUESS IT MUST BE *TRUE*, BECAUSE I REMEMBER EVERY MOMENT VERY CLEARLY.
THE GORGE LOOMED, A THOUSAND TIMES DEEPER THAN ANY ROLLER COASTER HILL.
I *KNEW* I WAS FALLING, BUT THERE WASN'T MUCH I COULD DO ABOUT IT.
I TRIED TO *SPIN*, TO *TURN* AWAY FROM THAT HORRIBLE DROP, SO I TWISTED MY SHOULDER AND MY HIPS, *FASTER* THAN I'D EVER DONE IN MY LIFE!
I MOVED SO FAST, I REMEMBER FEELING LIKE I'D SPRAINED A SHOULDER MUSCLE, THAT IT WAS GOING TO *HURT* PRETTY BAD WHEN I WOKE UP NEXT MORNING.
*IF* I WOKE UP NEXT MORNING.

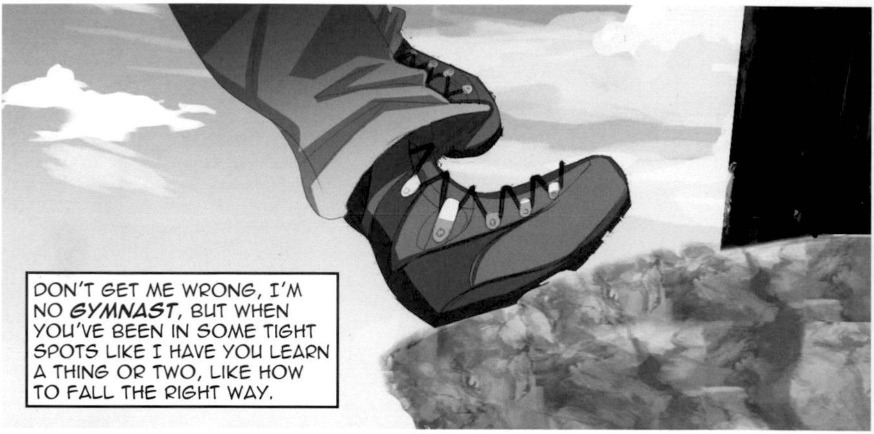
DON'T GET ME WRONG, I'M NO GYMNAST, BUT WHEN YOU'VE BEEN IN SOME TIGHT SPOTS LIKE I HAVE YOU LEARN A THING OR TWO, LIKE HOW TO FALL THE RIGHT WAY.

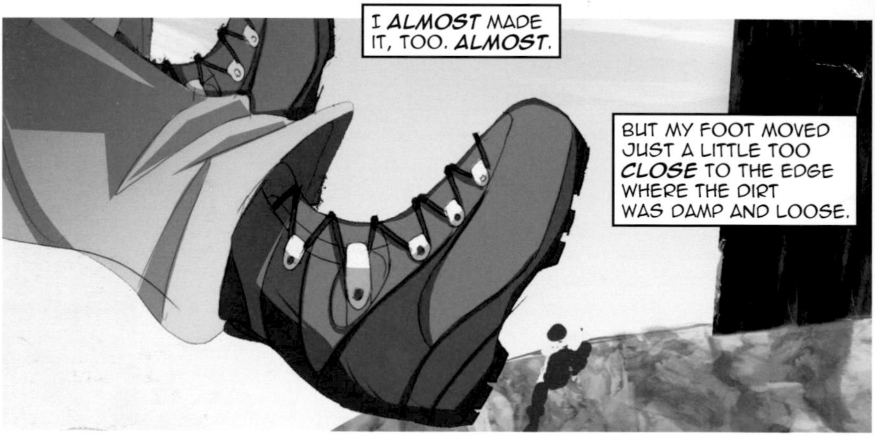
I ALMOST MADE IT, TOO. ALMOST.
BUT MY FOOT MOVED JUST A LITTLE TOO CLOSE TO THE EDGE WHERE THE DIRT WAS DAMP AND LOOSE.

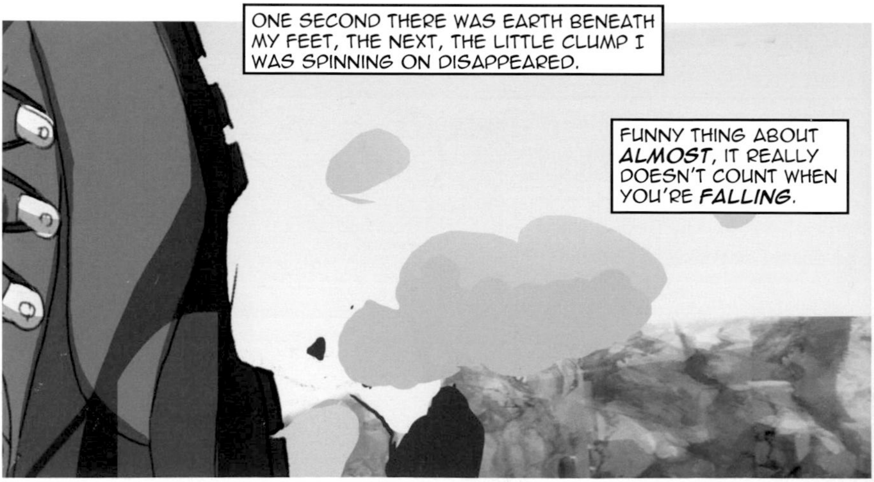
ONE SECOND THERE WAS EARTH BENEATH MY FEET, THE NEXT, THE LITTLE CLUMP I WAS SPINNING ON DISAPPEARED.
FUNNY THING ABOUT ALMOST, IT REALLY DOESN'T COUNT WHEN YOU'RE FALLING.

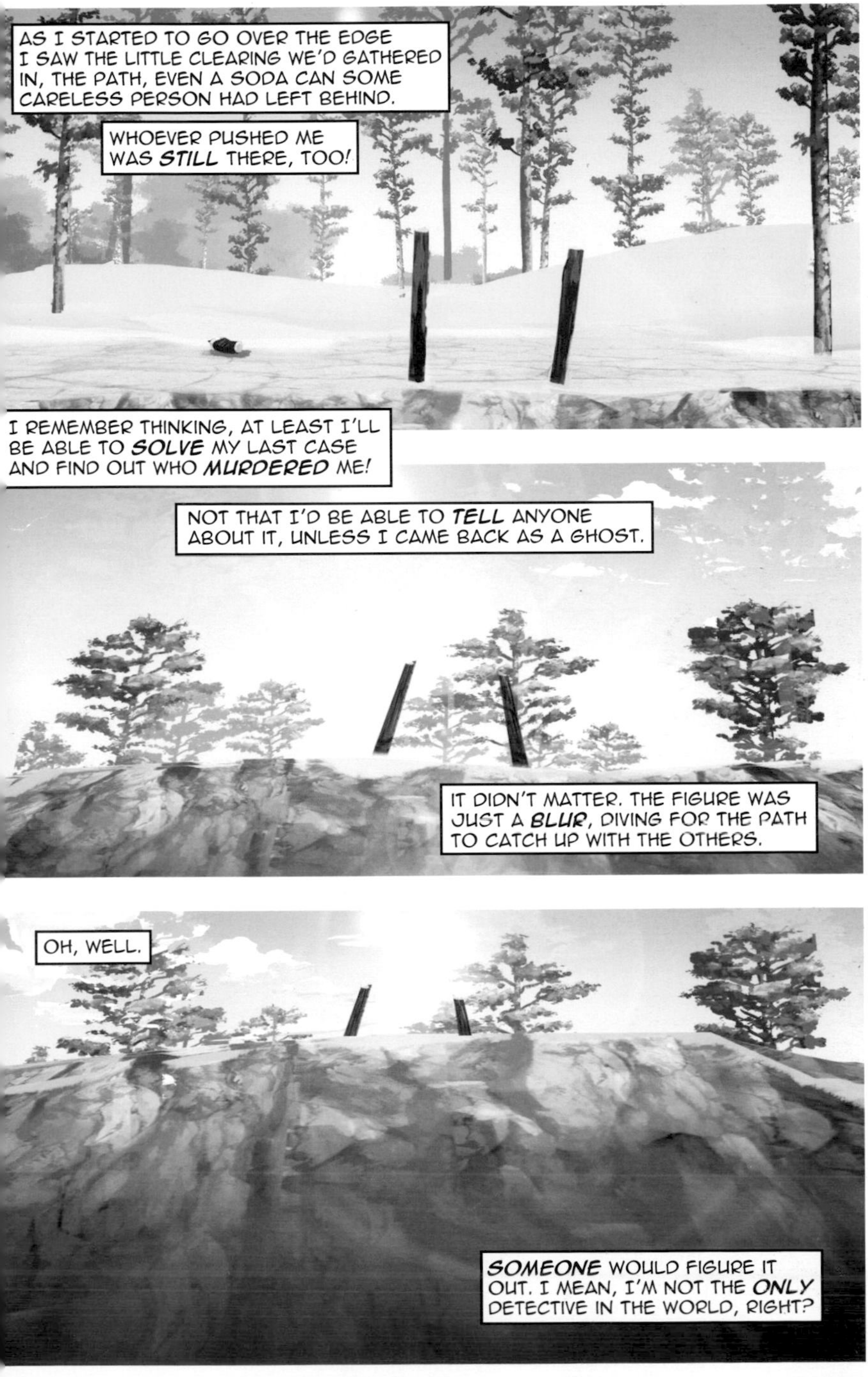
AS I STARTED TO GO OVER THE EDGE I SAW THE LITTLE CLEARING WE'D GATHERED IN, THE PATH, EVEN A SODA CAN SOME CARELESS PERSON HAD LEFT BEHIND.
WHOEVER PUSHED ME WAS STILL THERE, TOO!
I REMEMBER THINKING, AT LEAST I'LL BE ABLE TO SOLVE MY LAST CASE AND FIND OUT WHO MURDERED ME!
NOT THAT I'D BE ABLE TO TELL ANYONE ABOUT IT, UNLESS I CAME BACK AS A GHOST.
IT DIDN'T MATTER. THE FIGURE WAS JUST A BLUR, DIVING FOR THE PATH TO CATCH UP WITH THE OTHERS.
OH, WELL.
SOMEONE WOULD FIGURE IT OUT. I MEAN, I'M NOT THE ONLY DETECTIVE IN THE WORLD, RIGHT?

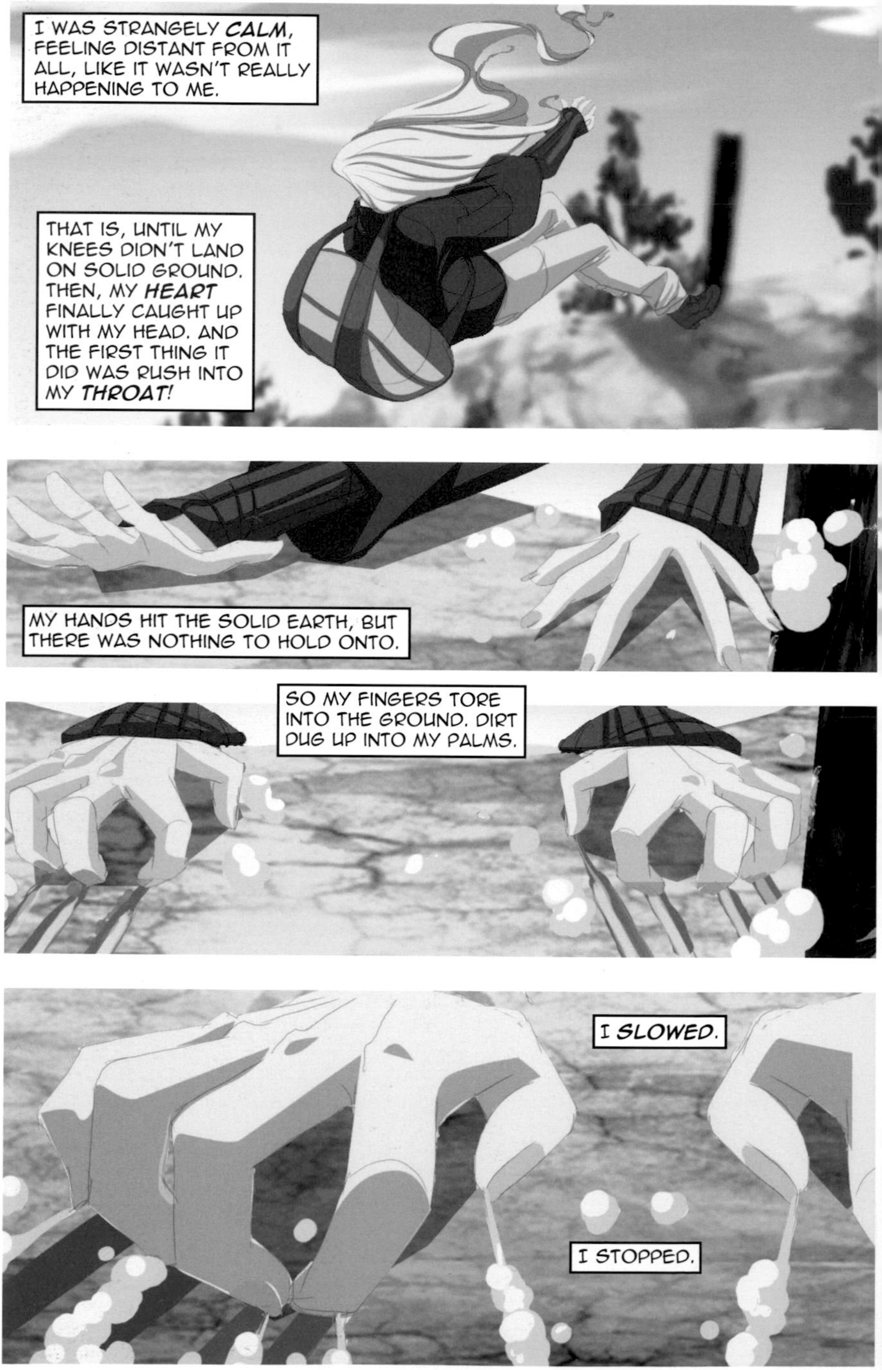
I WAS STRANGELY CALM, FEELING DISTANT FROM IT ALL, LIKE IT WASN'T REALLY HAPPENING TO ME.
THAT IS, UNTIL MY KNEES DIDN'T LAND ON SOLID GROUND. THEN, MY HEART FINALLY CAUGHT UP WITH MY HEAD. AND THE FIRST THING IT DID WAS RUSH INTO MY THROAT!
MY HANDS HIT THE SOLID EARTH, BUT THERE WAS NOTHING TO HOLD ONTO.
SO MY FINGERS TORE INTO THE GROUND. DIRT DUG UP INTO MY PALMS.
I SLOWED.
I STOPPED.

LET ME TELL YOU, I DON'T CARE *HOW* IT LOOKS, IT'S REALLY *NOT* EASY CLINGING TO SOMETHING BY YOUR FINGERTIPS.

FIRST THING I THOUGHT ABOUT, OF COURSE, WAS CALLING FOR *HELP*.

I'M NOT MUCH OF A *SCREAMER*, BUT UNDER THE CIRCUMSTANCES, I FIGURED I COULD SHOUT SO *LOUD, DAD* WOULD HEAR ME WAY BACK IN RIVER HEIGHTS.

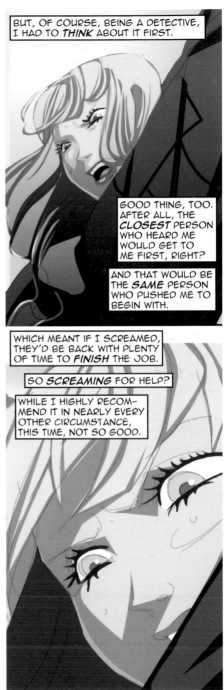

BUT, OF COURSE, BEING A DETECTIVE, I HAD TO *THINK* ABOUT IT FIRST.

GOOD THING, TOO. AFTER ALL, THE *CLOSEST* PERSON WHO HEARD ME WOULD GET TO ME FIRST, RIGHT?

AND THAT WOULD BE THE *SAME* PERSON WHO PUSHED ME TO BEGIN WITH.

WHICH MEANT IF I SCREAMED, THEY'D BE BACK WITH PLENTY OF TIME TO *FINISH* THE JOB.

SO *SCREAMING* FOR HELP?

WHILE I HIGHLY RECOM-MEND IT IN NEARLY EVERY OTHER CIRCUMSTANCE, THIS TIME, NOT SO GOOD.

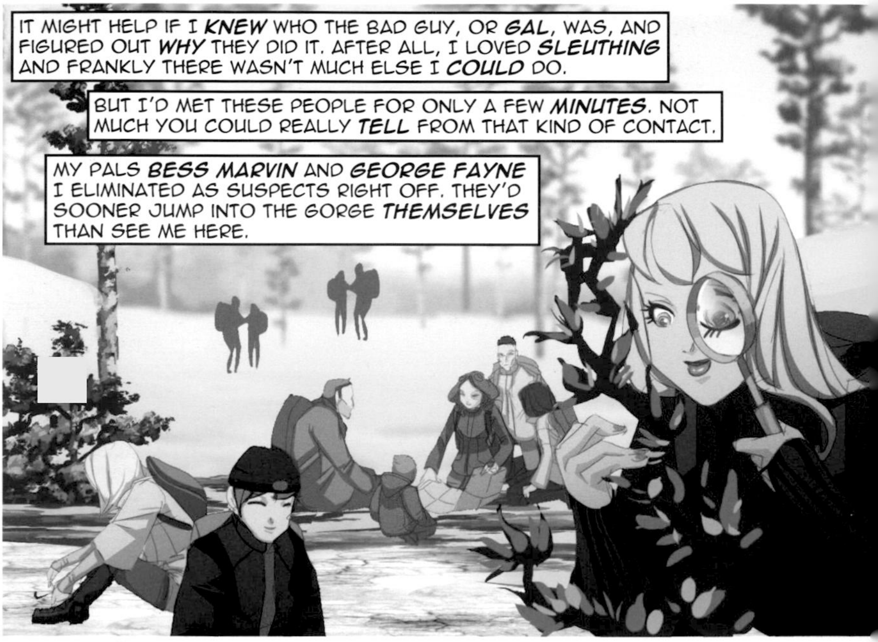
IT MIGHT HELP IF I KNEW WHO THE BAD GUY, OR GAL, WAS, AND FIGURED OUT WHY THEY DID IT. AFTER ALL, I LOVED SLEUTHING AND FRANKLY THERE WASN'T MUCH ELSE I COULD DO.
BUT I'D MET THESE PEOPLE FOR ONLY A FEW MINUTES. NOT MUCH YOU COULD REALLY TELL FROM THAT KIND OF CONTACT.
MY PALS BESS MARVIN AND GEORGE FAYNE I ELIMINATED AS SUSPECTS RIGHT OFF. THEY'D SOONER JUMP INTO THE GORGE THEMSELVES THAN SEE ME HERE.

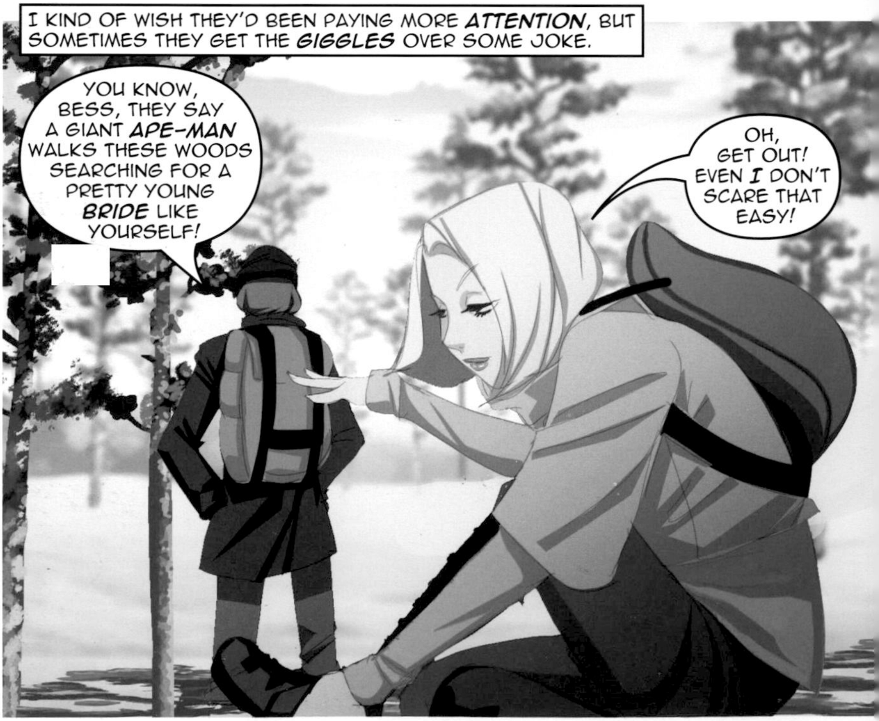
I KIND OF WISH THEY'D BEEN PAYING MORE ATTENTION, BUT SOMETIMES THEY GET THE GIGGLES OVER SOME JOKE.
YOU KNOW, BESS, THEY SAY A GIANT APE-MAN WALKS THESE WOODS SEARCHING FOR A PRETTY YOUNG BRIDE LIKE YOURSELF!
OH, GET OUT! EVEN I DON'T SCARE THAT EASY!

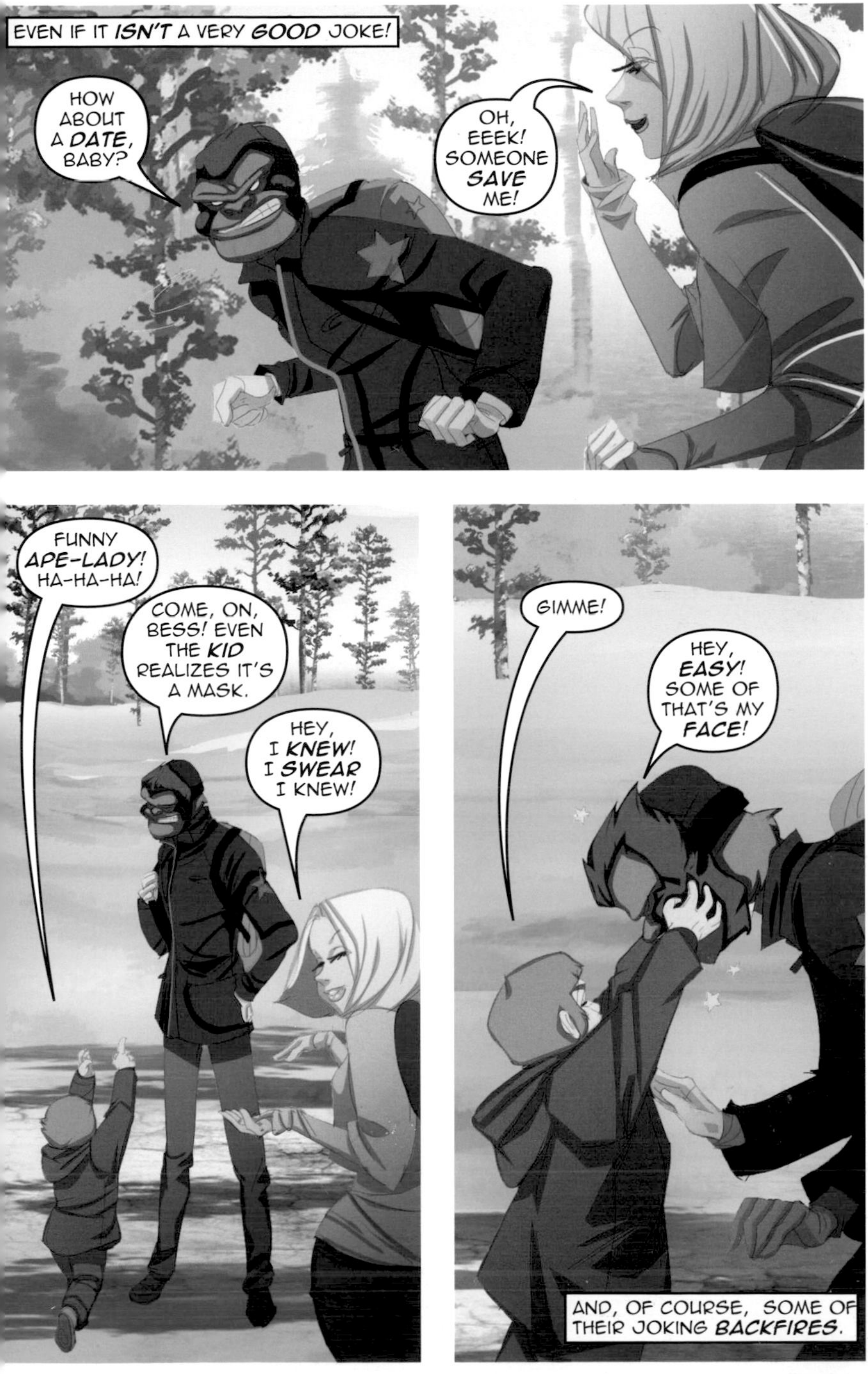
EVEN IF IT ISN'T A VERY GOOD JOKE!
HOW ABOUT A DATE, BABY?
OH, EEEK! SOMEONE SAVE ME!
FUNNY APE-LADY! HA-HA-HA!
COME, ON, BESS! EVEN THE KID REALIZES IT'S A MASK.
HEY, I KNEW! I SWEAR I KNEW!
GIMME!
HEY, EASY! SOME OF THAT'S MY FACE!
AND, OF COURSE, SOME OF THEIR JOKING BACKFIRES.

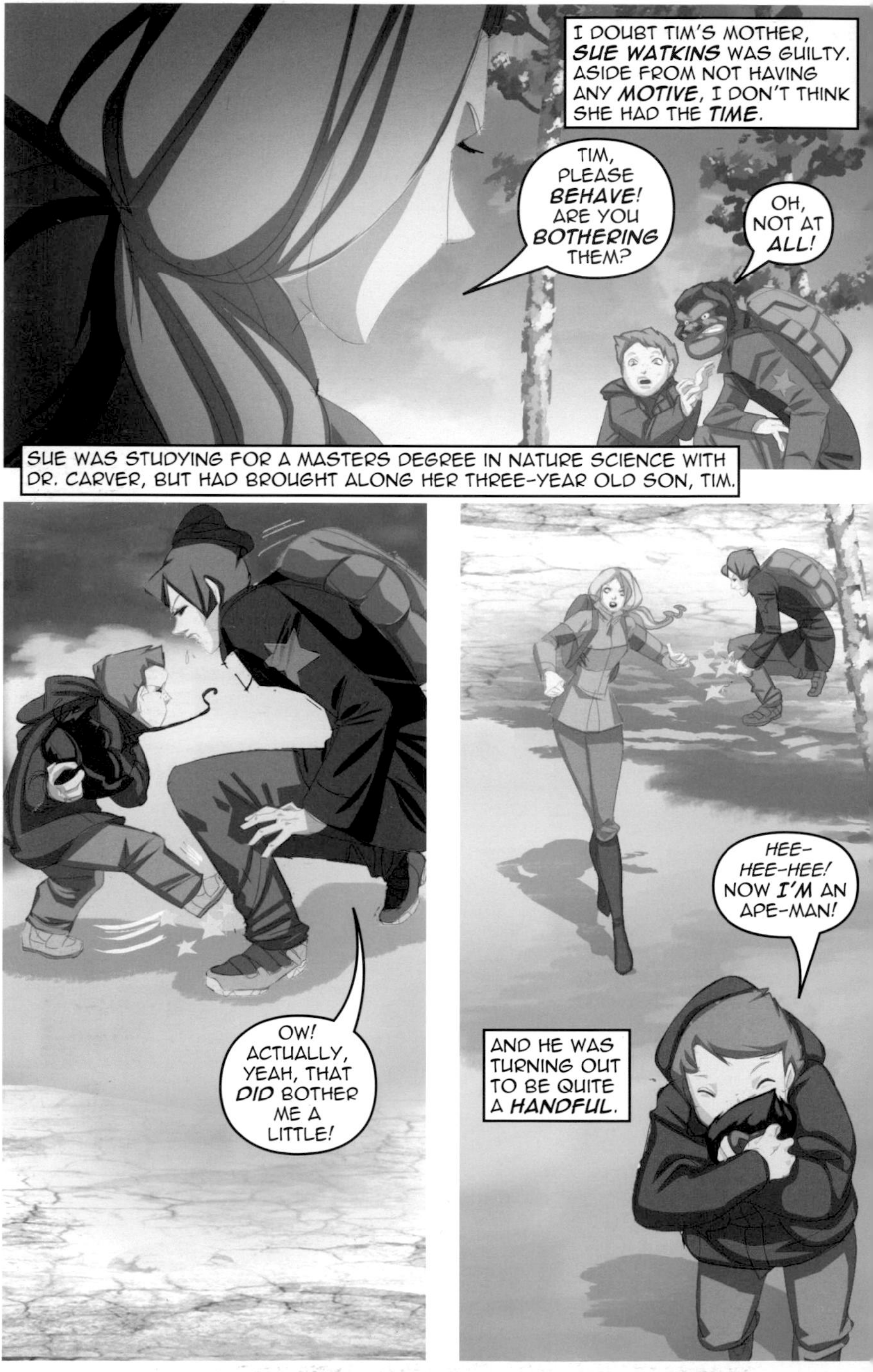

I DOUBT TIM'S MOTHER, SUE WATKINS WAS GUILTY. ASIDE FROM NOT HAVING ANY MOTIVE, I DON'T THINK SHE HAD THE TIME.
TIM, PLEASE BEHAVE! ARE YOU BOTHERING THEM?
OH, NOT AT ALL!
SUE WAS STUDYING FOR A MASTERS DEGREE IN NATURE SCIENCE WITH DR. CARVER, BUT HAD BROUGHT ALONG HER THREE-YEAR OLD SON, TIM.
OW! ACTUALLY, YEAH, THAT DID BOTHER ME A LITTLE!
HEE-HEE-HEE! NOW I'M AN APE-MAN!
AND HE WAS TURNING OUT TO BE QUITE A HANDFUL.

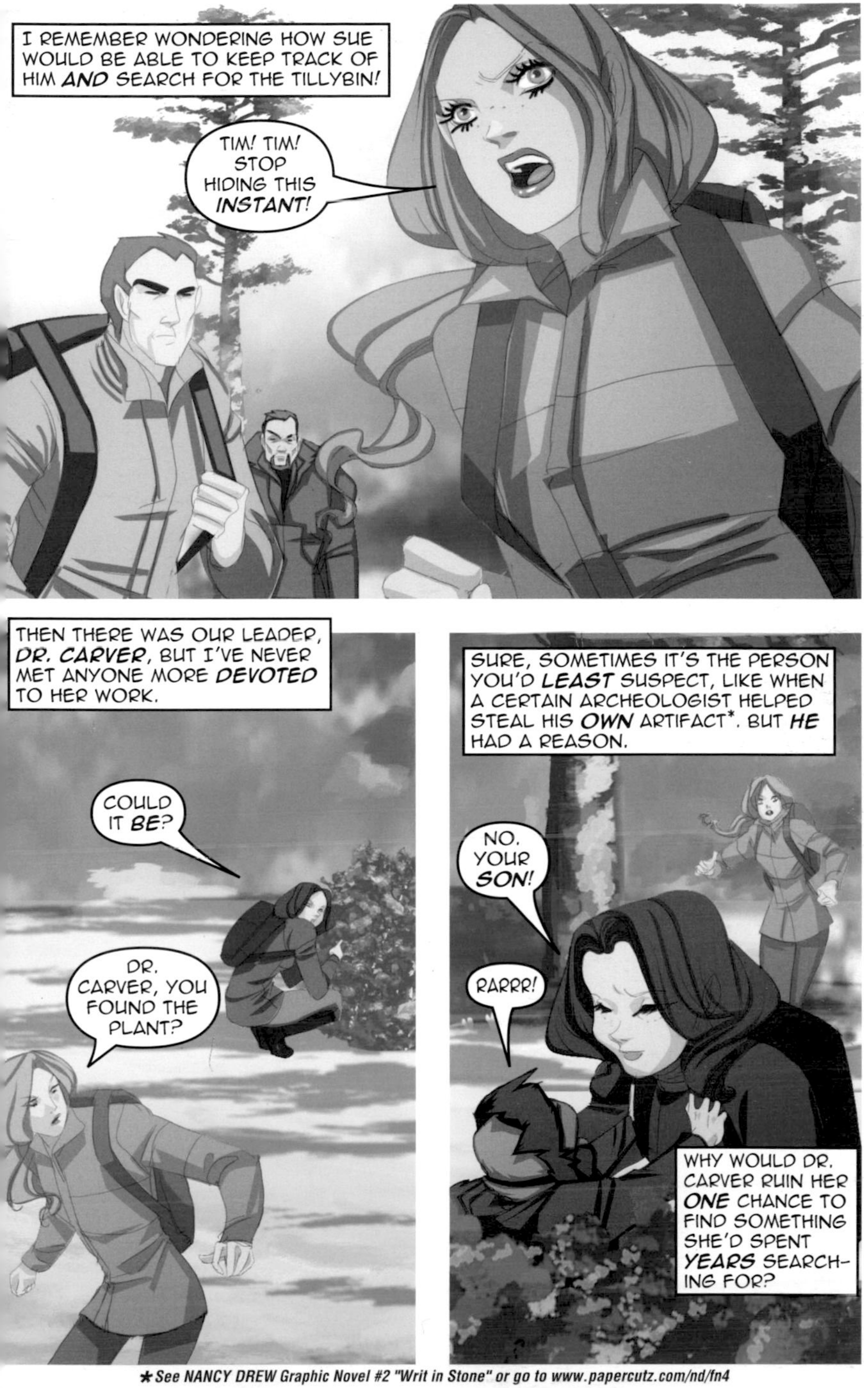
I REMEMBER WONDERING HOW SUE WOULD BE ABLE TO KEEP TRACK OF HIM AND SEARCH FOR THE TILLYBIN!
TIM! TIM! STOP HIDING THIS INSTANT!
THEN THERE WAS OUR LEADER, DR. CARVER, BUT I'VE NEVER MET ANYONE MORE DEVOTED TO HER WORK.
COULD IT BE?
DR. CARVER, YOU FOUND THE PLANT?
SURE, SOMETIMES IT'S THE PERSON YOU'D LEAST SUSPECT, LIKE WHEN A CERTAIN ARCHEOLOGIST HELPED STEAL HIS OWN ARTIFACT*. BUT HE HAD A REASON.
NO. YOUR SON!
RARRR!
WHY WOULD DR. CARVER RUIN HER ONE CHANCE TO FIND SOMETHING SHE'D SPENT YEARS SEARCHING FOR?

*See NANCY DREW Graphic Novel #2 "Writ in Stone" or go to www.papercutz.com/nd/fn4

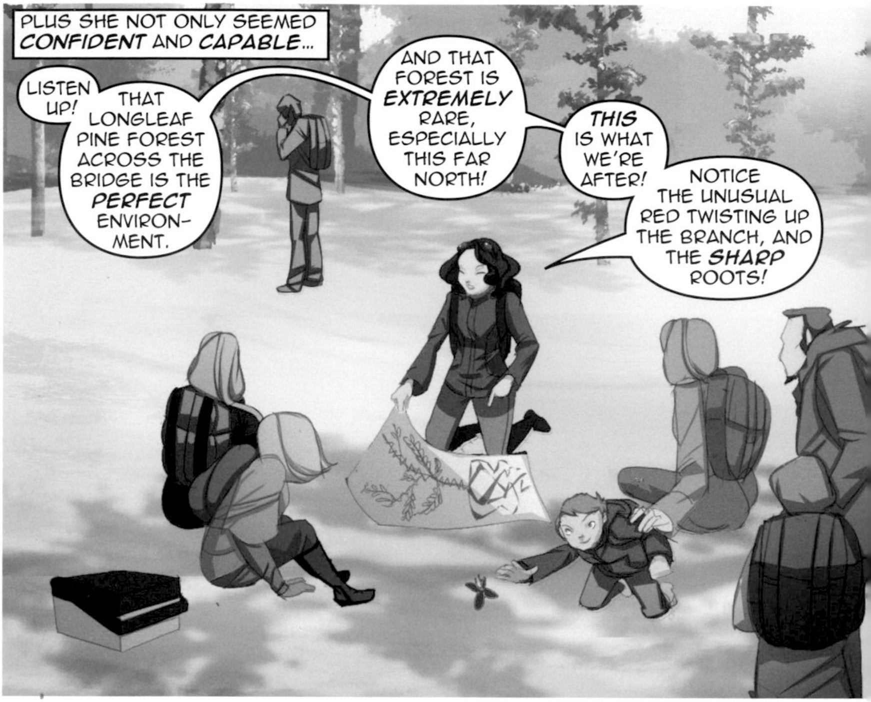
PLUS SHE NOT ONLY SEEMED CONFIDENT AND CAPABLE...
LISTEN UP!
THAT LONGLEAF PINE FOREST ACROSS THE BRIDGE IS THE PERFECT ENVIRONMENT.
AND THAT FOREST IS EXTREMELY RARE, ESPECIALLY THIS FAR NORTH!
THIS IS WHAT WE'RE AFTER!
NOTICE THE UNUSUAL RED TWISTING UP THE BRANCH, AND THE SHARP ROOTS!

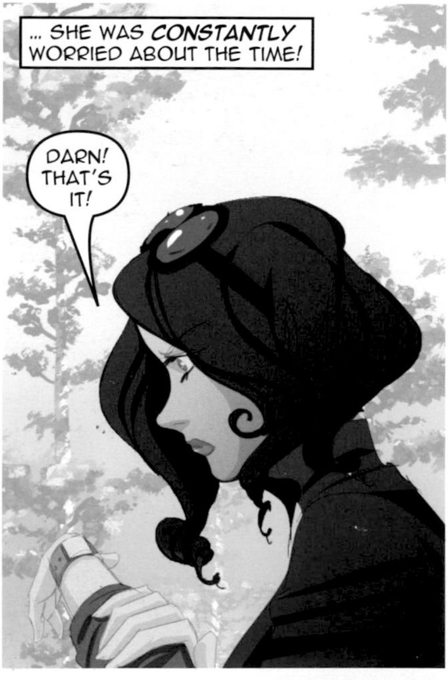
... SHE WAS CONSTANTLY WORRIED ABOUT THE TIME!
DARN! THAT'S IT!

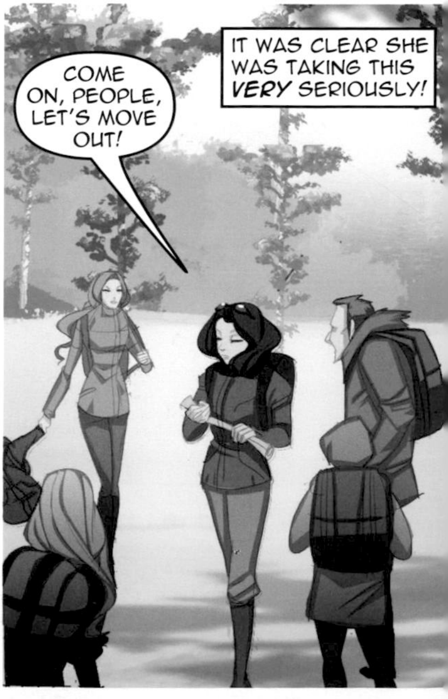
IT WAS CLEAR SHE WAS TAKING THIS VERY SERIOUSLY!
COME ON, PEOPLE, LET'S MOVE OUT!

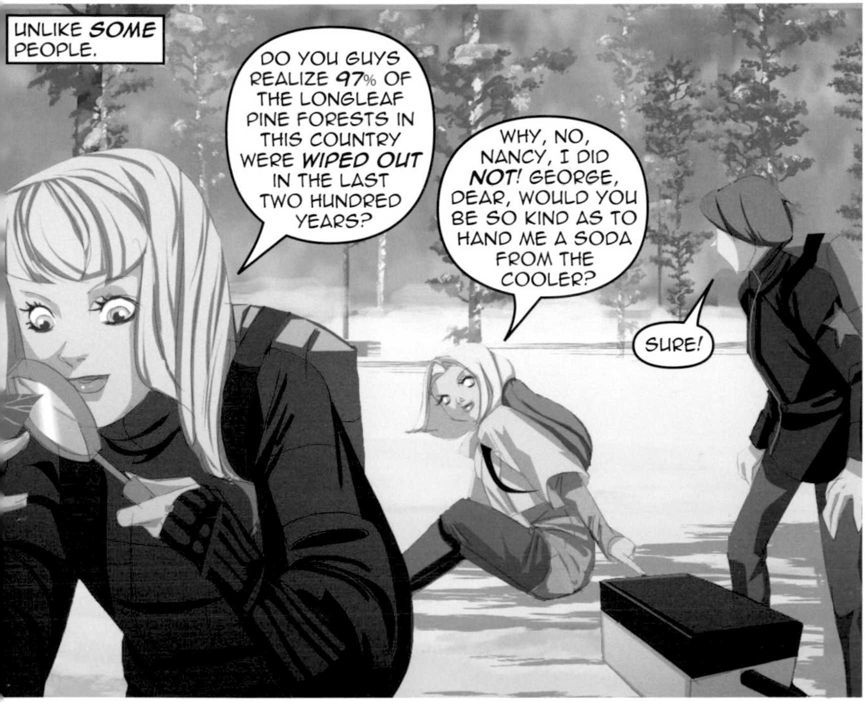
UNLIKE *SOME* PEOPLE.
DO YOU GUYS REALIZE **97%** OF THE LONGLEAF PINE FORESTS IN THIS COUNTRY WERE ***WIPED OUT*** IN THE LAST TWO HUNDRED YEARS?
WHY, NO, NANCY, I DID ***NOT***! GEORGE, DEAR, WOULD YOU BE SO KIND AS TO HAND ME A SODA FROM THE COOLER?
SURE!

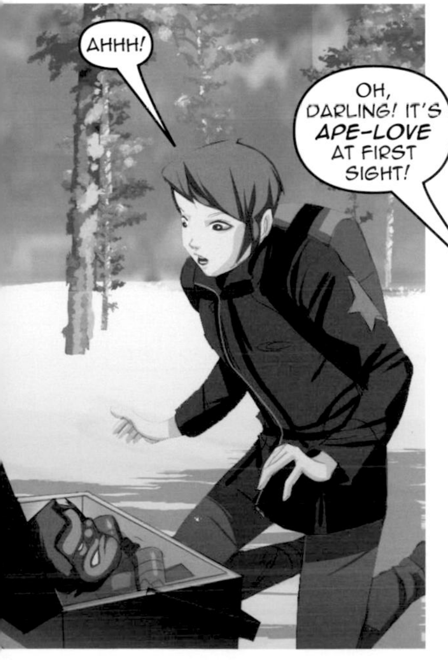
AHHH!
OH, DARLING! IT'S ***APE-LOVE*** AT FIRST SIGHT!

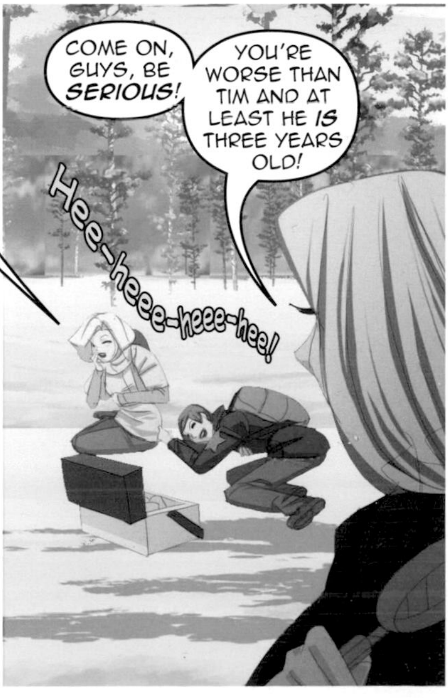
Hee-heee-heee-hee!
COME ON, GUYS, BE ***SERIOUS***!
YOU'RE WORSE THAN TIM AND AT LEAST HE ***IS*** THREE YEARS OLD!

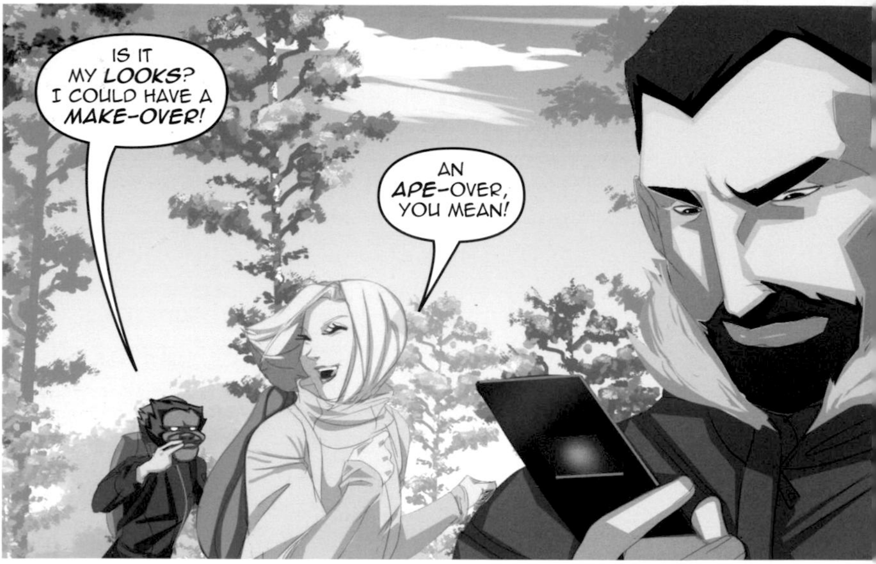
IS IT MY LOOKS? I COULD HAVE A MAKE-OVER!
AN APE-OVER, YOU MEAN!

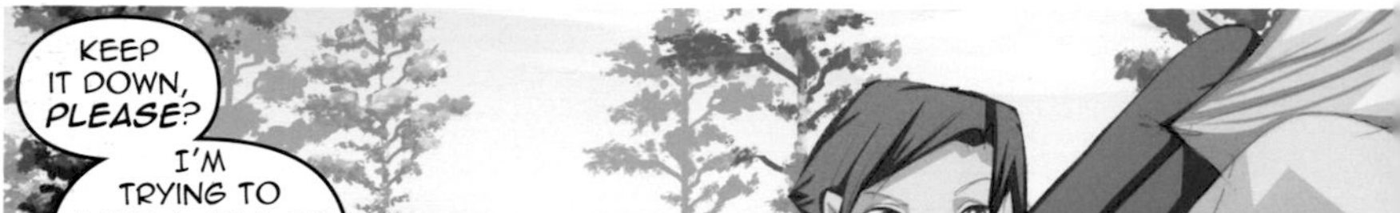
KEEP IT DOWN, PLEASE?
I'M TRYING TO MAKE A CALL TO MY... FAMILY BEFORE WE GET STARTED!
ADAM FINSTER WAS EASY TO REMEMBER. NICE ENOUGH, BUT HE SPENT ALL HIS TIME ON HIS PHONE.

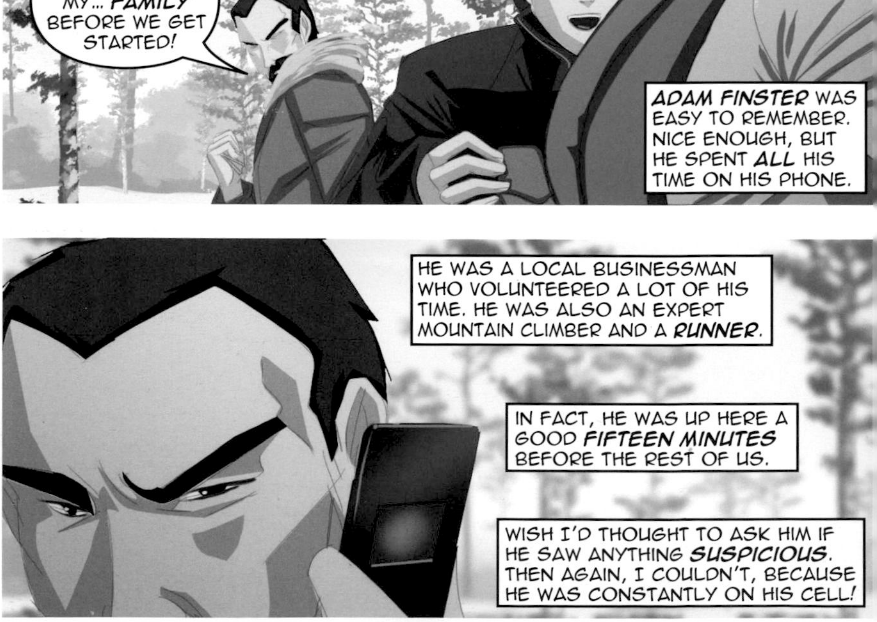
HE WAS A LOCAL BUSINESSMAN WHO VOLUNTEERED A LOT OF HIS TIME. HE WAS ALSO AN EXPERT MOUNTAIN CLIMBER AND A RUNNER.
IN FACT, HE WAS UP HERE A GOOD FIFTEEN MINUTES BEFORE THE REST OF US.
WISH I'D THOUGHT TO ASK HIM IF HE SAW ANYTHING SUSPICIOUS. THEN AGAIN, I COULDN'T, BECAUSE HE WAS CONSTANTLY ON HIS CELL!

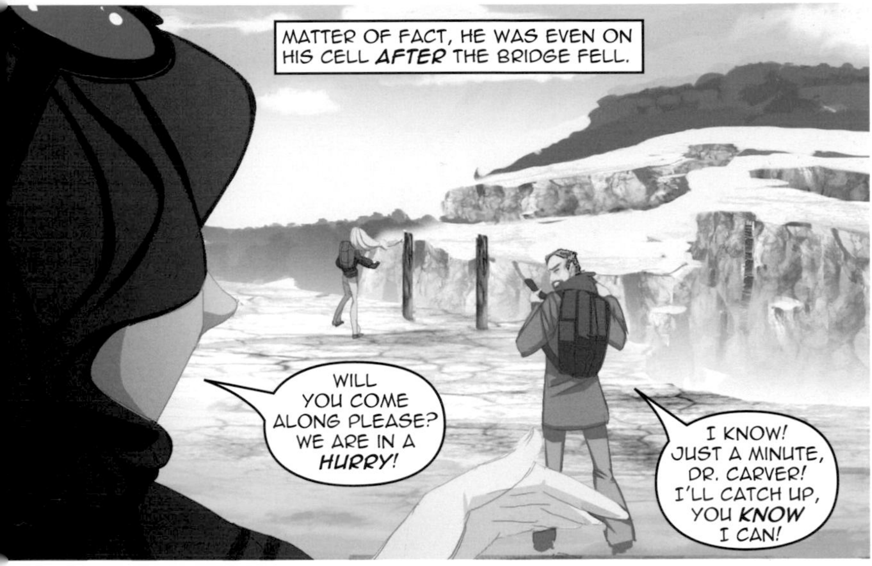
MATTER OF FACT, HE WAS EVEN ON HIS CELL AFTER THE BRIDGE FELL.
WILL YOU COME ALONG PLEASE? WE ARE IN A HURRY!
I KNOW! JUST A MINUTE, DR. CARVER! I'LL CATCH UP, YOU KNOW I CAN!

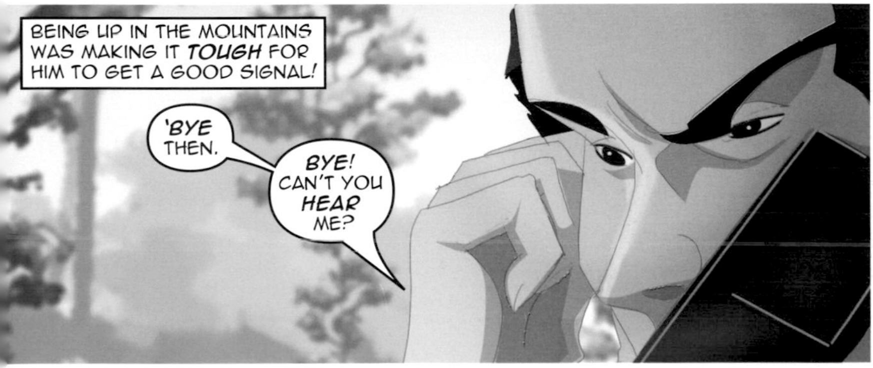
BEING UP IN THE MOUNTAINS WAS MAKING IT TOUGH FOR HIM TO GET A GOOD SIGNAL!
'BYE THEN.
BYE! CAN'T YOU HEAR ME?

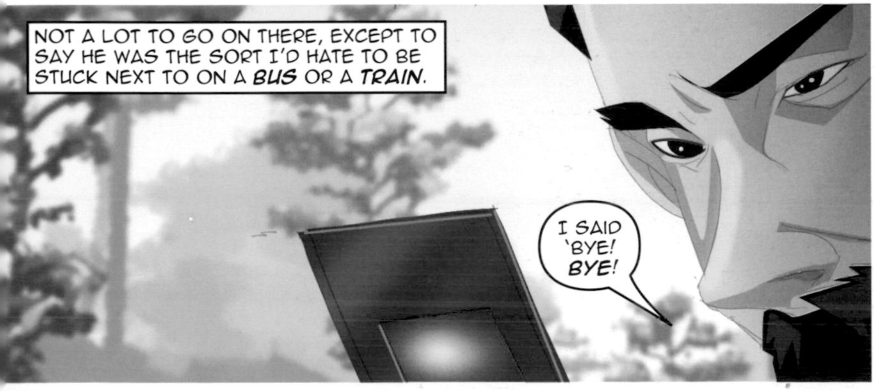
NOT A LOT TO GO ON THERE, EXCEPT TO SAY HE WAS THE SORT I'D HATE TO BE STUCK NEXT TO ON A BUS OR A TRAIN.
I SAID 'BYE! BYE!

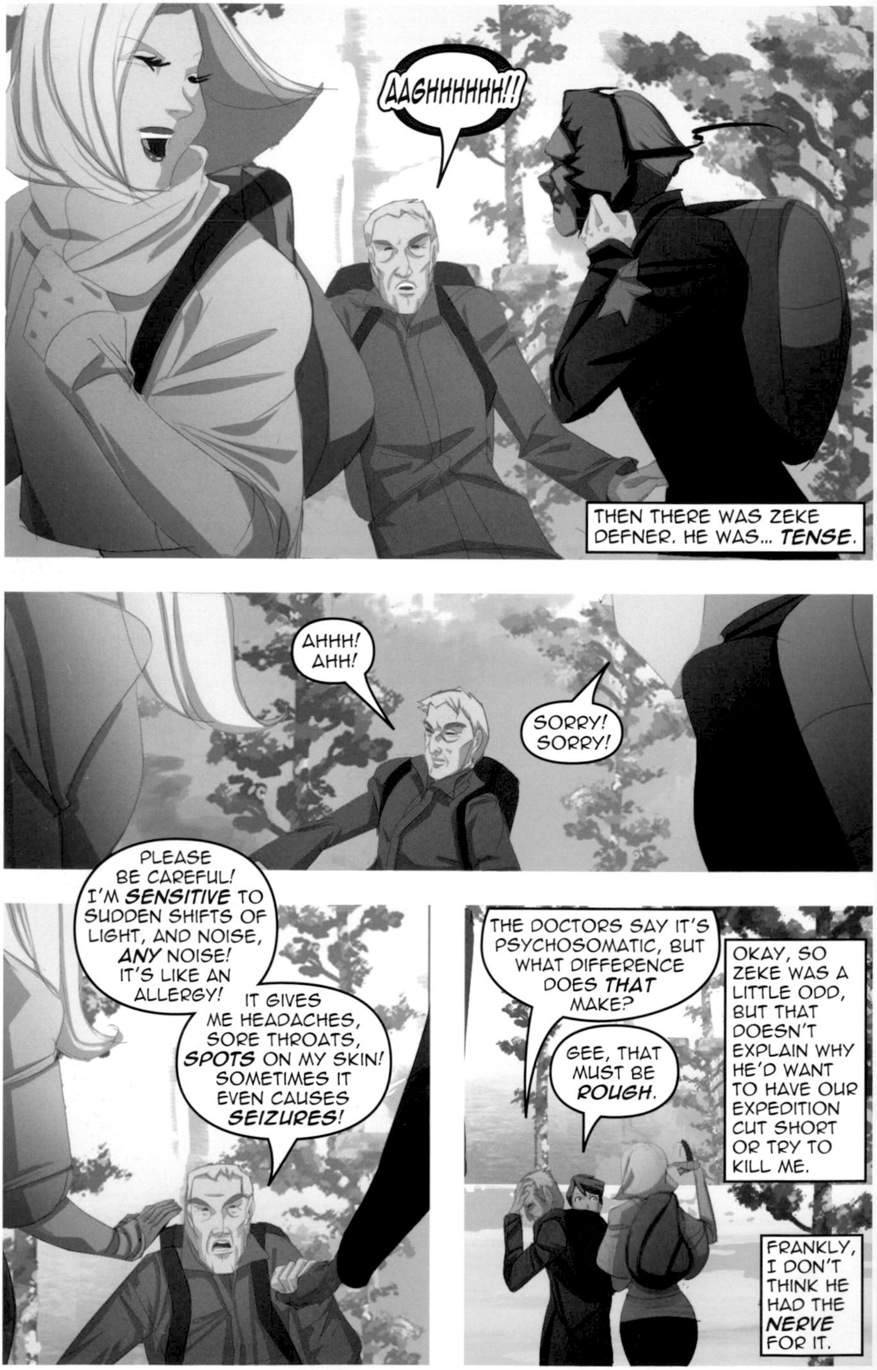

AAGHHHHHH!!
THEN THERE WAS ZEKE DEFNER. HE WAS... TENSE.
AHHH! AHH!
SORRY! SORRY!
PLEASE BE CAREFUL! I'M SENSITIVE TO SUDDEN SHIFTS OF LIGHT, AND NOISE, ANY NOISE! IT'S LIKE AN ALLERGY!
IT GIVES ME HEADACHES, SORE THROATS, SPOTS ON MY SKIN! SOMETIMES IT EVEN CAUSES SEIZURES!
THE DOCTORS SAY IT'S PSYCHOSOMATIC, BUT WHAT DIFFERENCE DOES THAT MAKE?
GEE, THAT MUST BE ROUGH.
OKAY, SO ZEKE WAS A LITTLE ODD, BUT THAT DOESN'T EXPLAIN WHY HE'D WANT TO HAVE OUR EXPEDITION CUT SHORT OR TRY TO KILL ME.
FRANKLY, I DON'T THINK HE HAD THE NERVE FOR IT.

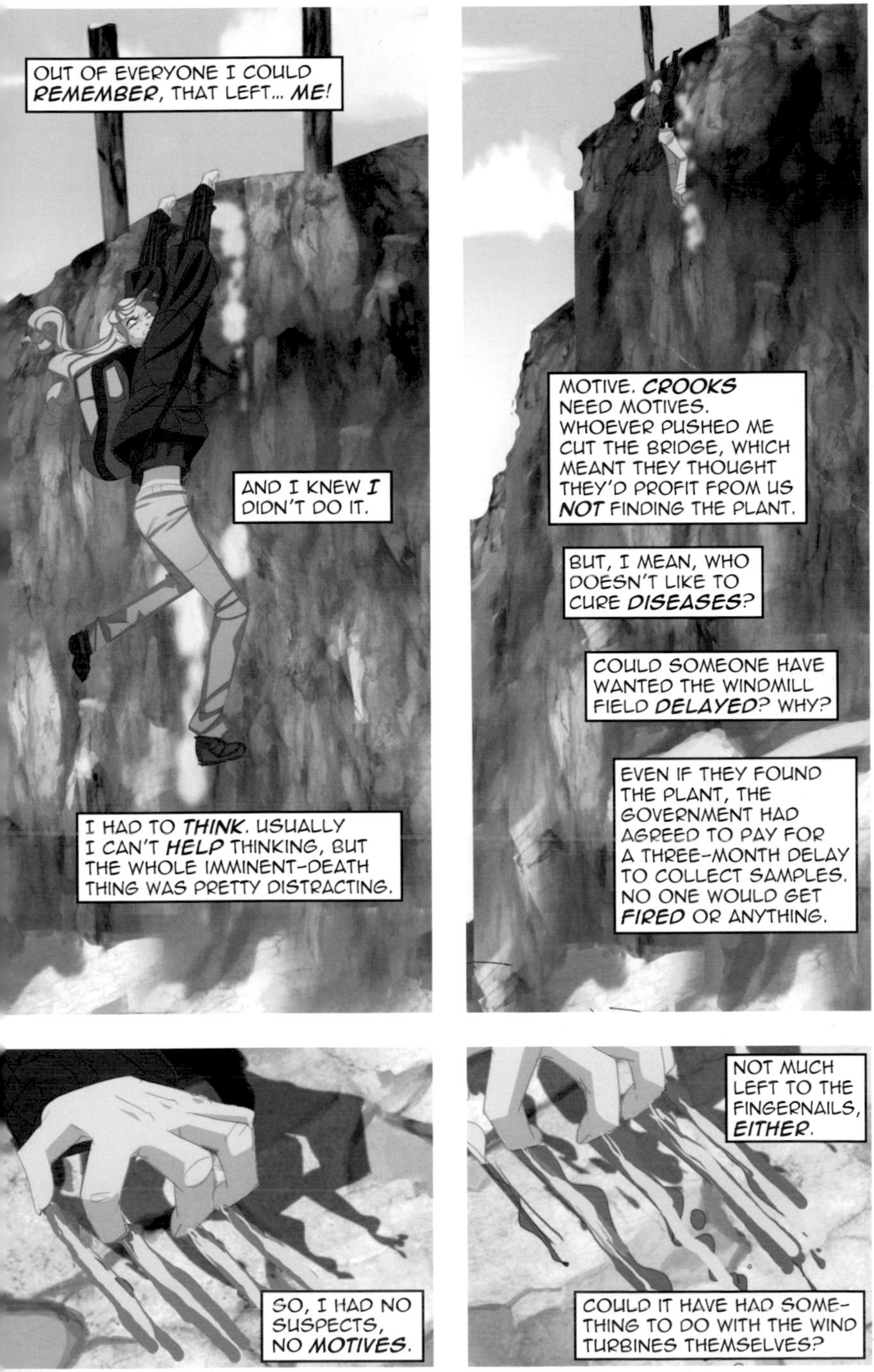
OUT OF EVERYONE I COULD REMEMBER, THAT LEFT... ME!
AND I KNEW I DIDN'T DO IT.
I HAD TO THINK. USUALLY I CAN'T HELP THINKING, BUT THE WHOLE IMMINENT-DEATH THING WAS PRETTY DISTRACTING.
MOTIVE. CROOKS NEED MOTIVES. WHOEVER PUSHED ME CUT THE BRIDGE, WHICH MEANT THEY THOUGHT THEY'D PROFIT FROM US NOT FINDING THE PLANT.
BUT, I MEAN, WHO DOESN'T LIKE TO CURE DISEASES?
COULD SOMEONE HAVE WANTED THE WINDMILL FIELD DELAYED? WHY?
EVEN IF THEY FOUND THE PLANT, THE GOVERNMENT HAD AGREED TO PAY FOR A THREE-MONTH DELAY TO COLLECT SAMPLES. NO ONE WOULD GET FIRED OR ANYTHING.
SO, I HAD NO SUSPECTS, NO MOTIVES.
NOT MUCH LEFT TO THE FINGERNAILS, EITHER.
COULD IT HAVE HAD SOMETHING TO DO WITH THE WIND TURBINES THEMSELVES?

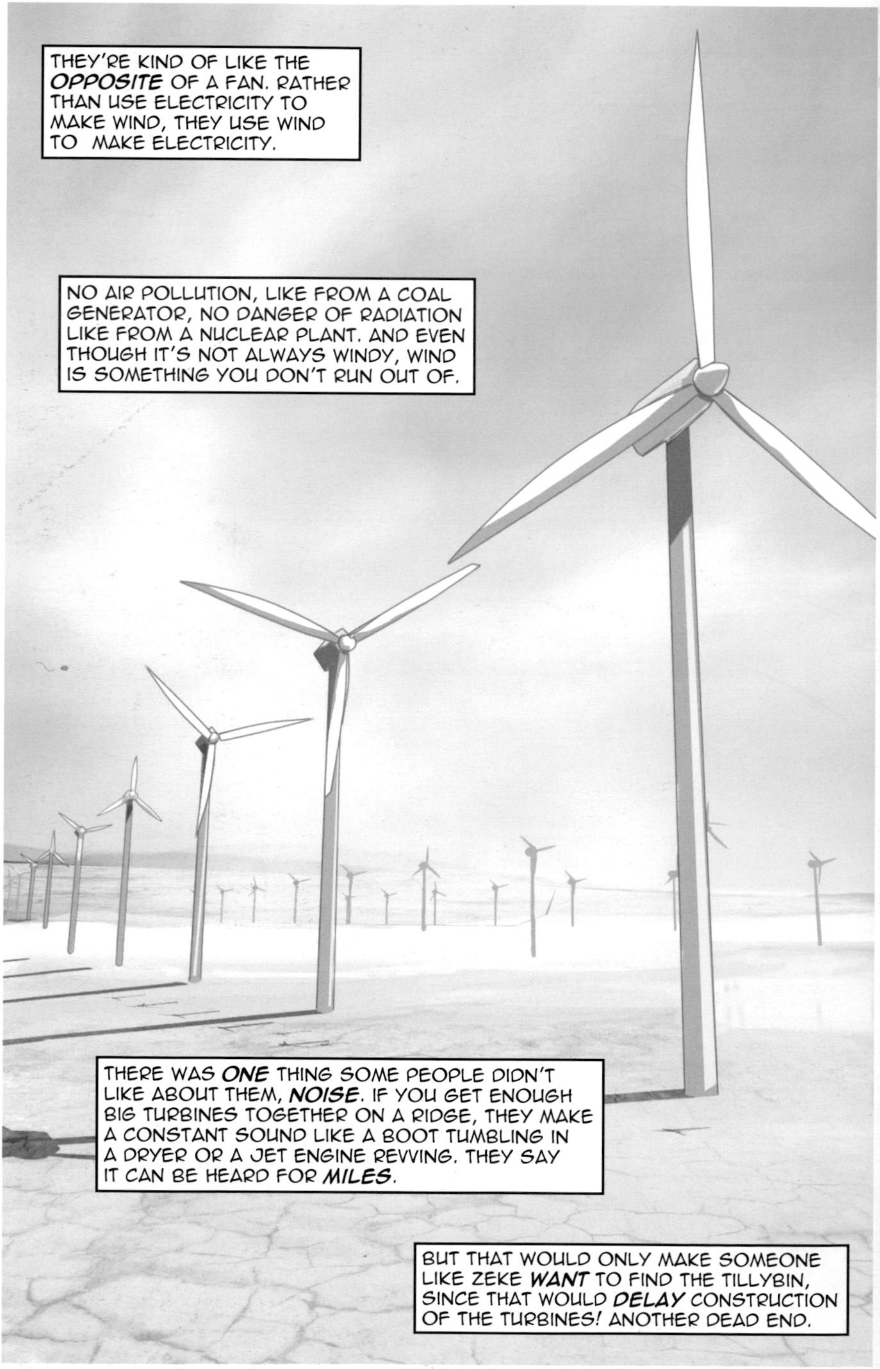
THEY'RE KIND OF LIKE THE OPPOSITE OF A FAN. RATHER THAN USE ELECTRICITY TO MAKE WIND, THEY USE WIND TO MAKE ELECTRICITY.
NO AIR POLLUTION, LIKE FROM A COAL GENERATOR, NO DANGER OF RADIATION LIKE FROM A NUCLEAR PLANT. AND EVEN THOUGH IT'S NOT ALWAYS WINDY, WIND IS SOMETHING YOU DON'T RUN OUT OF.
THERE WAS ONE THING SOME PEOPLE DIDN'T LIKE ABOUT THEM, NOISE. IF YOU GET ENOUGH BIG TURBINES TOGETHER ON A RIDGE, THEY MAKE A CONSTANT SOUND LIKE A BOOT TUMBLING IN A DRYER OR A JET ENGINE REVVING. THEY SAY IT CAN BE HEARD FOR MILES.
BUT THAT WOULD ONLY MAKE SOMEONE LIKE ZEKE WANT TO FIND THE TILLYBIN, SINCE THAT WOULD DELAY CONSTRUCTION OF THE TURBINES! ANOTHER DEAD END.

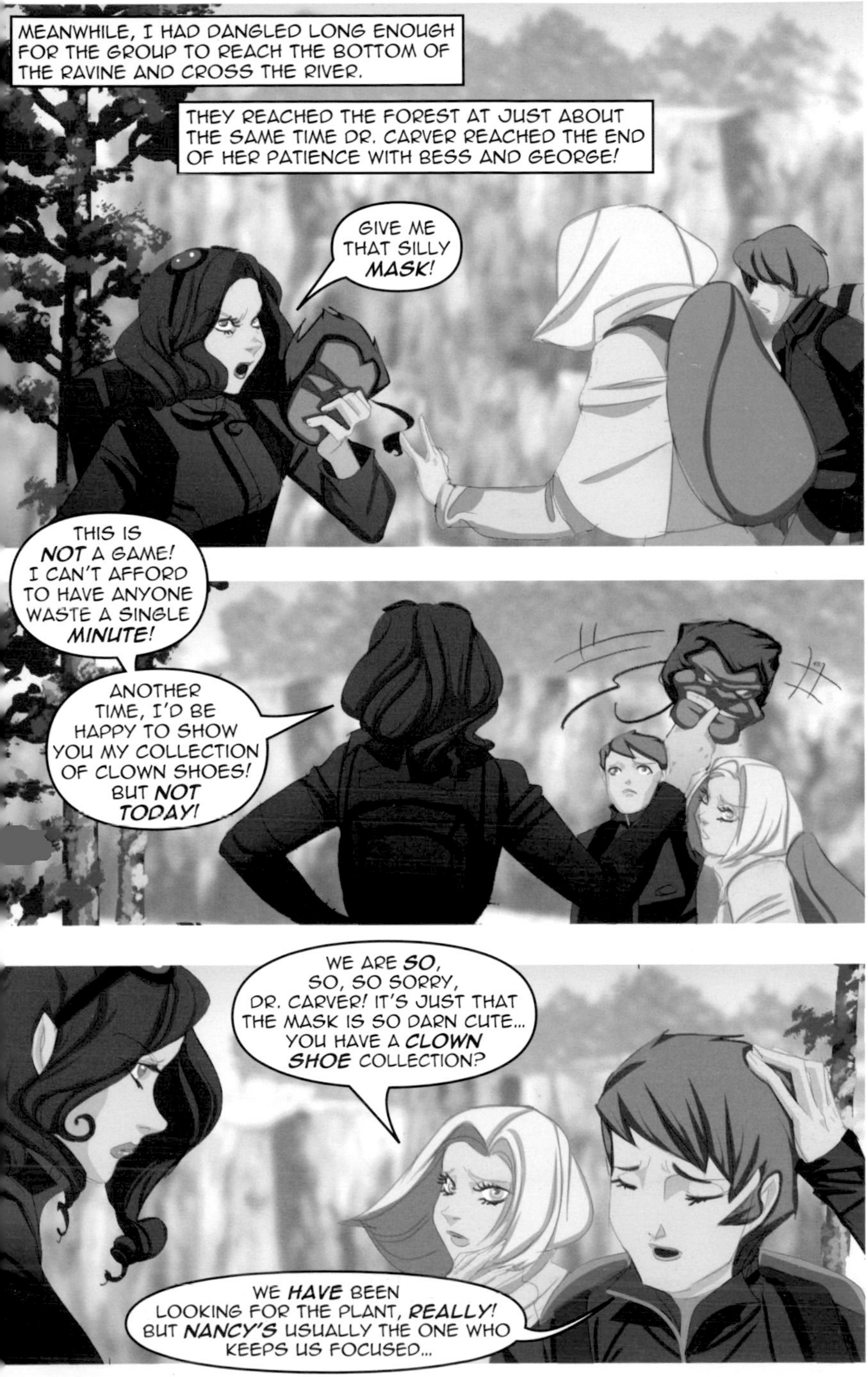
MEANWHILE, I HAD DANGLED LONG ENOUGH FOR THE GROUP TO REACH THE BOTTOM OF THE RAVINE AND CROSS THE RIVER.
THEY REACHED THE FOREST AT JUST ABOUT THE SAME TIME DR. CARVER REACHED THE END OF HER PATIENCE WITH BESS AND GEORGE!
GIVE ME THAT SILLY MASK!
THIS IS NOT A GAME! I CAN'T AFFORD TO HAVE ANYONE WASTE A SINGLE MINUTE!
ANOTHER TIME, I'D BE HAPPY TO SHOW YOU MY COLLECTION OF CLOWN SHOES! BUT NOT TODAY!
WE ARE SO, SO, SO SORRY, DR. CARVER! IT'S JUST THAT THE MASK IS SO DARN CUTE... YOU HAVE A CLOWN SHOE COLLECTION?
WE HAVE BEEN LOOKING FOR THE PLANT, REALLY! BUT NANCY'S USUALLY THE ONE WHO KEEPS US FOCUSED...

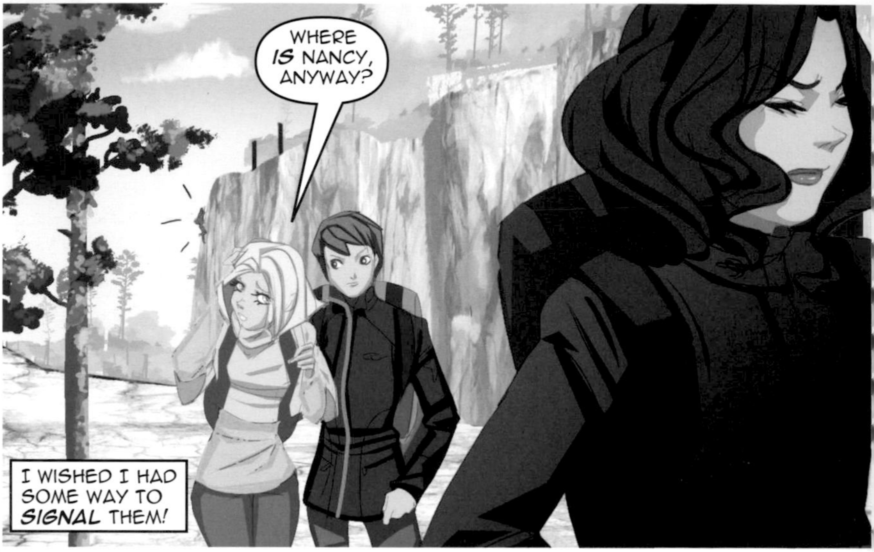
WHERE *IS* NANCY, ANYWAY?
I WISHED I HAD SOME WAY TO *SIGNAL* THEM!

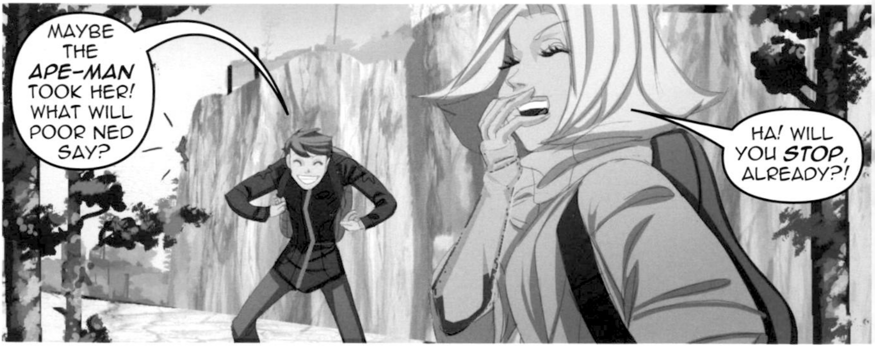
MAYBE THE *APE-MAN* TOOK HER! WHAT WILL POOR NED SAY?
HA! WILL YOU *STOP*, ALREADY?!

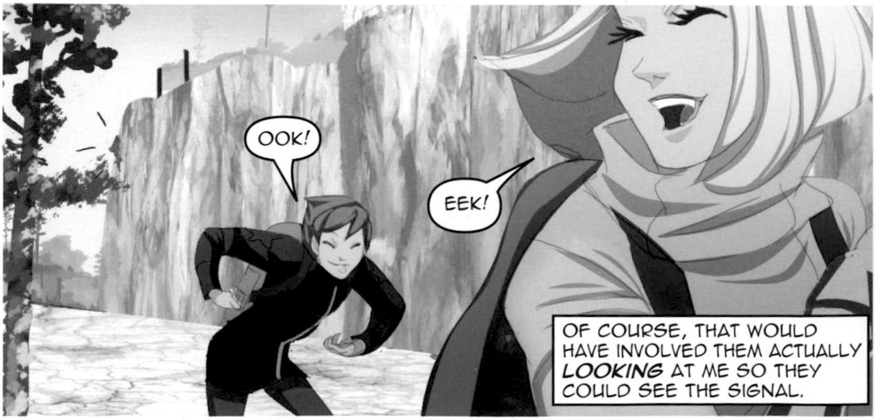
OOK!
EEK!
OF COURSE, THAT WOULD HAVE INVOLVED THEM ACTUALLY *LOOKING* AT ME SO THEY COULD SEE THE SIGNAL.

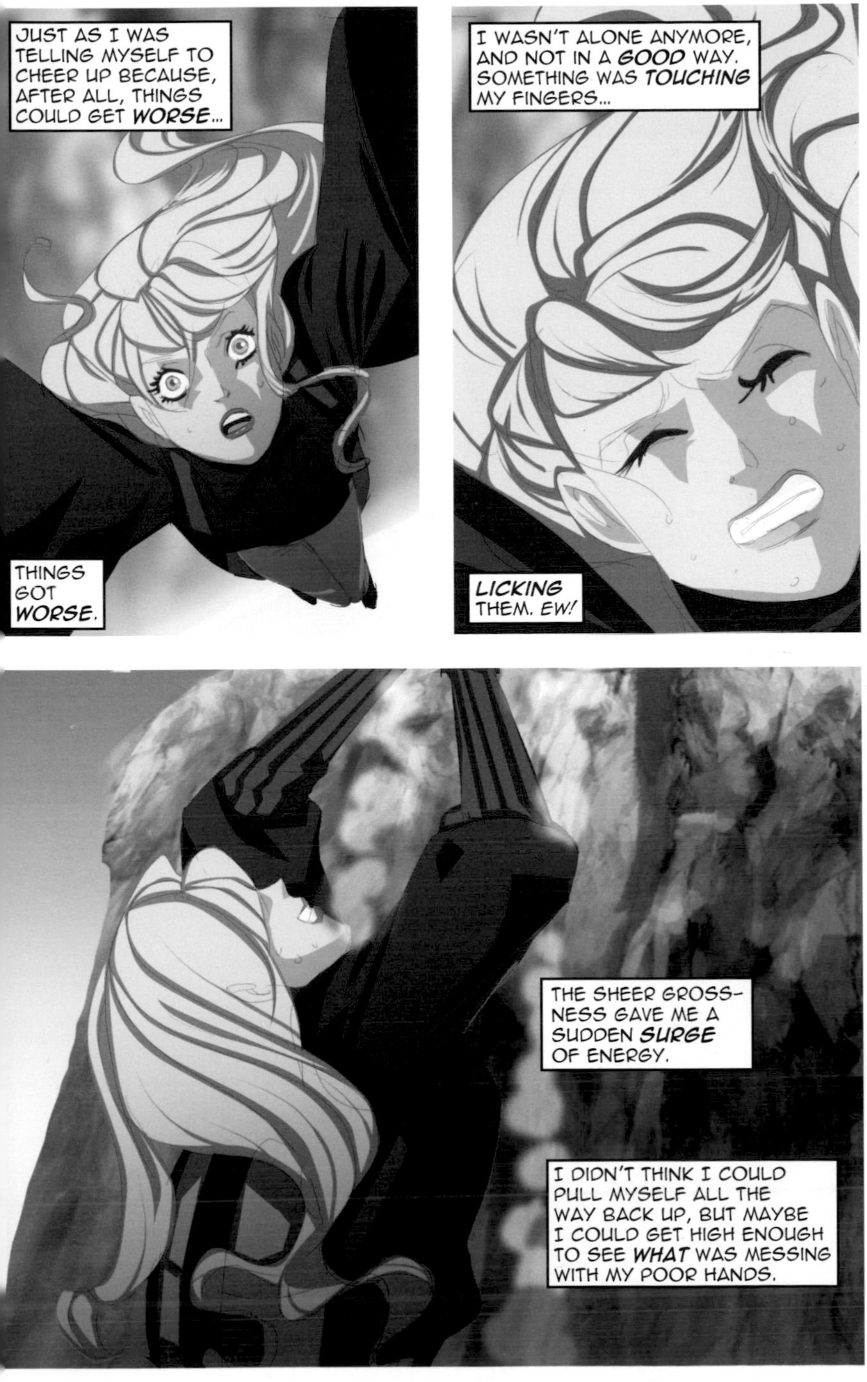
JUST AS I WAS TELLING MYSELF TO CHEER UP BECAUSE, AFTER ALL, THINGS COULD GET WORSE...
THINGS GOT WORSE.
I WASN'T ALONE ANYMORE, AND NOT IN A GOOD WAY. SOMETHING WAS TOUCHING MY FINGERS...
LICKING THEM. EW!
THE SHEER GROSS-NESS GAVE ME A SUDDEN SURGE OF ENERGY.
I DIDN'T THINK I COULD PULL MYSELF ALL THE WAY BACK UP, BUT MAYBE I COULD GET HIGH ENOUGH TO SEE WHAT WAS MESSING WITH MY POOR HANDS.

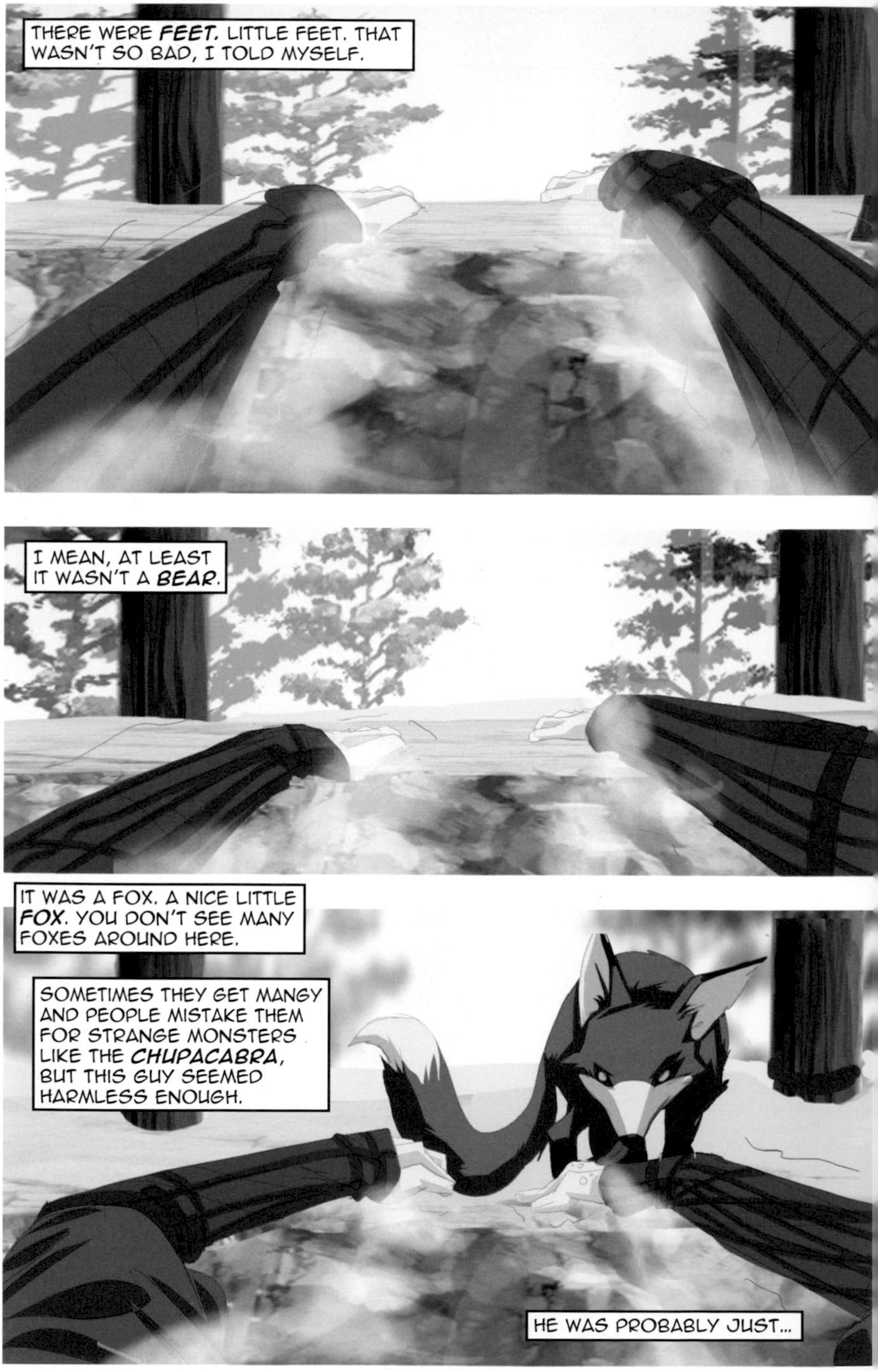
THERE WERE FEET. LITTLE FEET. THAT WASN'T SO BAD, I TOLD MYSELF.
I MEAN, AT LEAST IT WASN'T A BEAR.
IT WAS A FOX. A NICE LITTLE FOX. YOU DON'T SEE MANY FOXES AROUND HERE.
SOMETIMES THEY GET MANGY AND PEOPLE MISTAKE THEM FOR STRANGE MONSTERS LIKE THE CHUPACABRA, BUT THIS GUY SEEMED HARMLESS ENOUGH.
HE WAS PROBABLY JUST...

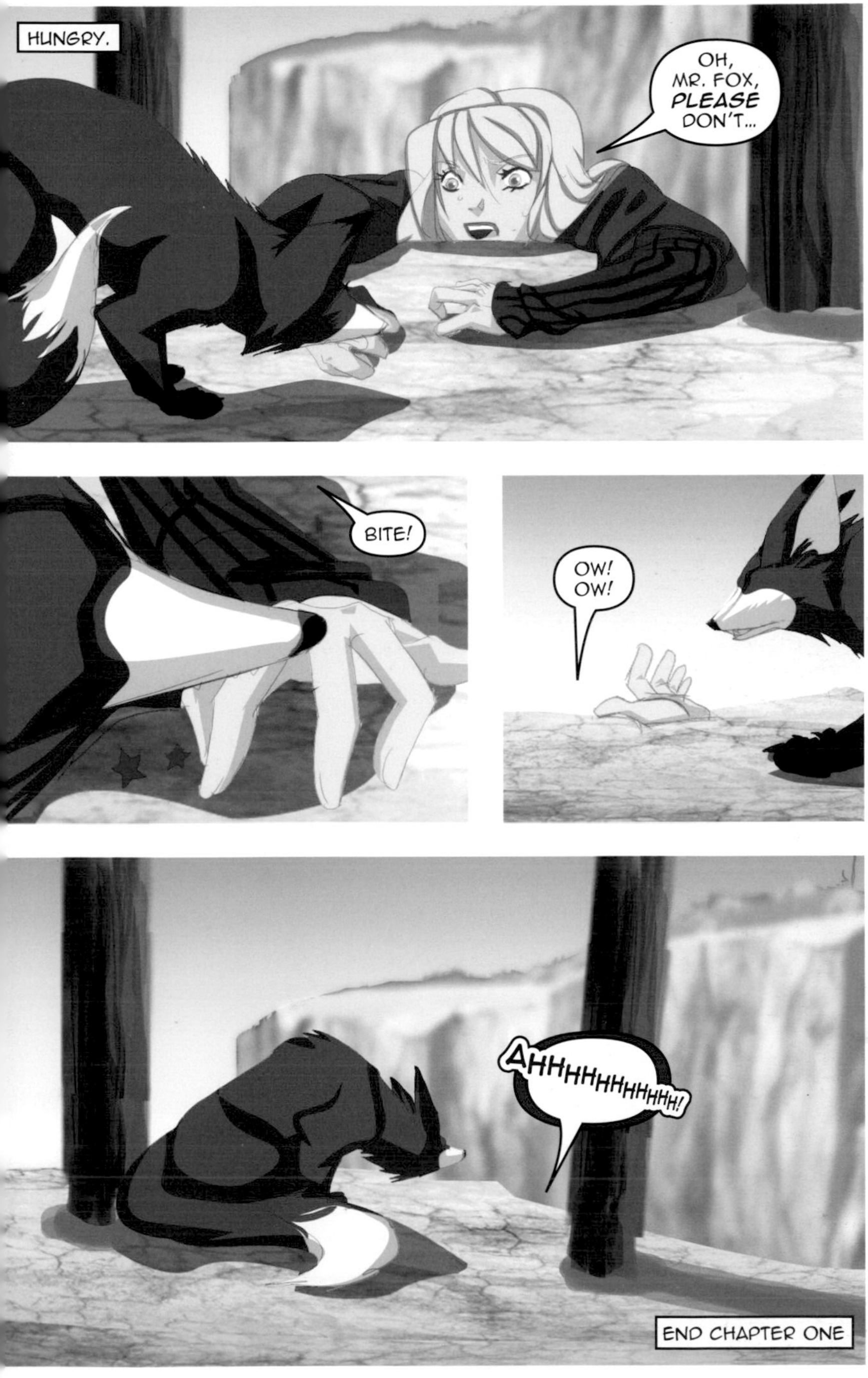
HUNGRY.
OH, MR. FOX, PLEASE DON'T...
BITE!
OW! OW!
AHHHHHHHHHHH!
END CHAPTER ONE

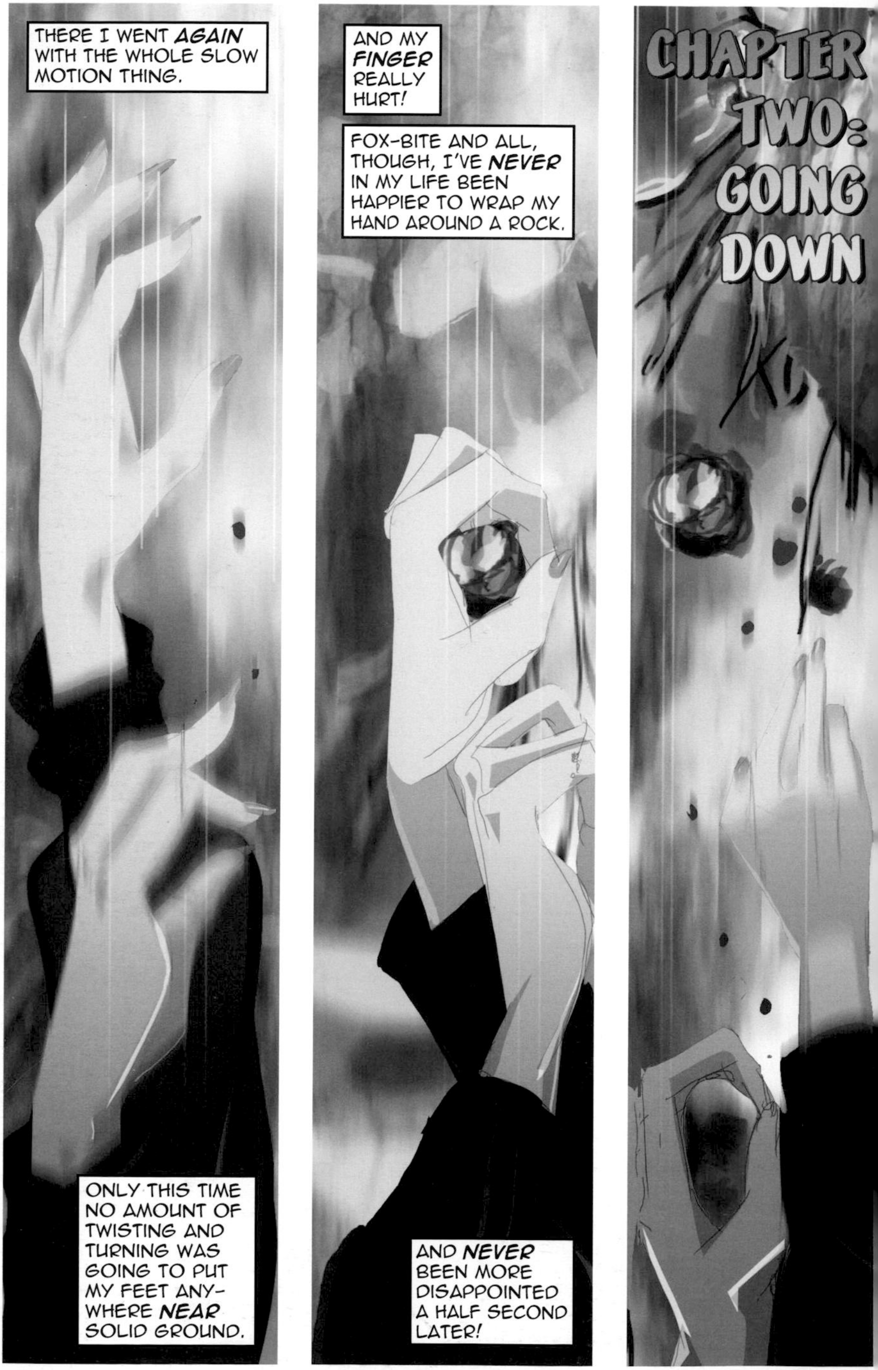
THERE I WENT AGAIN WITH THE WHOLE SLOW MOTION THING.
ONLY THIS TIME NO AMOUNT OF TWISTING AND TURNING WAS GOING TO PUT MY FEET ANY-WHERE NEAR SOLID GROUND.
AND MY FINGER REALLY HURT!
FOX-BITE AND ALL, THOUGH, I'VE NEVER IN MY LIFE BEEN HAPPIER TO WRAP MY HAND AROUND A ROCK.
AND NEVER BEEN MORE DISAPPOINTED A HALF SECOND LATER!
CHAPTER TWO: GOING DOWN

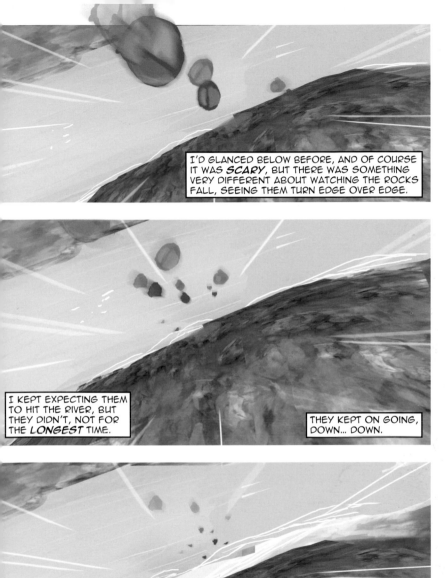

I'D GLANCED BELOW BEFORE, AND OF COURSE IT WAS *SCARY*, BUT THERE WAS SOMETHING VERY DIFFERENT ABOUT WATCHING THE ROCKS FALL, SEEING THEM TURN EDGE OVER EDGE.

I KEPT EXPECTING THEM TO HIT THE RIVER, BUT THEY DIDN'T, NOT FOR THE *LONGEST* TIME.

THEY KEPT ON GOING, DOWN... DOWN.

WHEN THEY FINALLY DID HIT, BARELY PEBBLES, AND MADE A SPLASH I COULDN'T EVEN HEAR, I *FELT* IT, FIRST IN MY STOMACH THEN IN MY WHOLE BODY.

AS I WAS FINALLY REALIZING THOSE ROCKS WERE GOING TO BE *ME*.

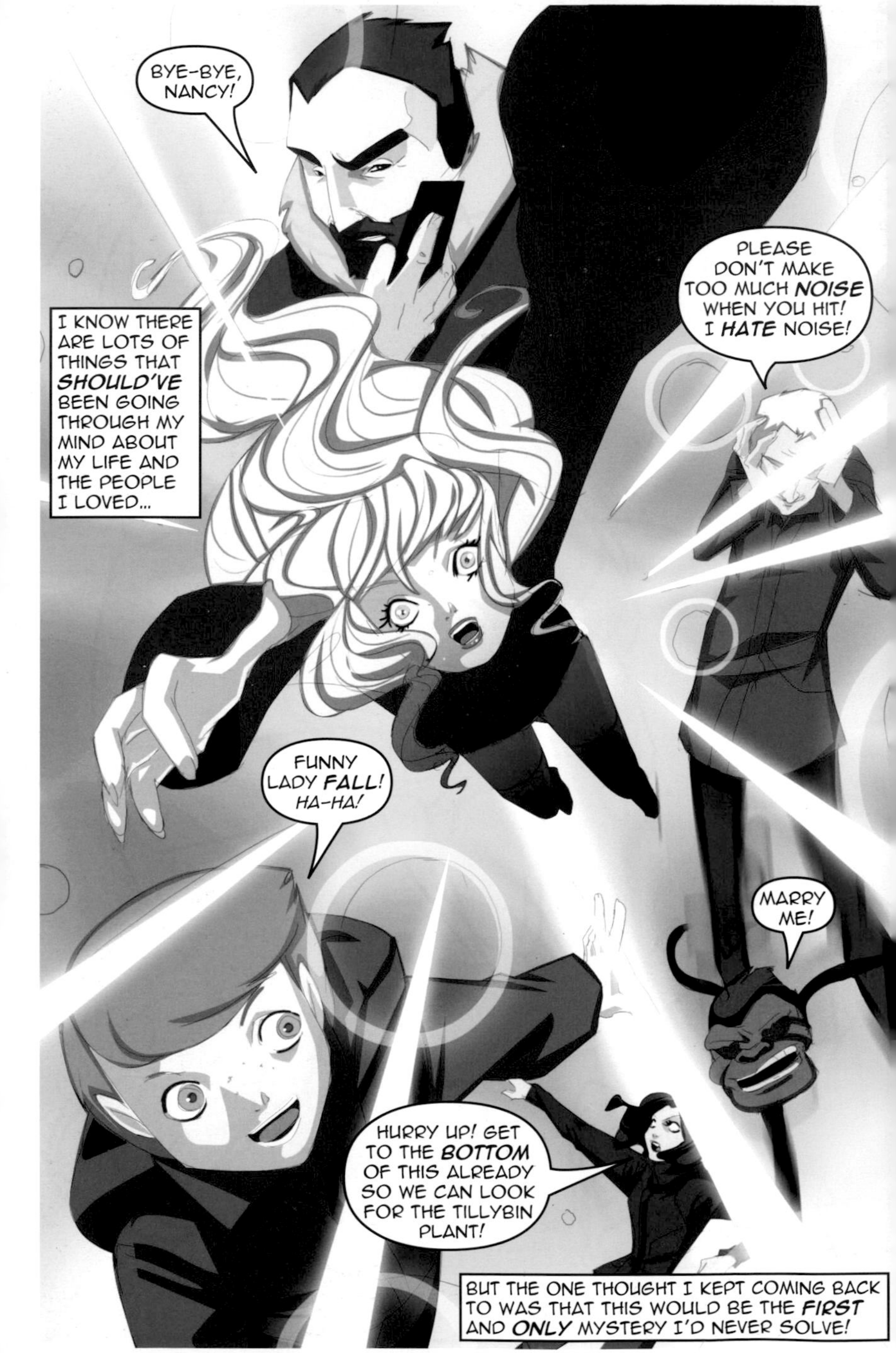
BYE-BYE, NANCY!
I KNOW THERE ARE LOTS OF THINGS THAT SHOULD'VE BEEN GOING THROUGH MY MIND ABOUT MY LIFE AND THE PEOPLE I LOVED...
PLEASE DON'T MAKE TOO MUCH NOISE WHEN YOU HIT! I HATE NOISE!
FUNNY LADY FALL! HA-HA!
MARRY ME!
HURRY UP! GET TO THE BOTTOM OF THIS ALREADY SO WE CAN LOOK FOR THE TILLYBIN PLANT!
BUT THE ONE THOUGHT I KEPT COMING BACK TO WAS THAT THIS WOULD BE THE FIRST AND ONLY MYSTERY I'D NEVER SOLVE!

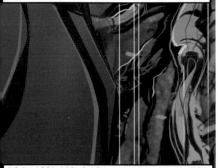

TURNS OUT THAT EVEN WHEN YOU'RE THINKING ABOUT SOMETHING ELSE, YOUR BODY CAN STILL ACT ALL ON ITS OWN.

FOR INSTANCE, I REALLY, REALLY WANTED TO HOLD ONTO THE LEDGE WHEN THE FOX BIT ME, BUT MY BODY JUST SAID *NO*.

THIS IS CALLED A *SOMATIC REFLEX.*

WHEN YOUR NERVES SENSE SOMETHING THAT NEEDS A REALLY *QUICK* RESPONSE, YOUR SPINAL CORD CAN MAKE YOUR MUSCLES MOVE BEFORE YOUR BRAIN EVEN KNOWS ABOUT IT!

SOMETIMES THAT DOESN'T WORK OUT TO YOUR BEST ADVANTAGE.

BUT SOMETIMES, IT *DOES!*

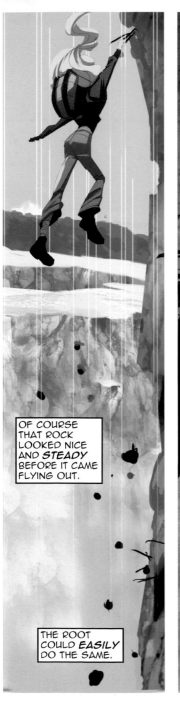

AND IT DIDN'T LOOK LIKE THERE WAS ANYTHING ELSE FOR ME *OR* MY SOMATIC REFLEXES TO GRAB ONTO.

OF COURSE THAT ROCK LOOKED NICE AND *STEADY* BEFORE IT CAME FLYING OUT.

THE ROOT COULD *EASILY* DO THE SAME.

FORTUNATELY ROOTS ARE MORE *FLEXIBLE* THAN ROCKS. THEY BEND A LOT BEFORE THEY BREAK.

EVEN IF THIS ONE WAS A LITTLE ON THE *SHARP* SIDE, REALLY, I HAD *NOTHING* TO COMPLAIN ABOUT.

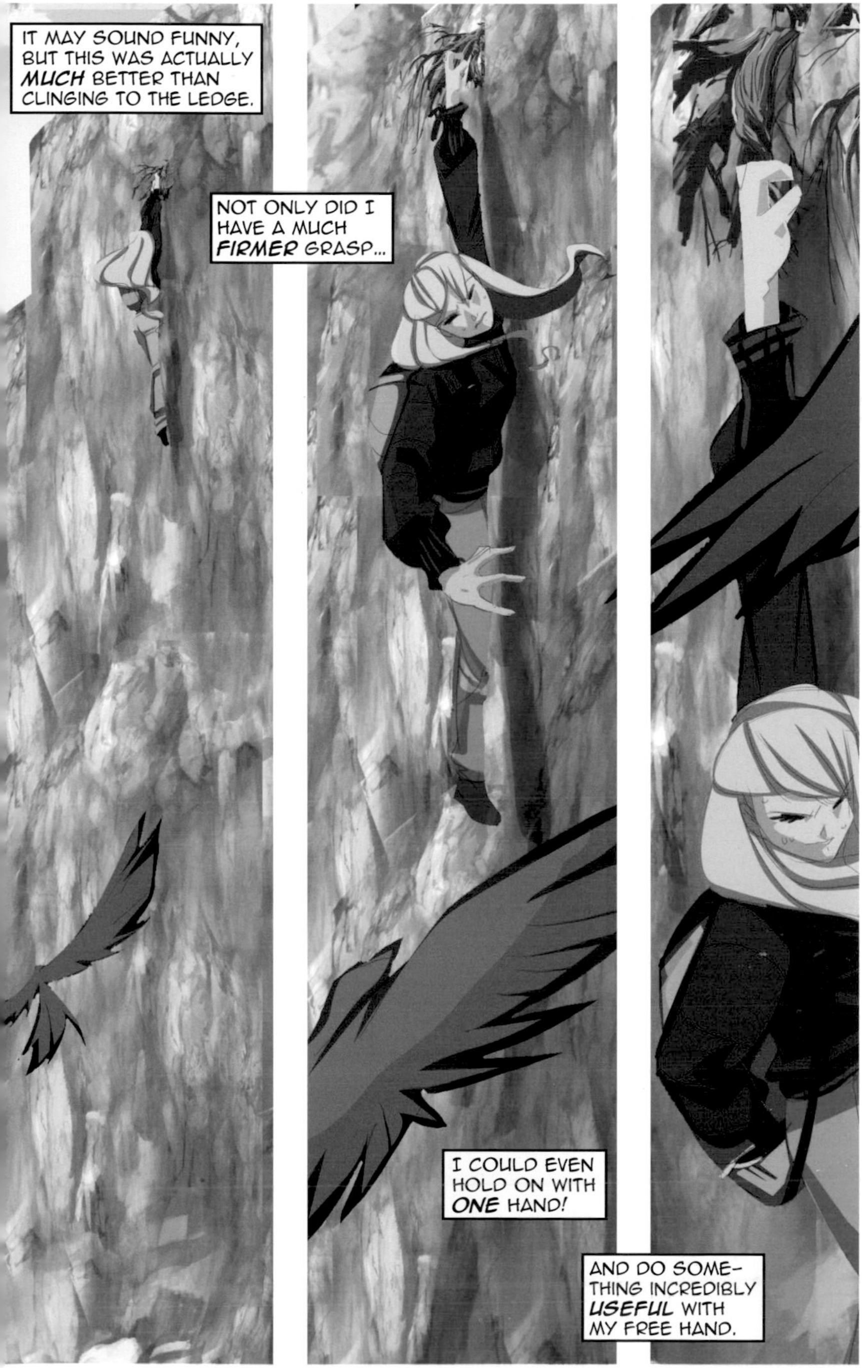
IT MAY SOUND FUNNY, BUT THIS WAS ACTUALLY MUCH BETTER THAN CLINGING TO THE LEDGE.
NOT ONLY DID I HAVE A MUCH FIRMER GRASP...
I COULD EVEN HOLD ON WITH ONE HAND!
AND DO SOME-THING INCREDIBLY USEFUL WITH MY FREE HAND.

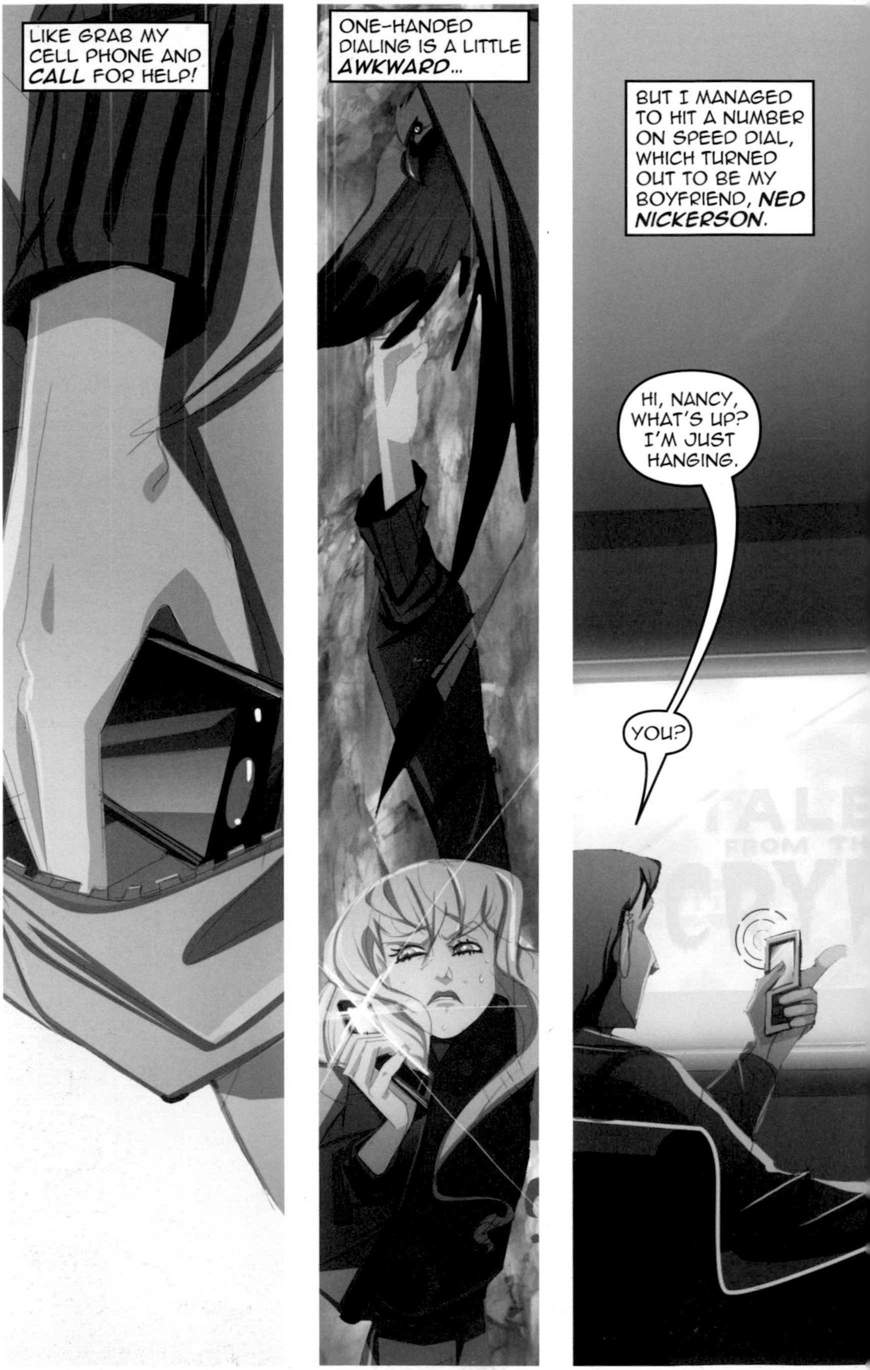
LIKE GRAB MY CELL PHONE AND CALL FOR HELP!
ONE-HANDED DIALING IS A LITTLE AWKWARD...
BUT I MANAGED TO HIT A NUMBER ON SPEED DIAL, WHICH TURNED OUT TO BE MY BOYFRIEND, NED NICKERSON.
HI, NANCY, WHAT'S UP? I'M JUST HANGING.
YOU?

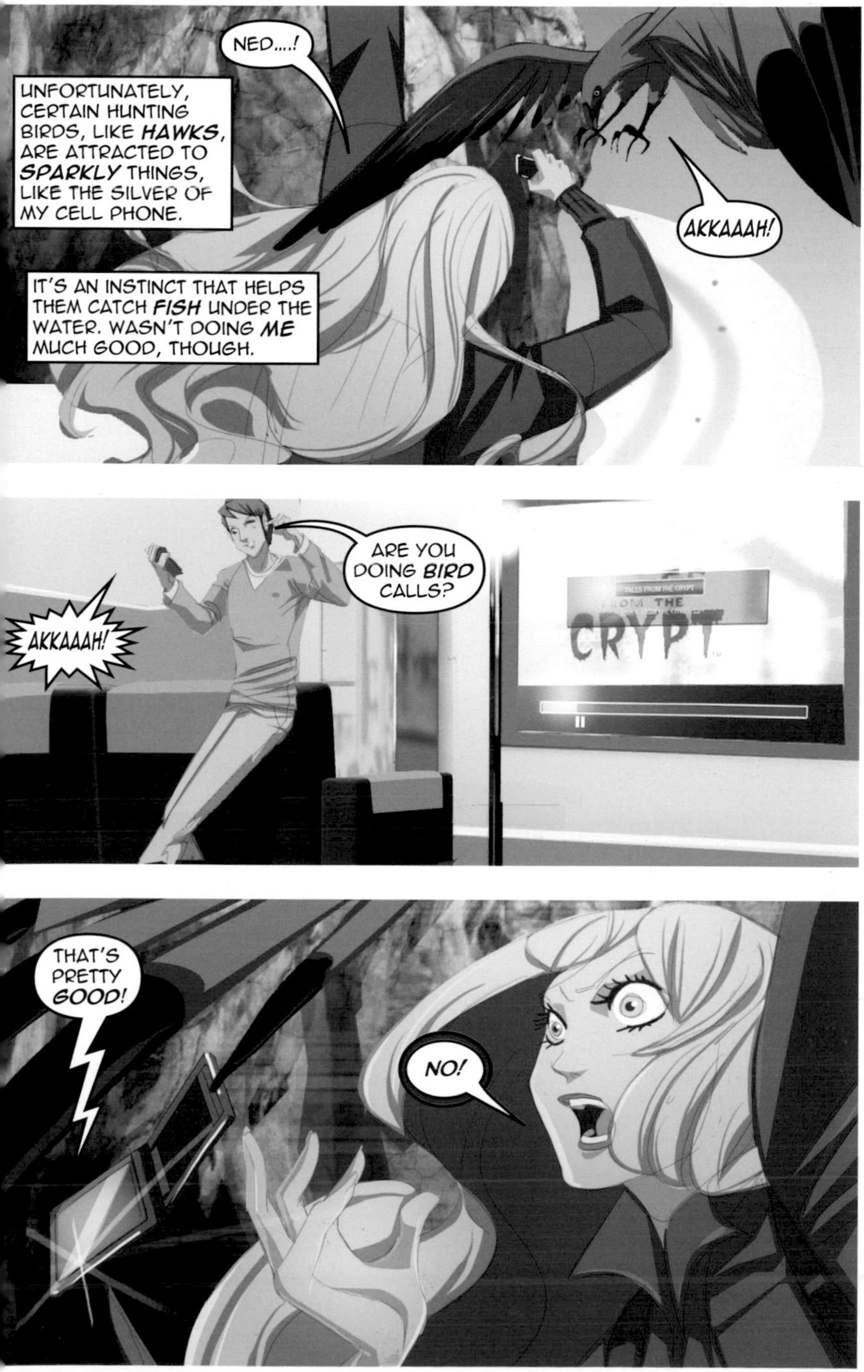
NED....!
UNFORTUNATELY, CERTAIN HUNTING BIRDS, LIKE HAWKS, ARE ATTRACTED TO SPARKLY THINGS, LIKE THE SILVER OF MY CELL PHONE.
AKKAAAH!
IT'S AN INSTINCT THAT HELPS THEM CATCH FISH UNDER THE WATER. WASN'T DOING ME MUCH GOOD, THOUGH.
AKKAAAH!
ARE YOU DOING BIRD CALLS?
FROM THE CRYPT
THAT'S PRETTY GOOD!
NO!

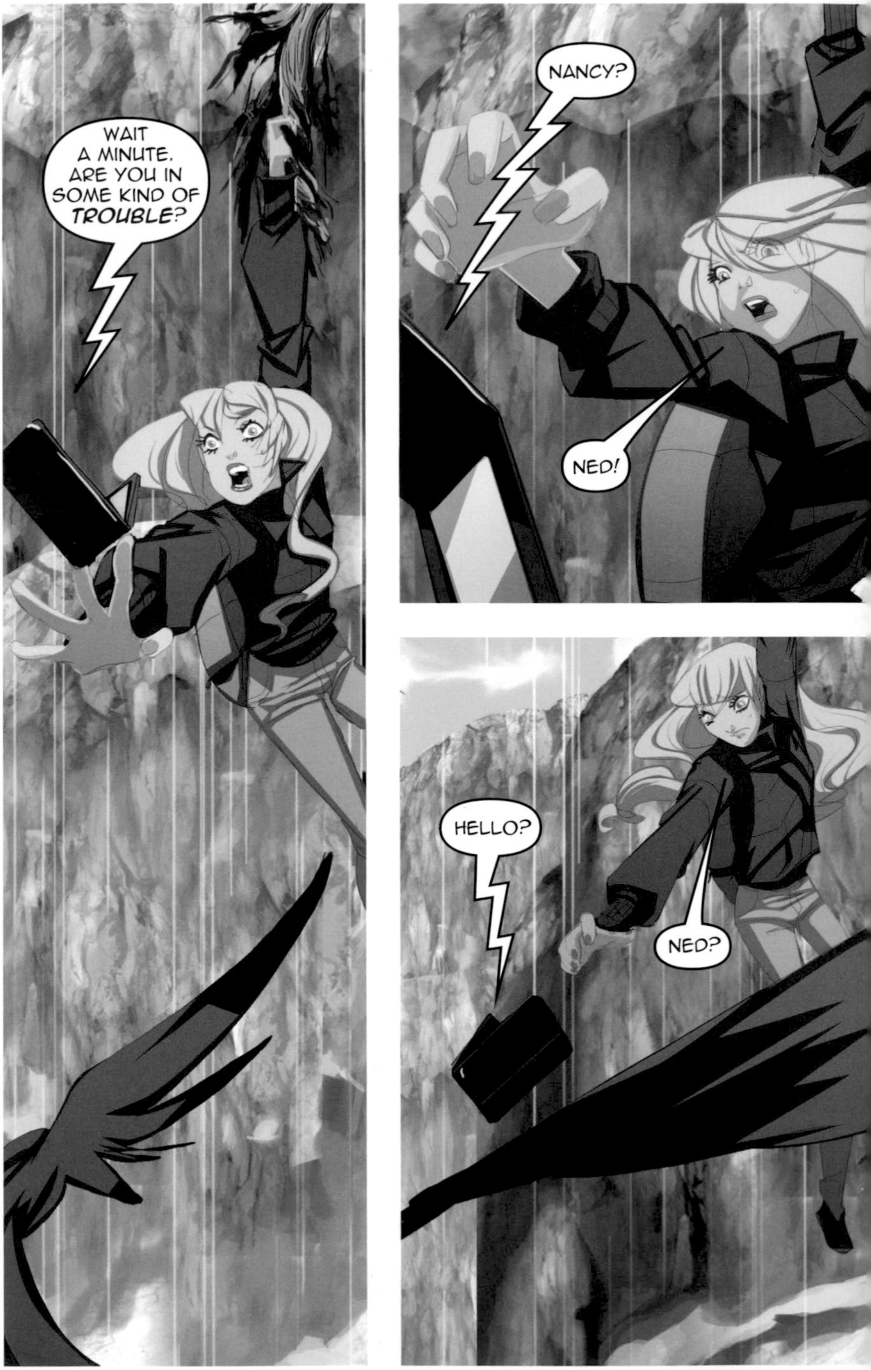
WAIT A MINUTE. ARE YOU IN SOME KIND OF *TROUBLE*?
NANCY?
NED!
HELLO?
NED?

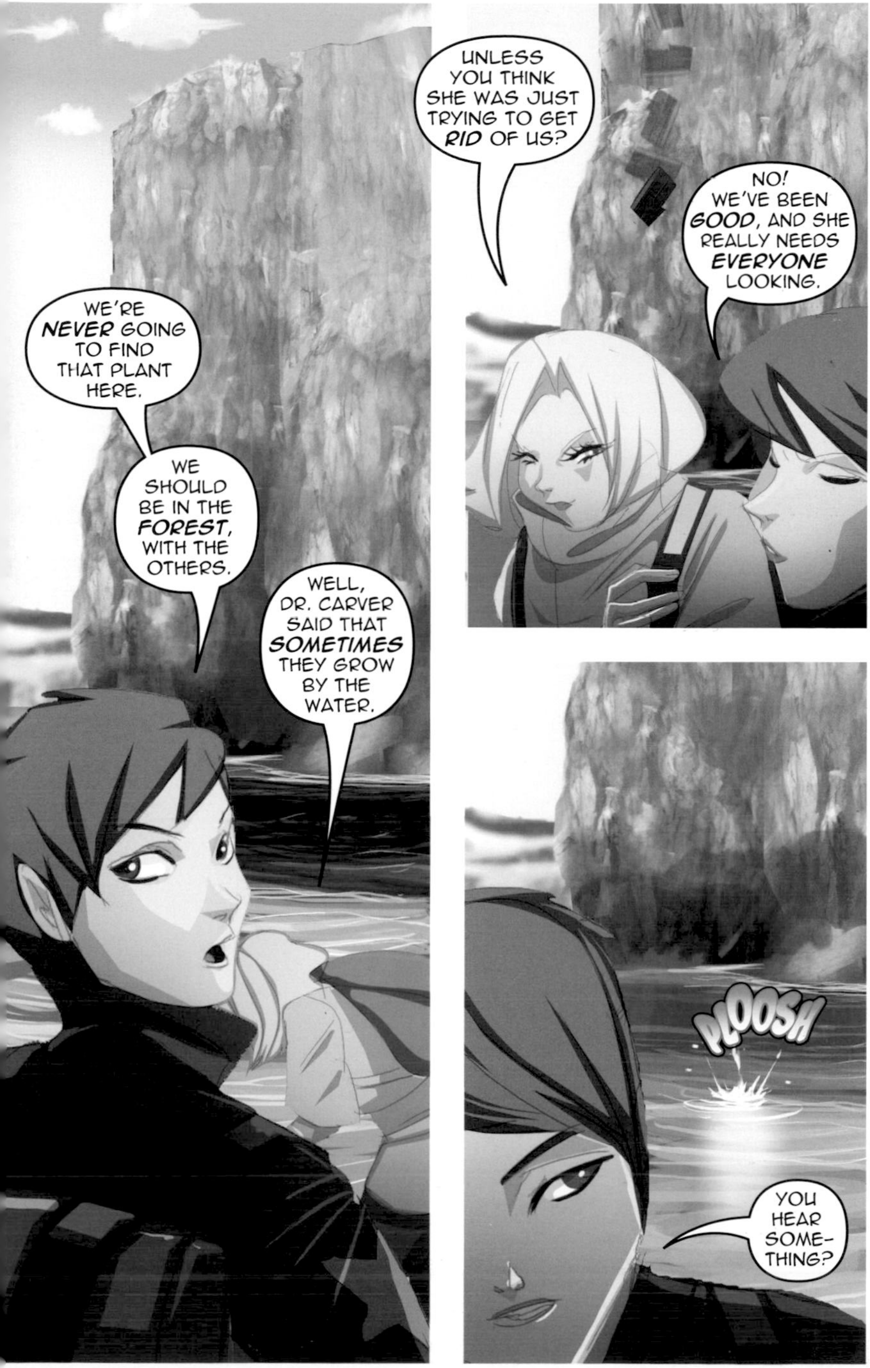
WE'RE NEVER GOING TO FIND THAT PLANT HERE.
WE SHOULD BE IN THE FOREST, WITH THE OTHERS.
WELL, DR. CARVER SAID THAT SOMETIMES THEY GROW BY THE WATER.
UNLESS YOU THINK SHE WAS JUST TRYING TO GET RID OF US?
NO! WE'VE BEEN GOOD, AND SHE REALLY NEEDS EVERYONE LOOKING.
PLOOSH
YOU HEAR SOME-THING?

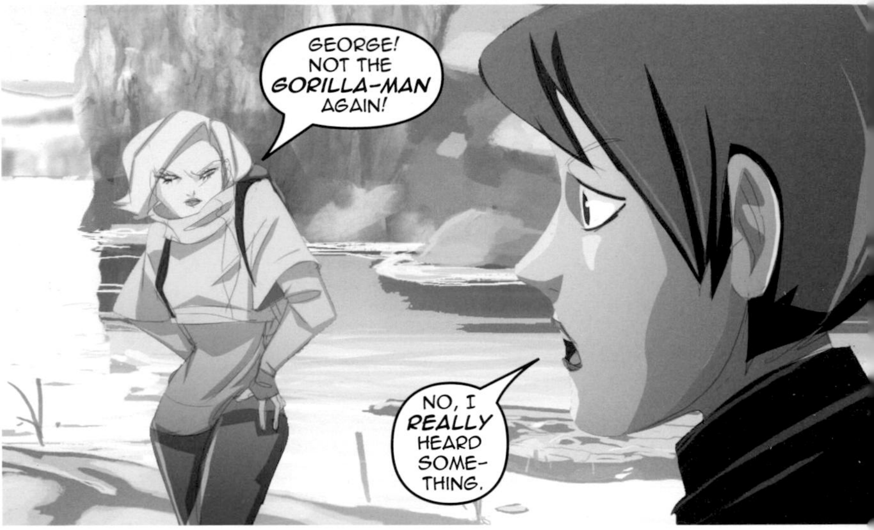
GEORGE! NOT THE GORILLA-MAN AGAIN!
NO, I REALLY HEARD SOME-THING.

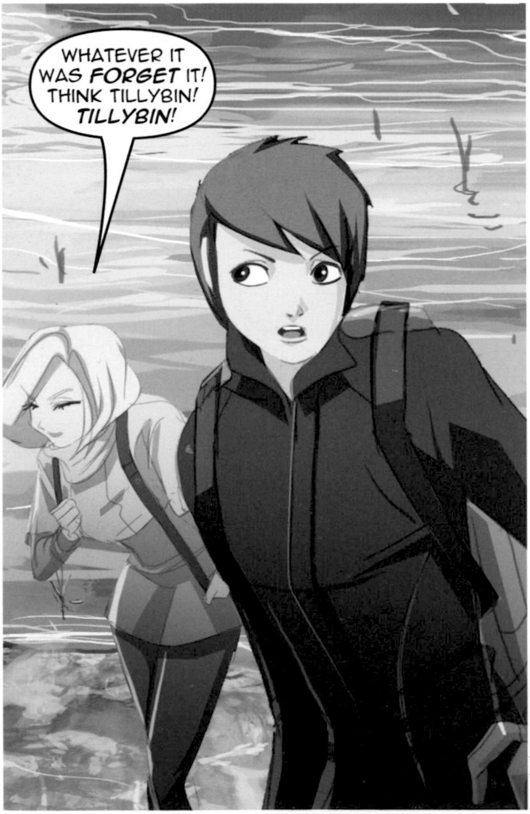
WHATEVER IT WAS FORGET IT! THINK TILLYBIN! TILLYBIN!

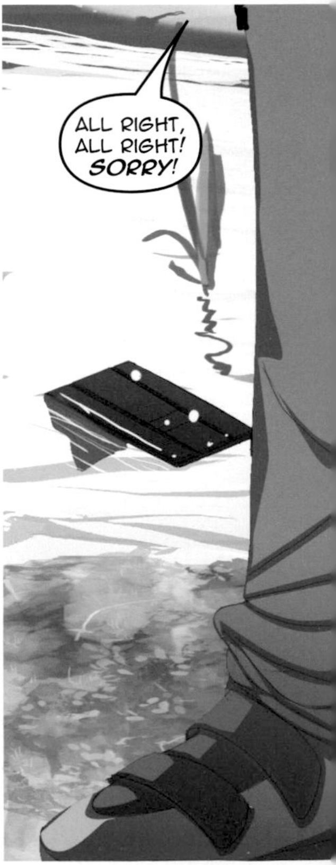
ALL RIGHT, ALL RIGHT! SORRY!

I'M NOT THE TYPE TO *EVER* GIVE UP, BUT LOSING THE CELL PHONE WAS PRETTY DEPRESSING.

MY ARMS WERE *ACHING*, I WAS TIRED, AND REALLY, I HAD *NO* IDEA WHAT I COULD DO NEXT.

THEN I HEARD *SOMETHING* ABOVE, FOOTSTEPS. NOT LIKE A FOX, BUT NOT VERY *HEAVY* EITHER.

AT THAT POINT I REALLY DIDN'T CARE *WHO* IT WAS. I JUST WANTED SOMEONE TO *FIND* ME!

HELLO? HELP?

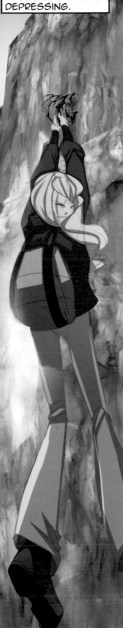

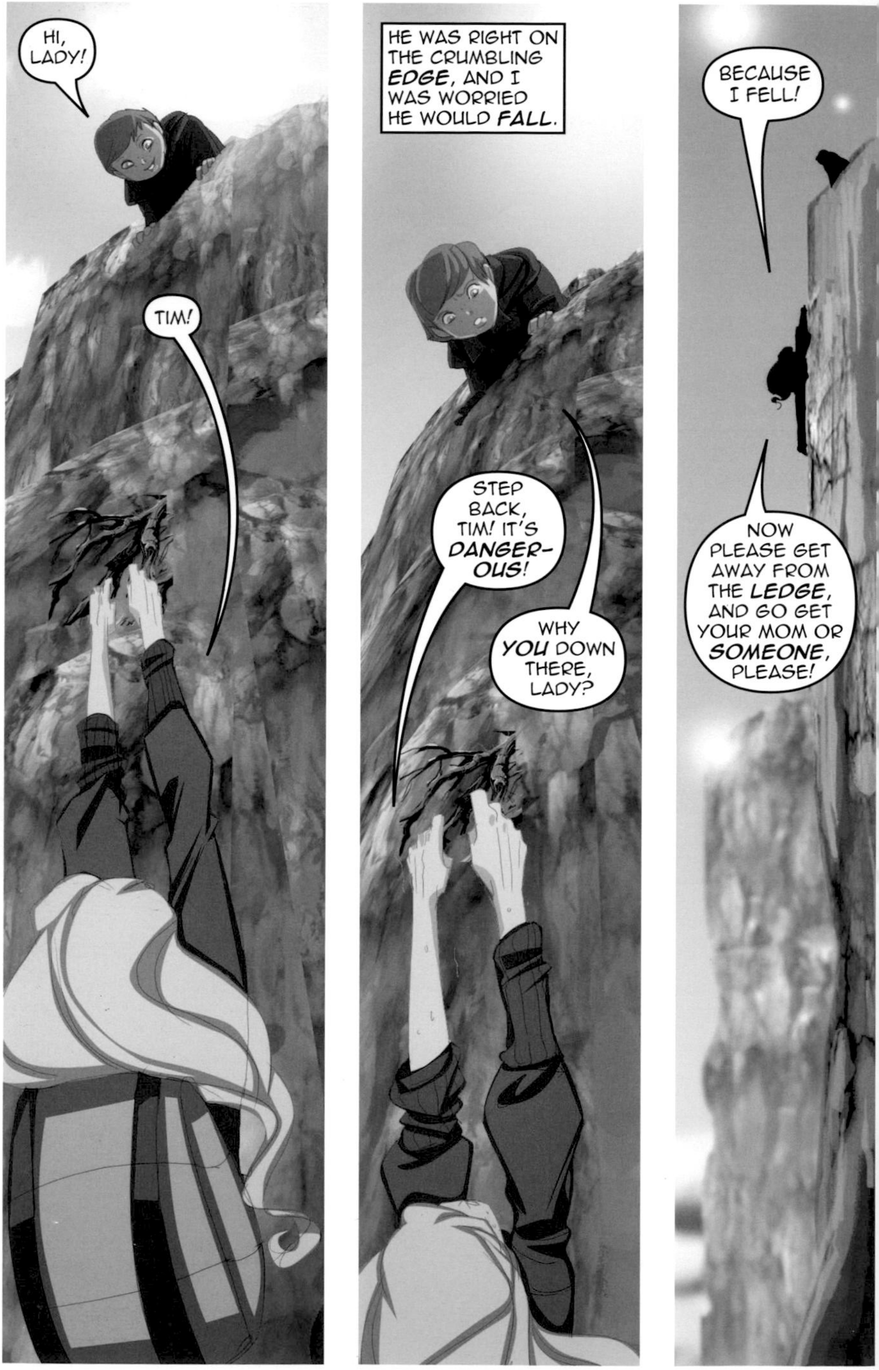
HI, LADY!
TIM!
HE WAS RIGHT ON THE CRUMBLING EDGE, AND I WAS WORRIED HE WOULD FALL.
STEP BACK, TIM! IT'S DANGER-OUS!
WHY YOU DOWN THERE, LADY?
BECAUSE I FELL!
NOW PLEASE GET AWAY FROM THE LEDGE, AND GO GET YOUR MOM OR SOMEONE, PLEASE!

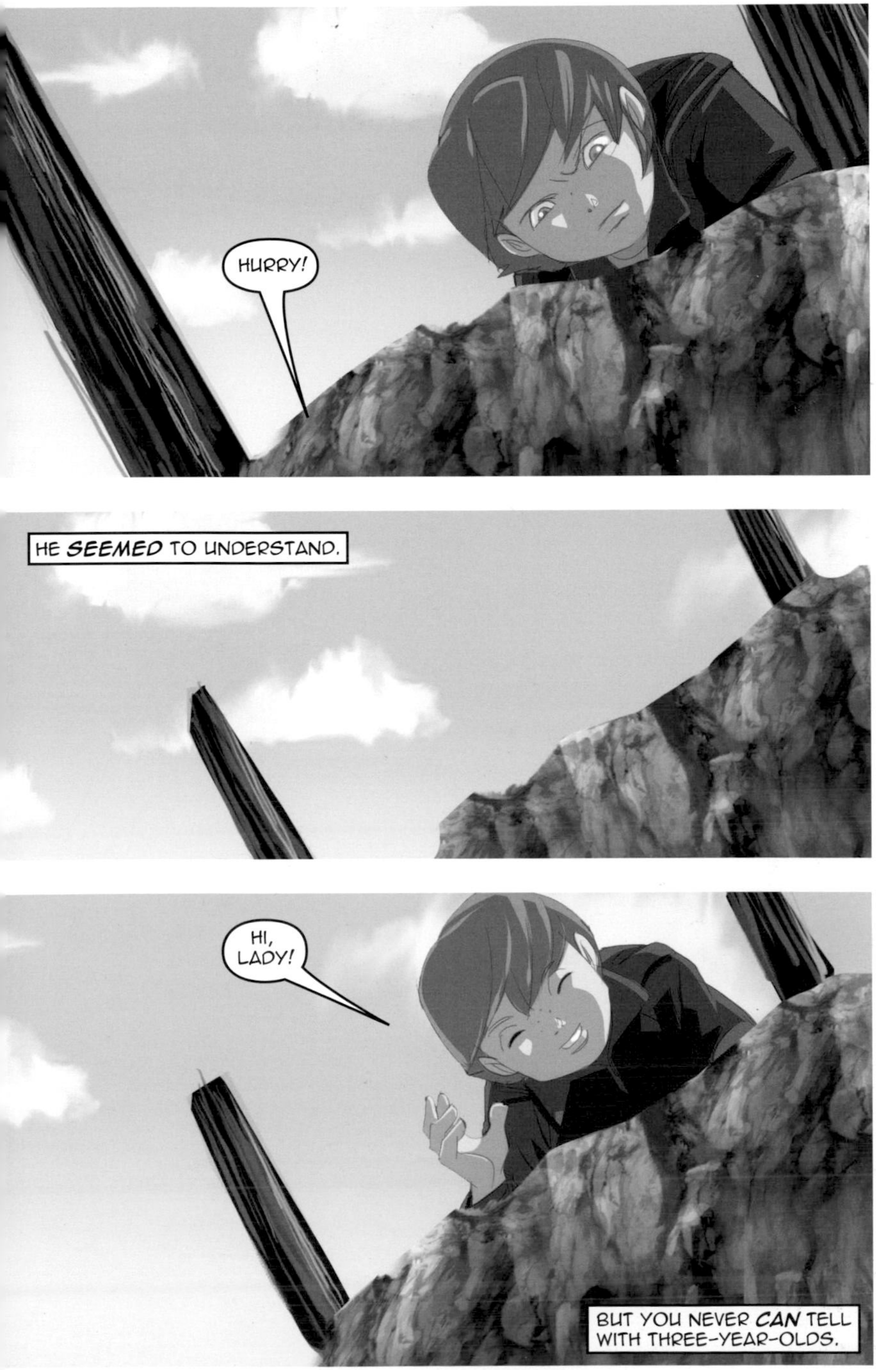
HURRY!
HE SEEMED TO UNDERSTAND.
HI, LADY!
BUT YOU NEVER CAN TELL WITH THREE-YEAR-OLDS.

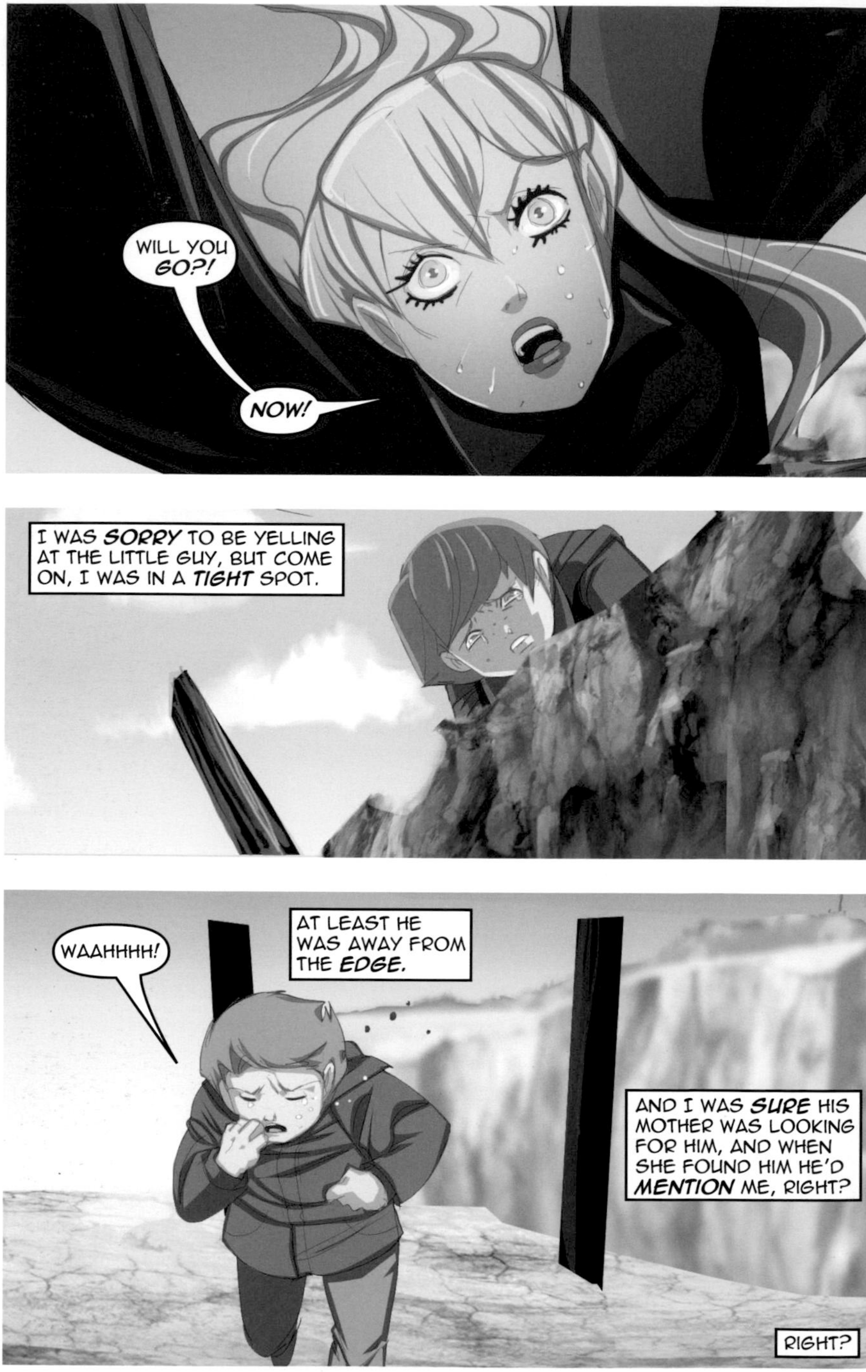
WILL YOU GO?!
NOW!
I WAS SORRY TO BE YELLING AT THE LITTLE GUY, BUT COME ON, I WAS IN A TIGHT SPOT.
WAAHHHH!
AT LEAST HE WAS AWAY FROM THE EDGE.
AND I WAS SURE HIS MOTHER WAS LOOKING FOR HIM, AND WHEN SHE FOUND HIM HE'D MENTION ME, RIGHT?
RIGHT?

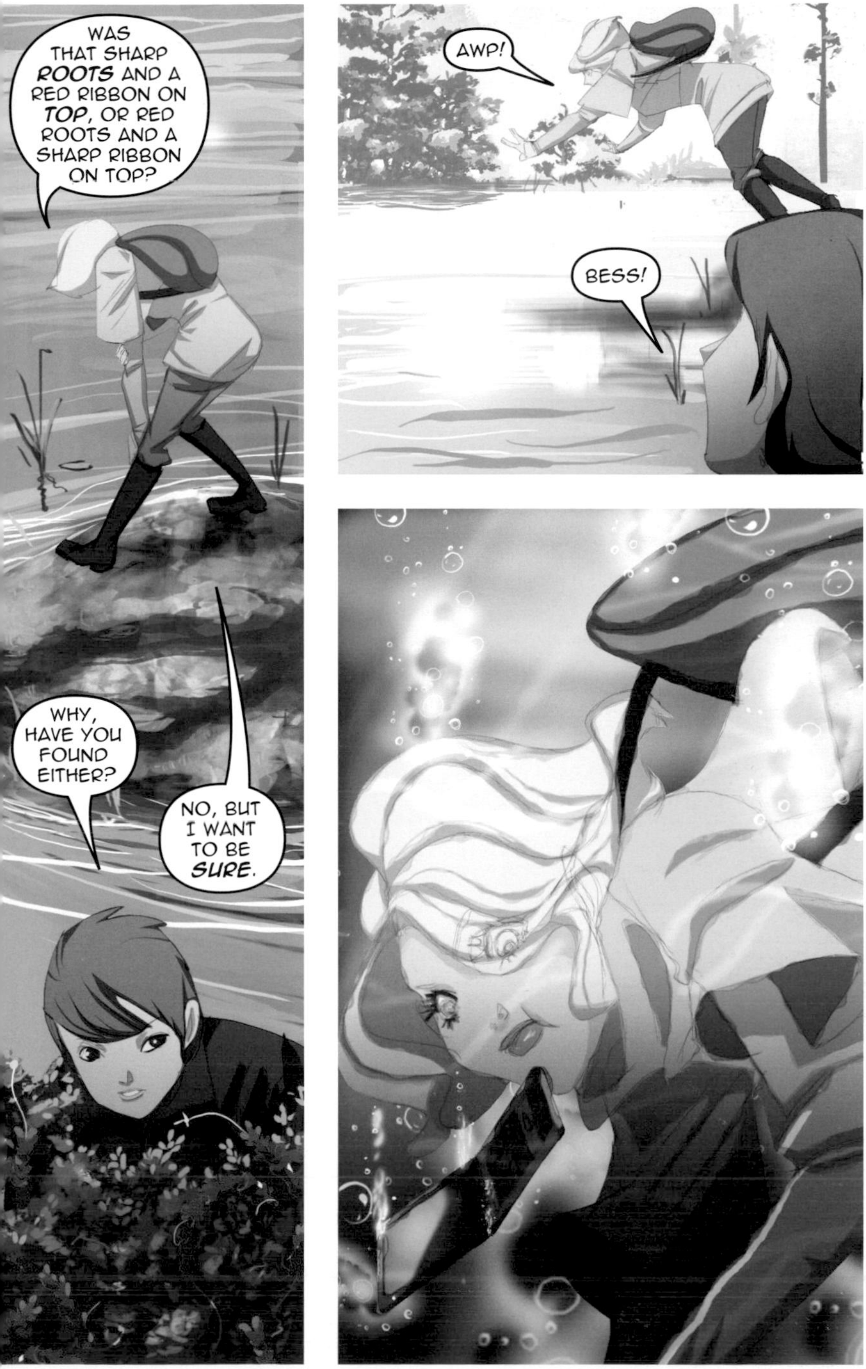
WAS THAT SHARP ROOTS AND A RED RIBBON ON TOP, OR RED ROOTS AND A SHARP RIBBON ON TOP?
AWP!
BESS!
WHY, HAVE YOU FOUND EITHER?
NO, BUT I WANT TO BE SURE.

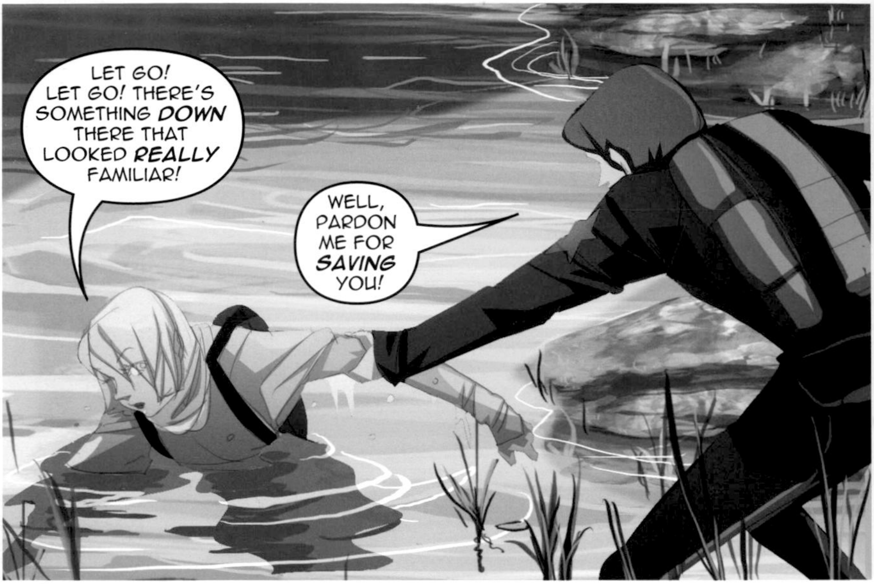
LET GO! LET GO! THERE'S SOMETHING **DOWN** THERE THAT LOOKED **REALLY** FAMILIAR!
WELL, PARDON ME FOR **SAVING** YOU!

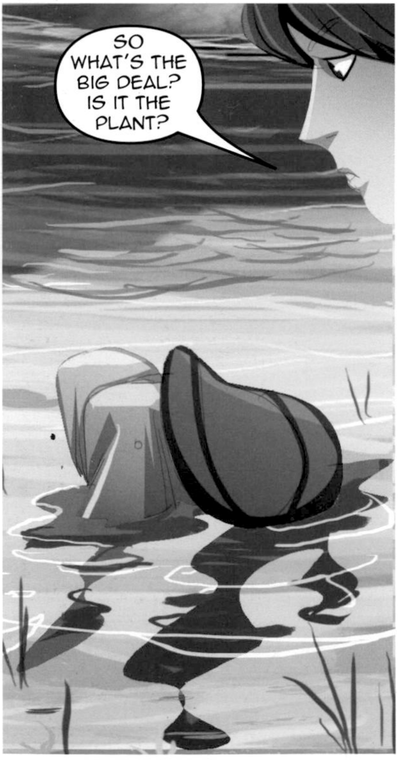
SO WHAT'S THE BIG DEAL? IS IT THE PLANT?

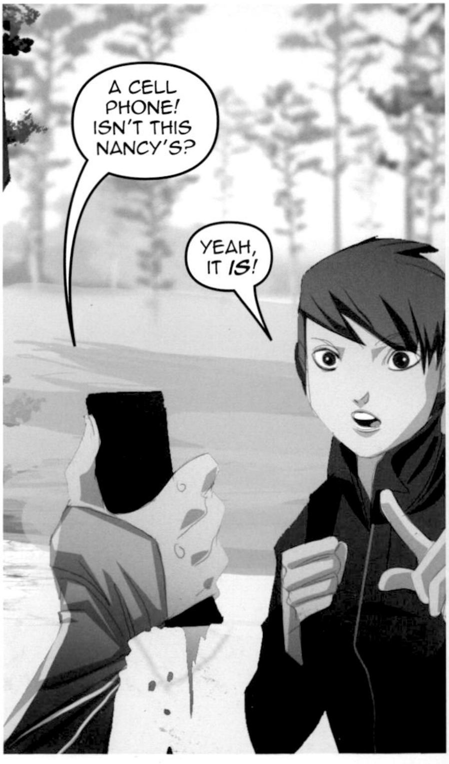
A CELL PHONE! ISN'T THIS NANCY'S?
YEAH, IT **IS**!

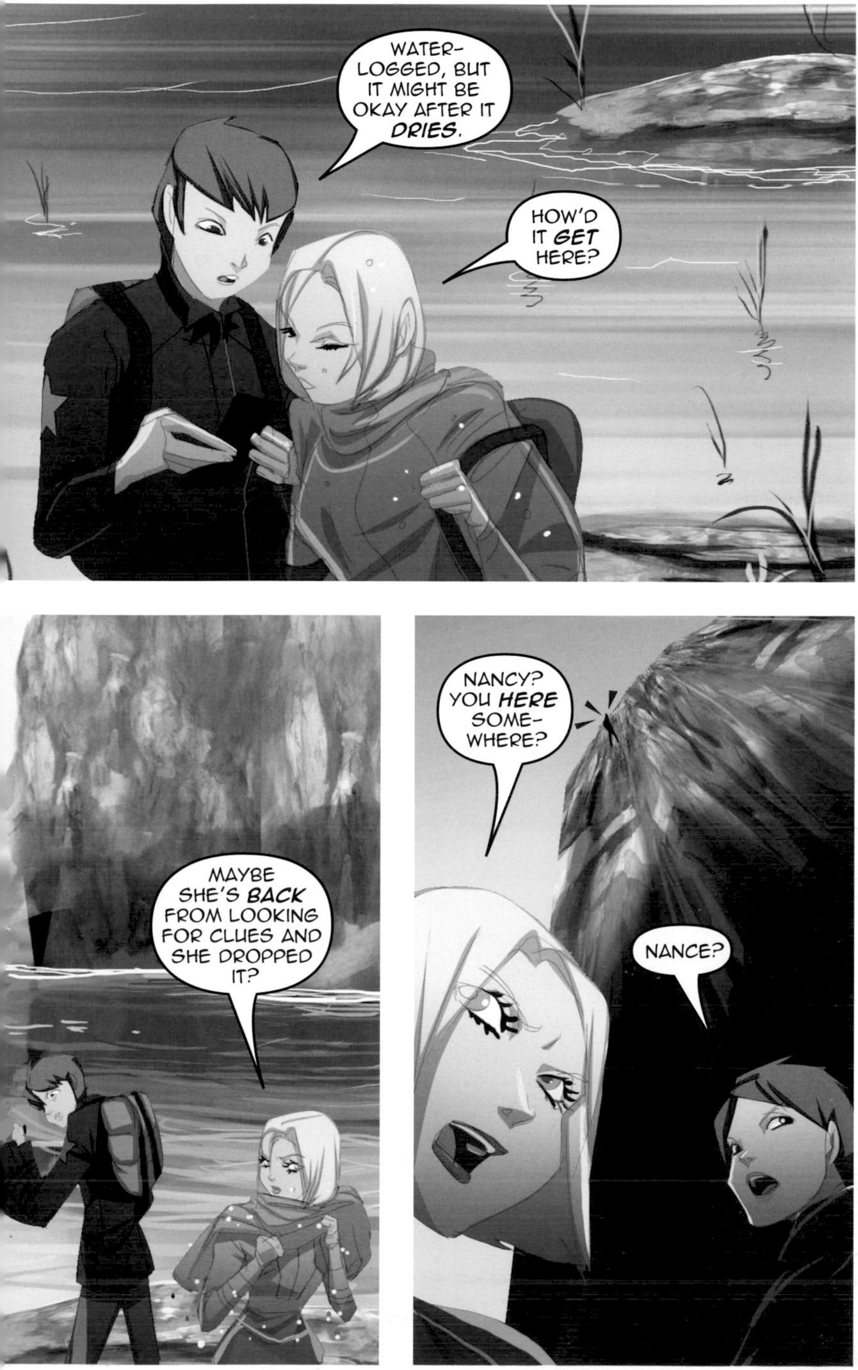
WATER-LOGGED, BUT IT MIGHT BE OKAY AFTER IT DRIES.
HOW'D IT GET HERE?
MAYBE SHE'S BACK FROM LOOKING FOR CLUES AND SHE DROPPED IT?
NANCY? YOU HERE SOME-WHERE?
NANCE?

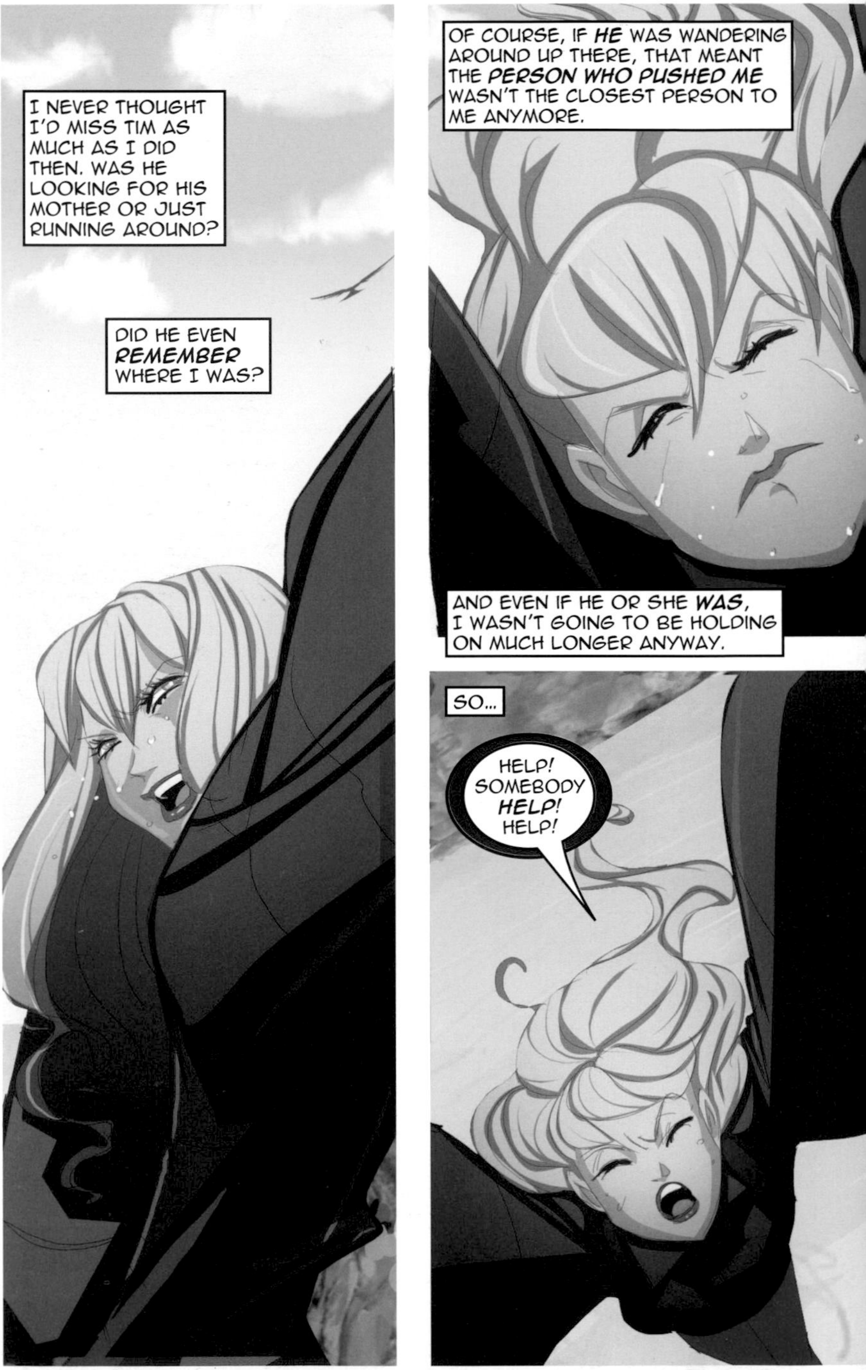
I NEVER THOUGHT I'D MISS TIM AS MUCH AS I DID THEN. WAS HE LOOKING FOR HIS MOTHER OR JUST RUNNING AROUND?
DID HE EVEN ***REMEMBER*** WHERE I WAS?
OF COURSE, IF ***HE*** WAS WANDERING AROUND UP THERE, THAT MEANT THE ***PERSON WHO PUSHED ME*** WASN'T THE CLOSEST PERSON TO ME ANYMORE.
AND EVEN IF HE OR SHE ***WAS***, I WASN'T GOING TO BE HOLDING ON MUCH LONGER ANYWAY.
SO...
HELP! SOMEBODY ***HELP!*** HELP!

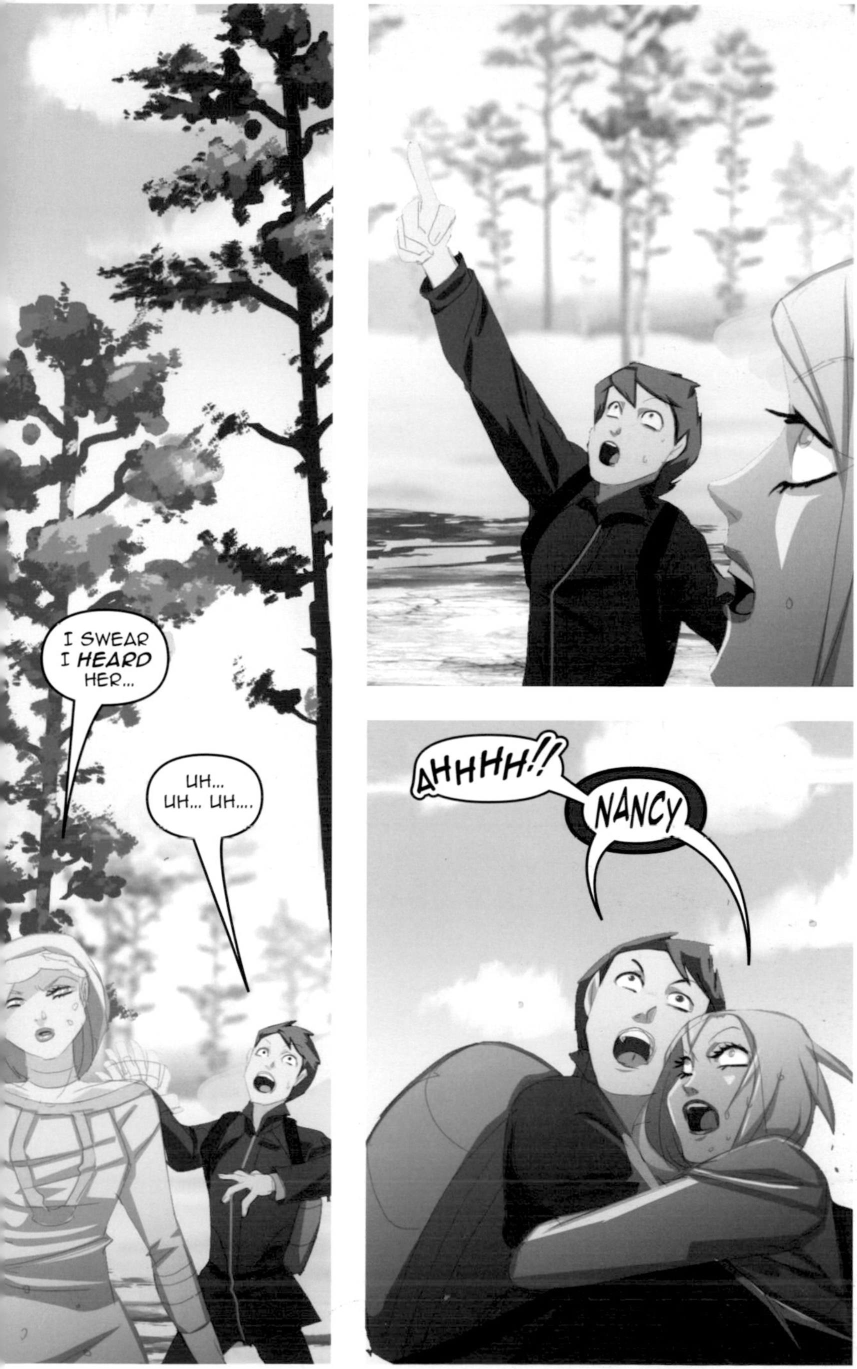
I SWEAR I **HEARD** HER...
UH... UH... UH....
AHHHH!!
NANCY

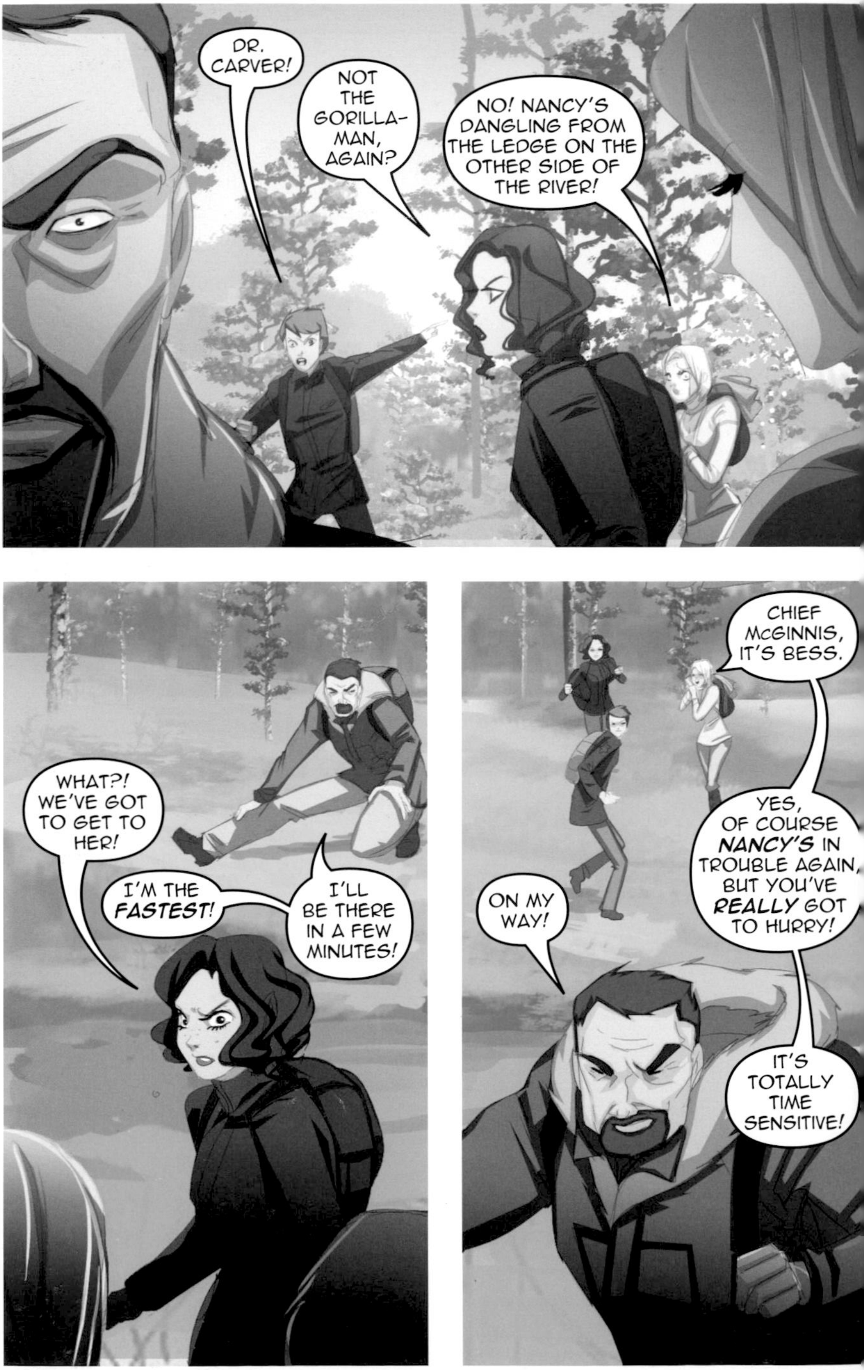
DR. CARVER!
NOT THE GORILLA-MAN, AGAIN?
NO! NANCY'S DANGLING FROM THE LEDGE ON THE OTHER SIDE OF THE RIVER!
WHAT?! WE'VE GOT TO GET TO HER!
I'M THE *FASTEST*!
I'LL BE THERE IN A FEW MINUTES!
CHIEF McGINNIS, IT'S BESS.
YES, OF COURSE ***NANCY'S*** IN TROUBLE AGAIN, BUT YOU'VE ***REALLY*** GOT TO HURRY!
ON MY WAY!
IT'S TOTALLY TIME SENSITIVE!

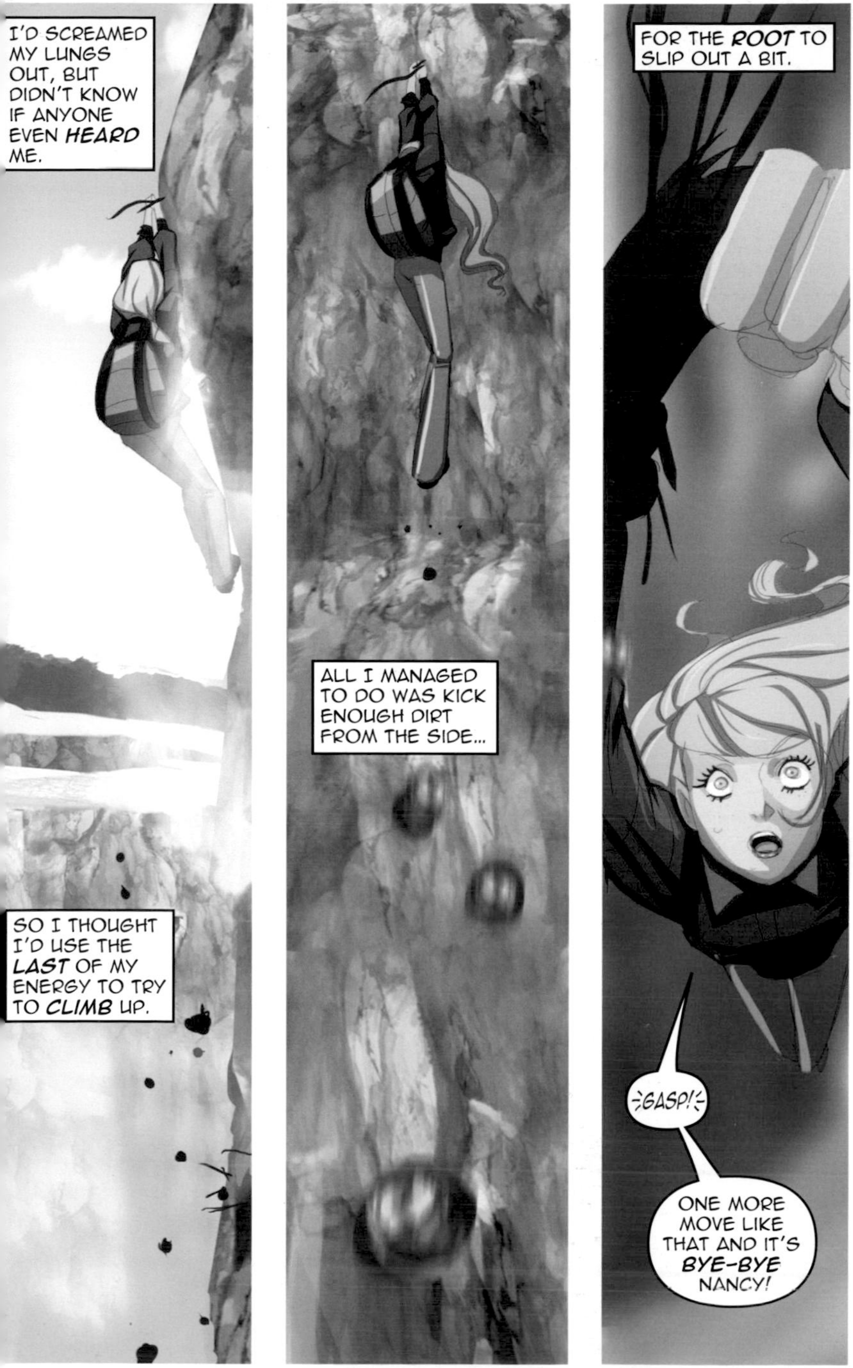
I'D SCREAMED MY LUNGS OUT, BUT DIDN'T KNOW IF ANYONE EVEN HEARD ME.
SO I THOUGHT I'D USE THE LAST OF MY ENERGY TO TRY TO CLIMB UP.
ALL I MANAGED TO DO WAS KICK ENOUGH DIRT FROM THE SIDE...
FOR THE ROOT TO SLIP OUT A BIT.
GASP!
ONE MORE MOVE LIKE THAT AND IT'S BYE-BYE NANCY!

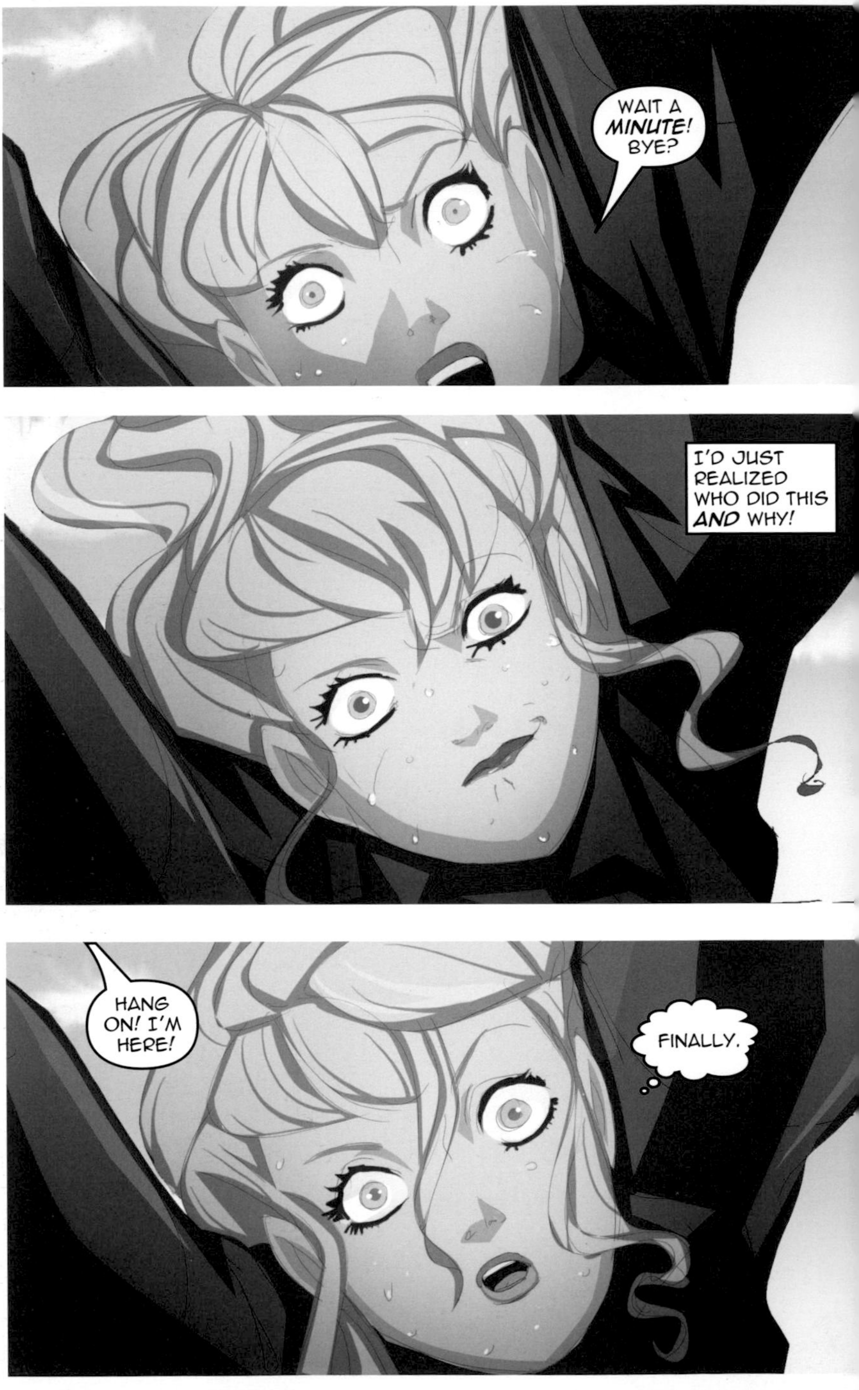
WAIT A MINUTE! BYE?
I'D JUST REALIZED WHO DID THIS AND WHY!
HANG ON! I'M HERE!
FINALLY.

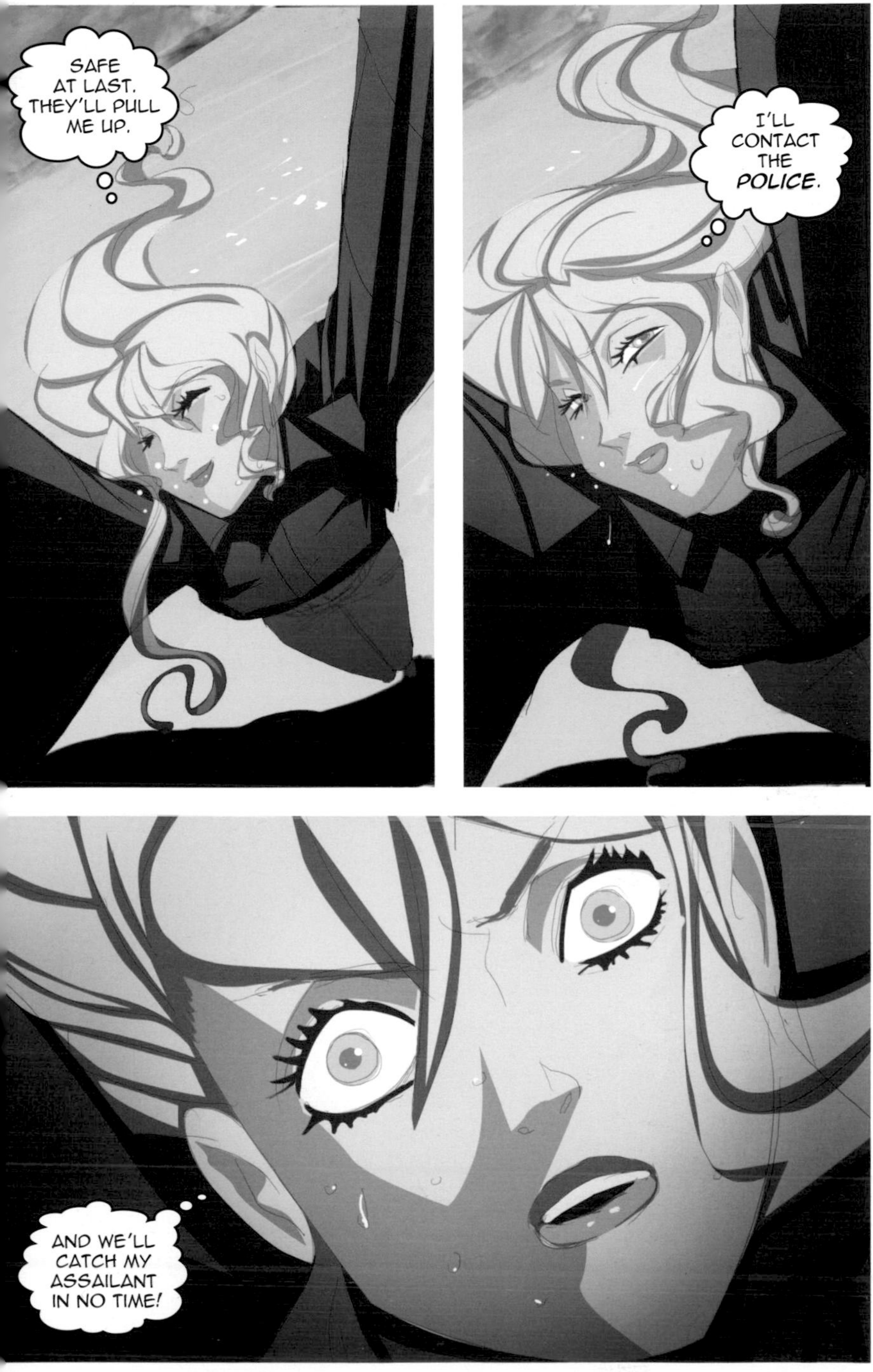
SAFE AT LAST. THEY'LL PULL ME UP.
I'LL CONTACT THE *POLICE*.
AND WE'LL CATCH MY ASSAILANT IN NO TIME!

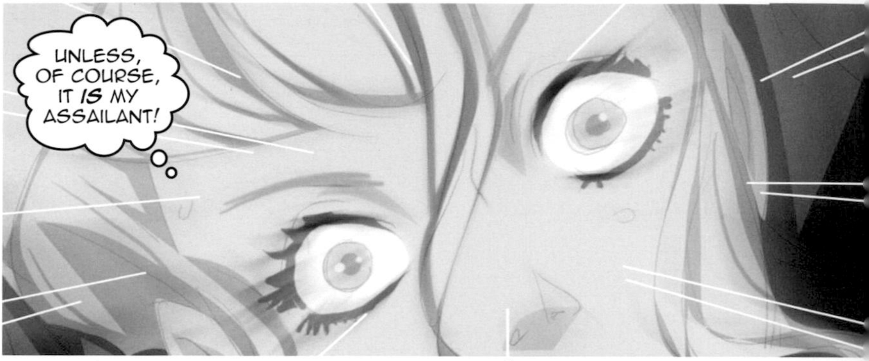
UNLESS, OF COURSE, IT IS MY ASSAILANT!

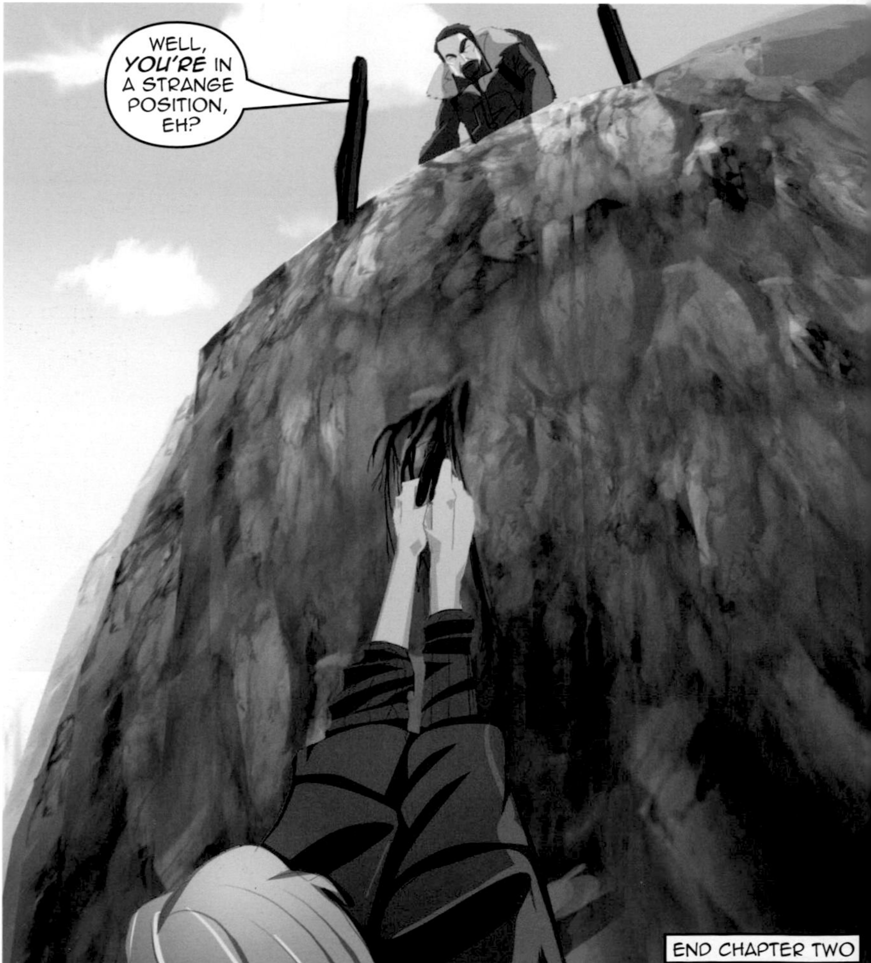
WELL, YOU'RE IN A STRANGE POSITION, EH?
END CHAPTER TWO

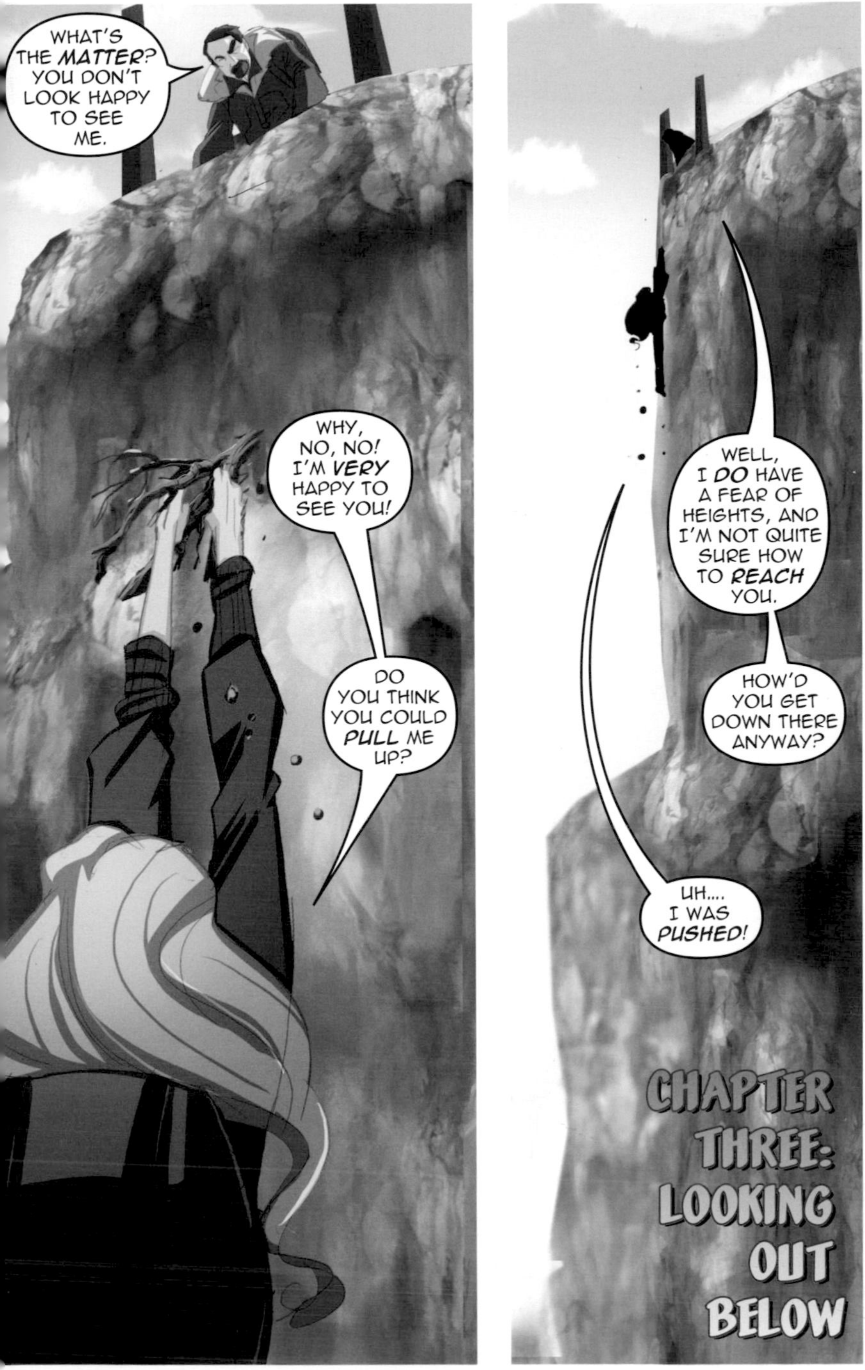
WHAT'S THE MATTER? YOU DON'T LOOK HAPPY TO SEE ME.
WHY, NO, NO! I'M VERY HAPPY TO SEE YOU!
DO YOU THINK YOU COULD PULL ME UP?
WELL, I DO HAVE A FEAR OF HEIGHTS, AND I'M NOT QUITE SURE HOW TO REACH YOU.
HOW'D YOU GET DOWN THERE ANYWAY?
UH.... I WAS PUSHED!
CHAPTER THREE: LOOKING OUT BELOW

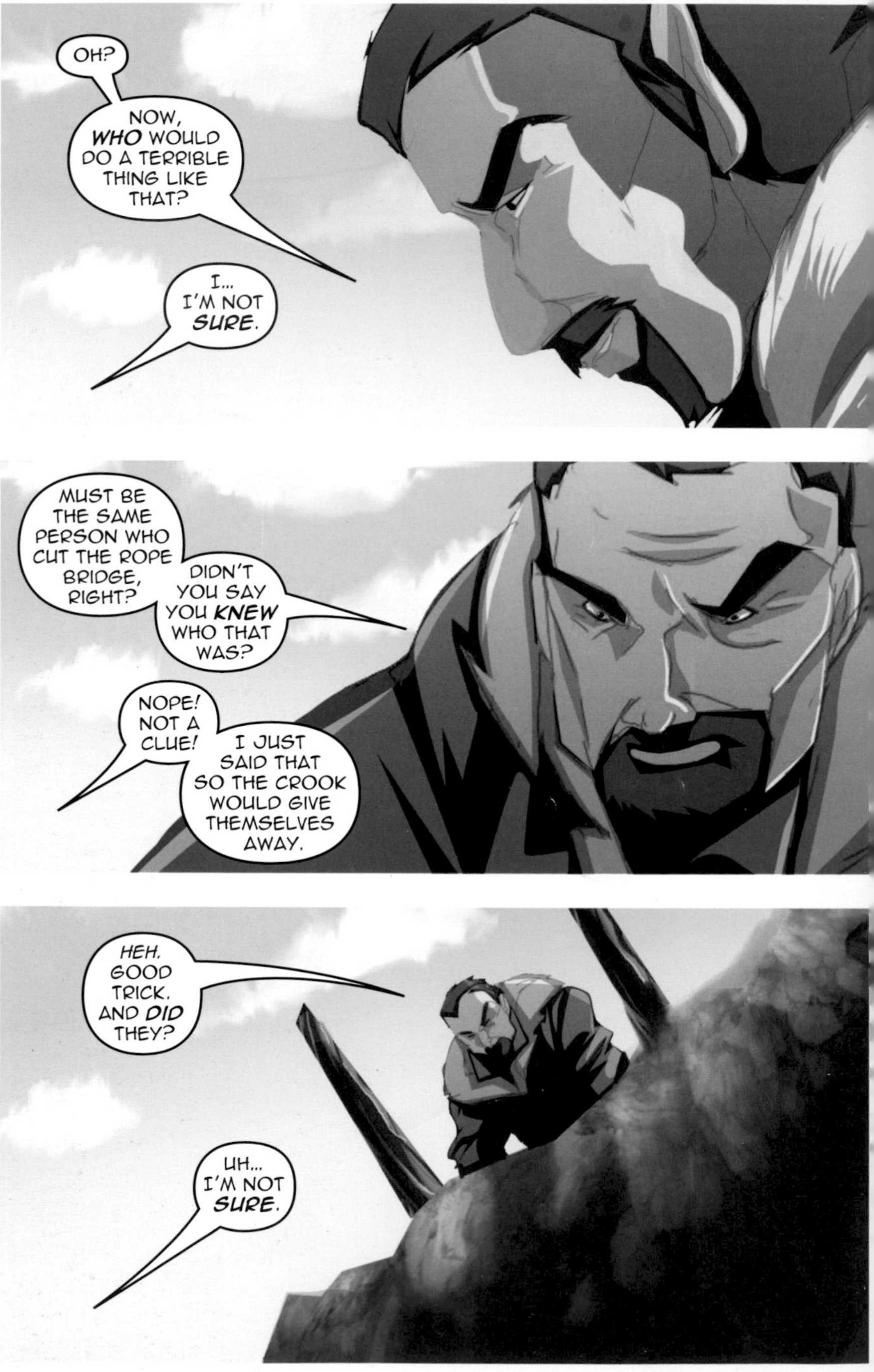
OH?
NOW, WHO WOULD DO A TERRIBLE THING LIKE THAT?
I... I'M NOT SURE.
MUST BE THE SAME PERSON WHO CUT THE ROPE BRIDGE, RIGHT?
DIDN'T YOU SAY YOU KNEW WHO THAT WAS?
NOPE! NOT A CLUE!
I JUST SAID THAT SO THE CROOK WOULD GIVE THEMSELVES AWAY.
HEH. GOOD TRICK. AND DID THEY?
UH... I'M NOT SURE.

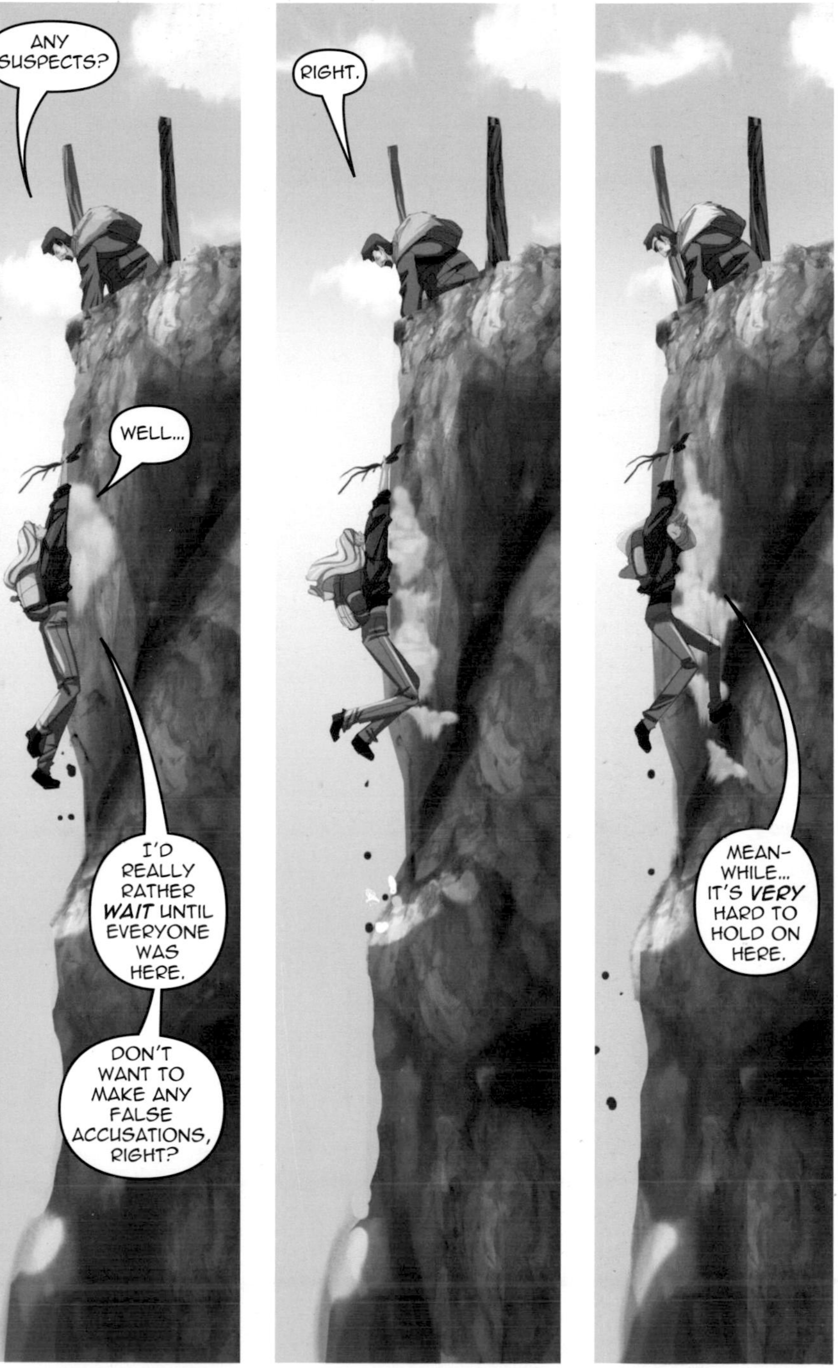
ANY SUSPECTS?
WELL...
I'D REALLY RATHER *WAIT* UNTIL EVERYONE WAS HERE.
DON'T WANT TO MAKE ANY FALSE ACCUSATIONS, RIGHT?
RIGHT.
MEAN-WHILE... IT'S *VERY* HARD TO HOLD ON HERE.

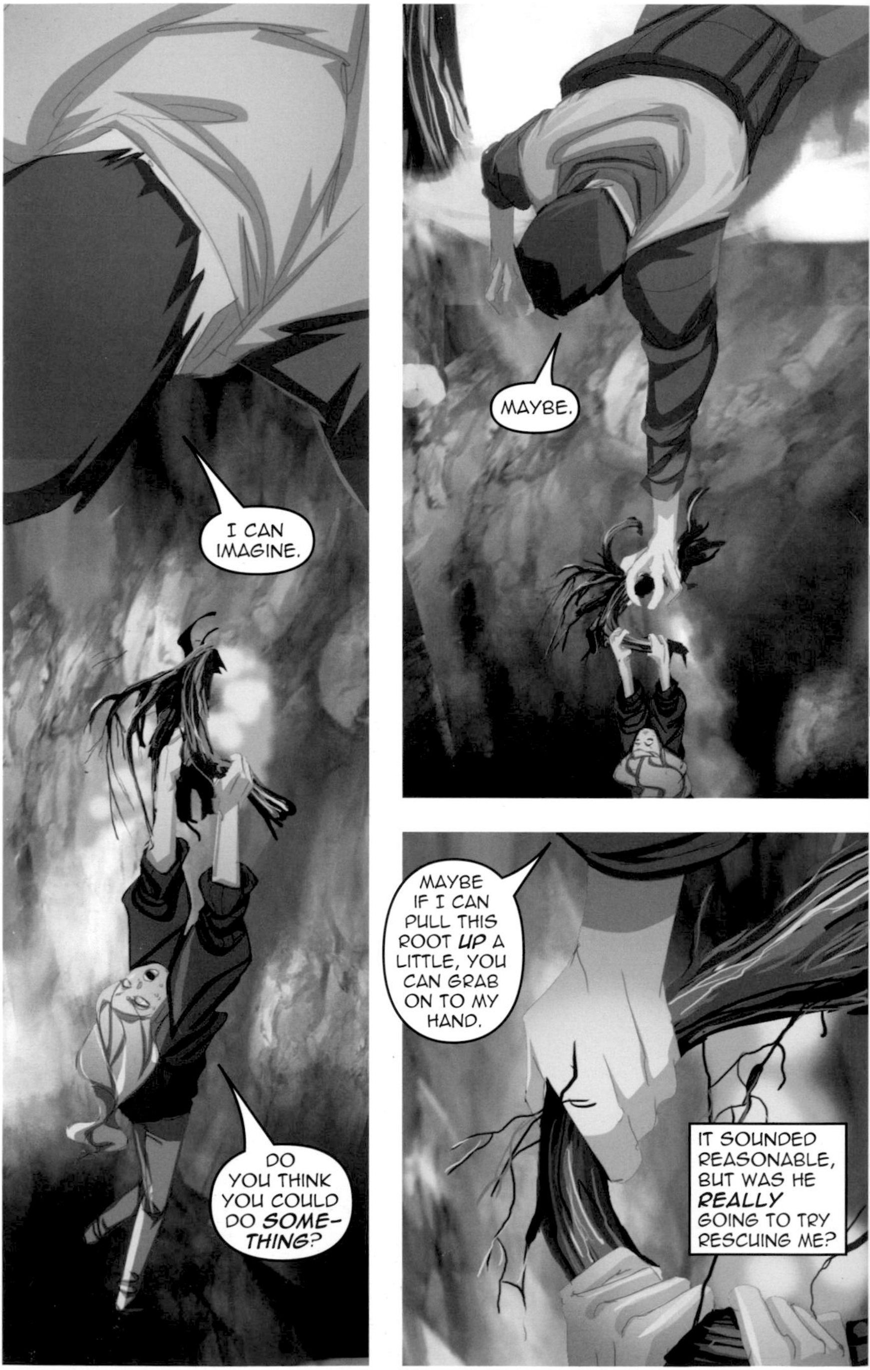
I CAN IMAGINE.
DO YOU THINK YOU COULD DO SOMETHING?
MAYBE.
MAYBE IF I CAN PULL THIS ROOT UP A LITTLE, YOU CAN GRAB ON TO MY HAND.
IT SOUNDED REASONABLE, BUT WAS HE REALLY GOING TO TRY RESCUING ME?

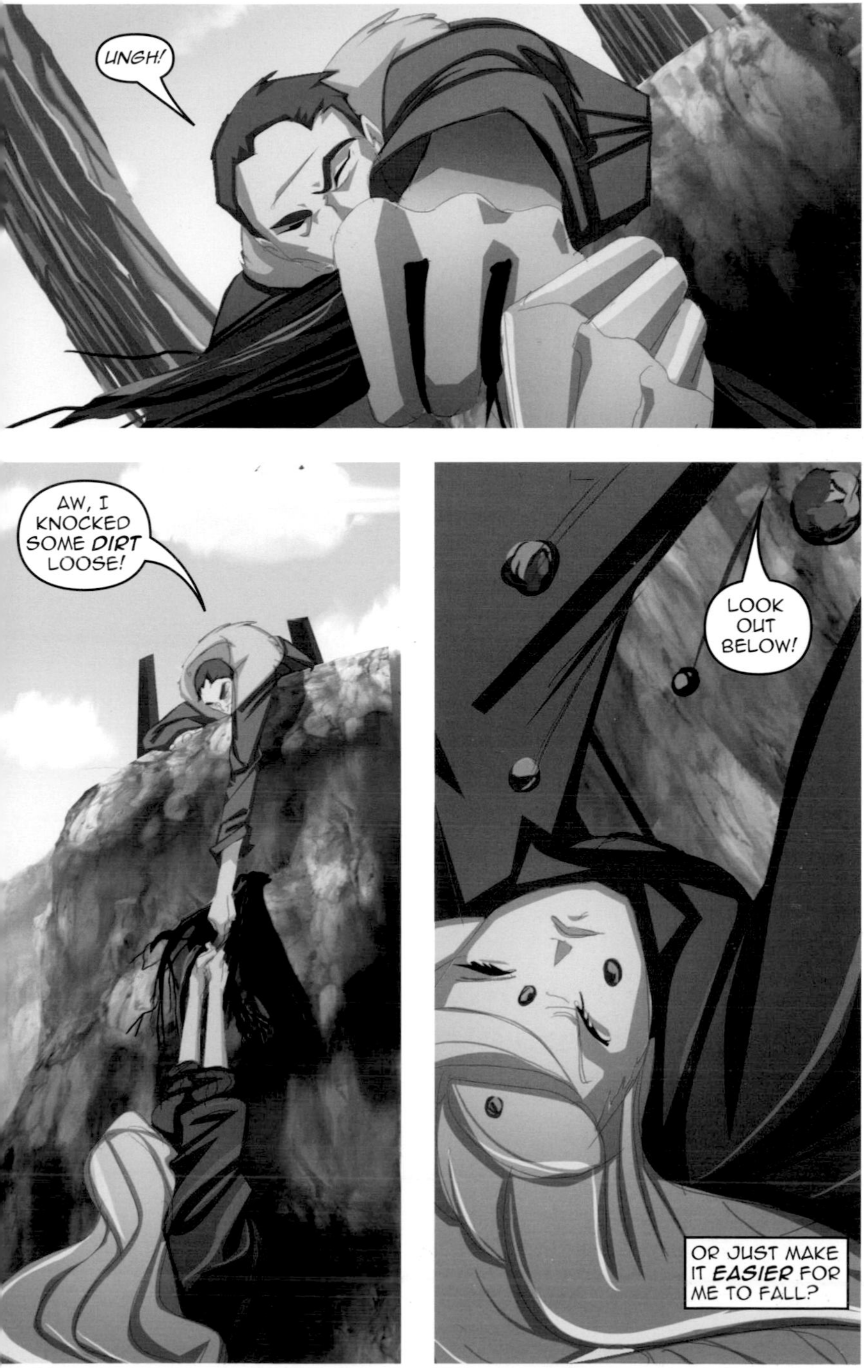
UNGH!
AW, I KNOCKED SOME *DIRT* LOOSE!
LOOK OUT BELOW!
OR JUST MAKE IT ***EASIER*** FOR ME TO FALL?

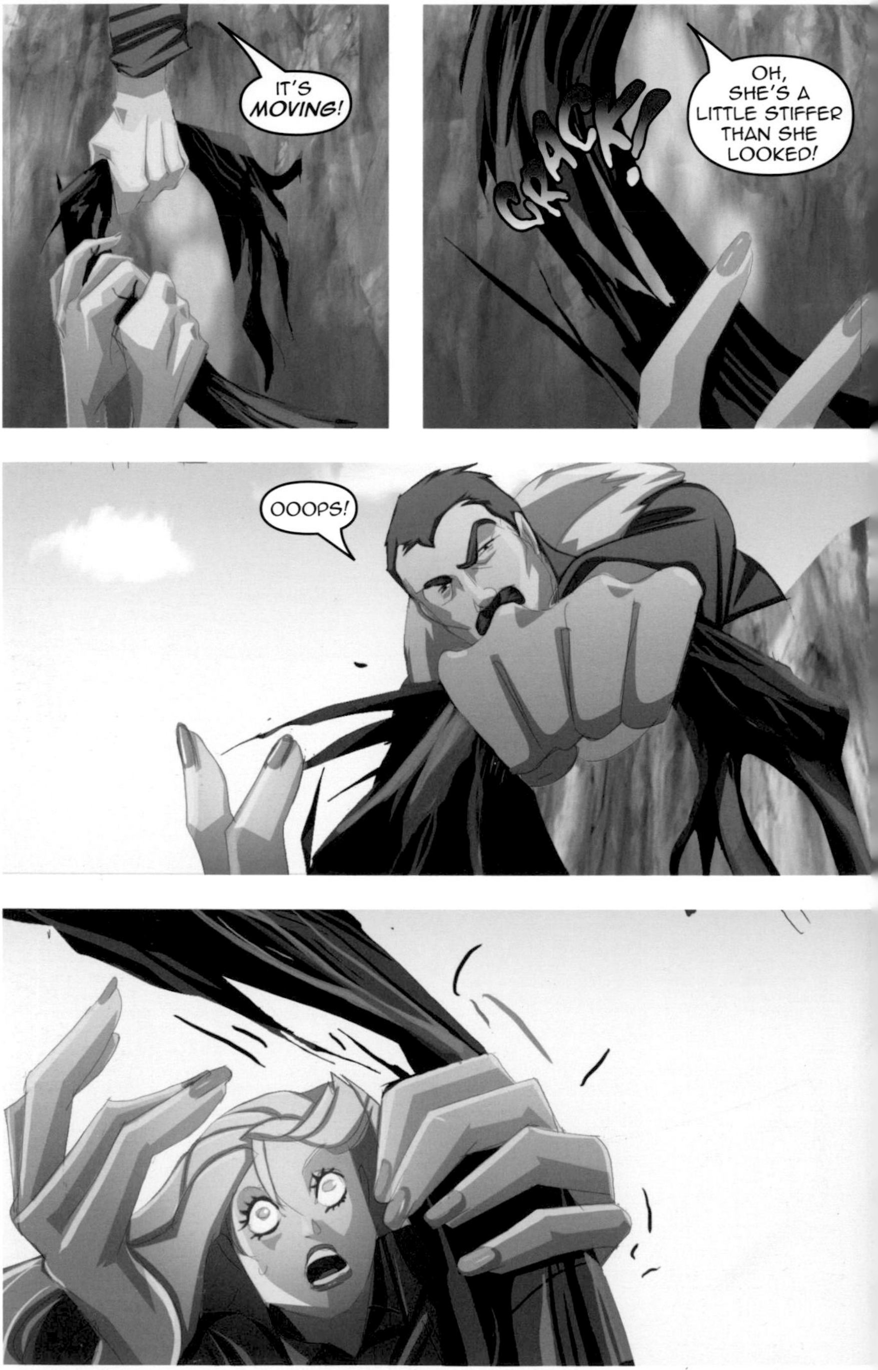
IT'S MOVING!
CRACK!
OH, SHE'S A LITTLE STIFFER THAN SHE LOOKED!
OOOPS!

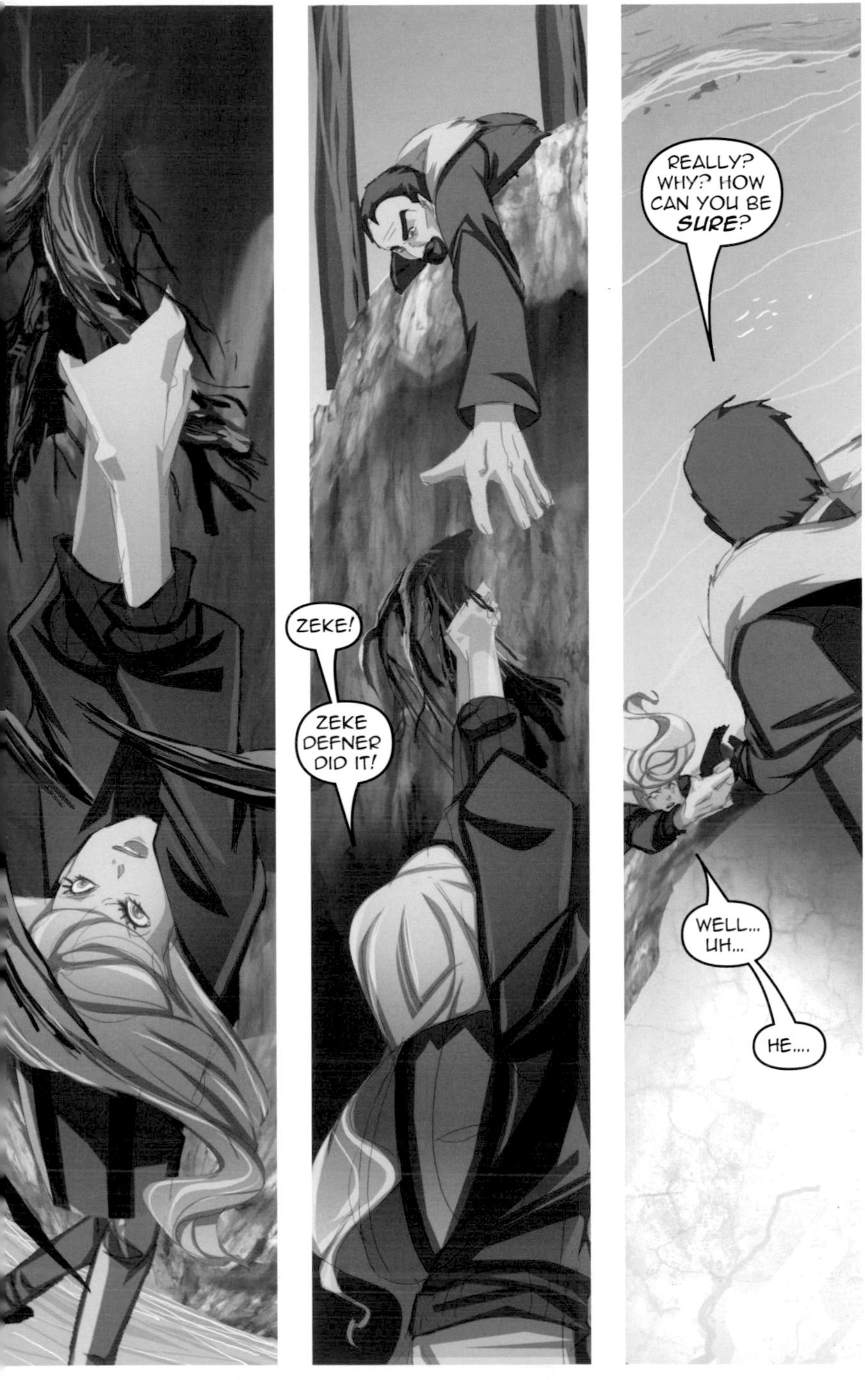
ZEKE!
ZEKE DEFNER DID IT!
REALLY? WHY? HOW CAN YOU BE SURE?
WELL... UH...
HE....

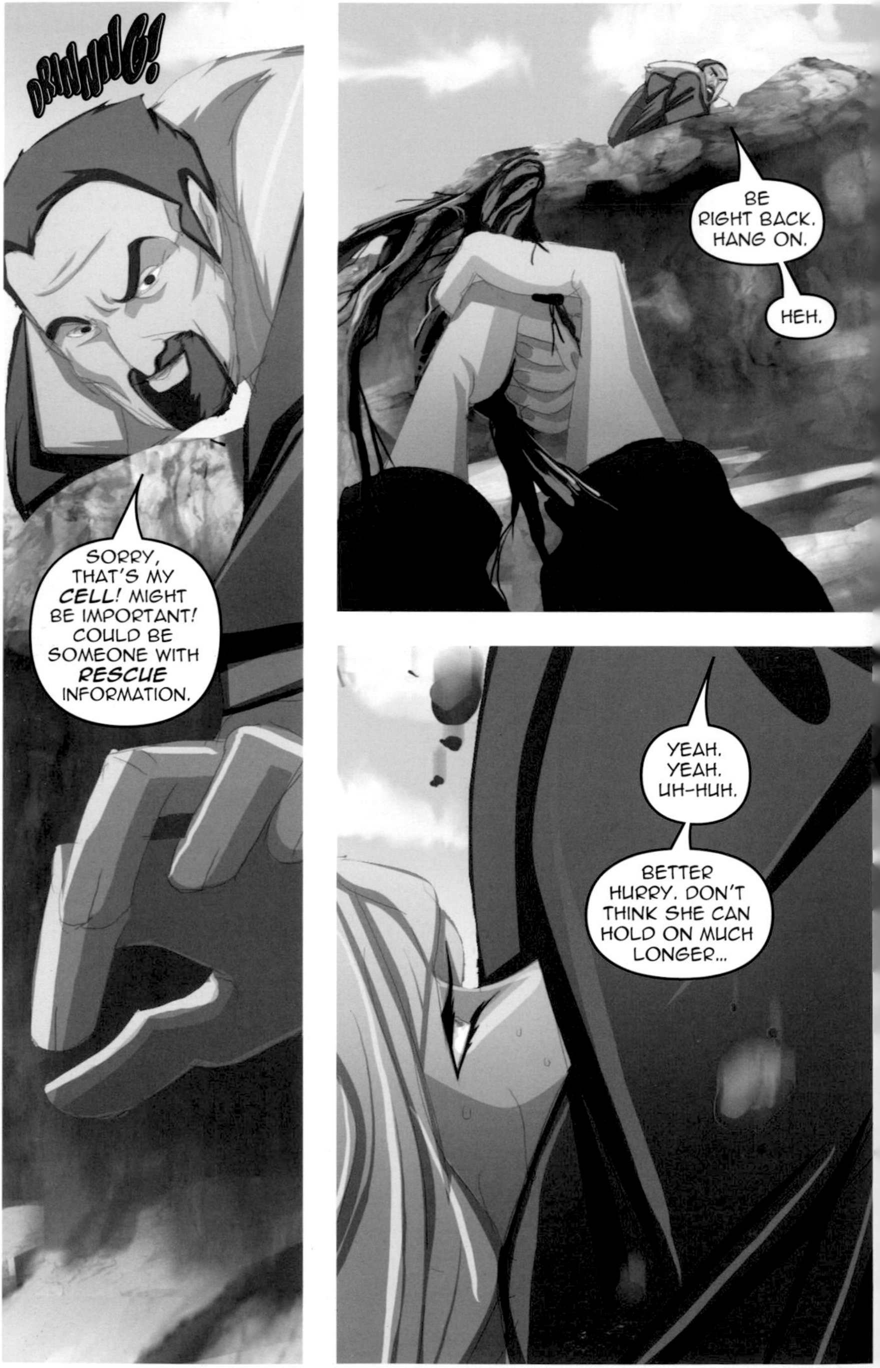
DRINNNG!
SORRY, THAT'S MY CELL! MIGHT BE IMPORTANT! COULD BE SOMEONE WITH RESCUE INFORMATION.
BE RIGHT BACK. HANG ON.
HEH.
YEAH. YEAH. UH-HUH.
BETTER HURRY. DON'T THINK SHE CAN HOLD ON MUCH LONGER...

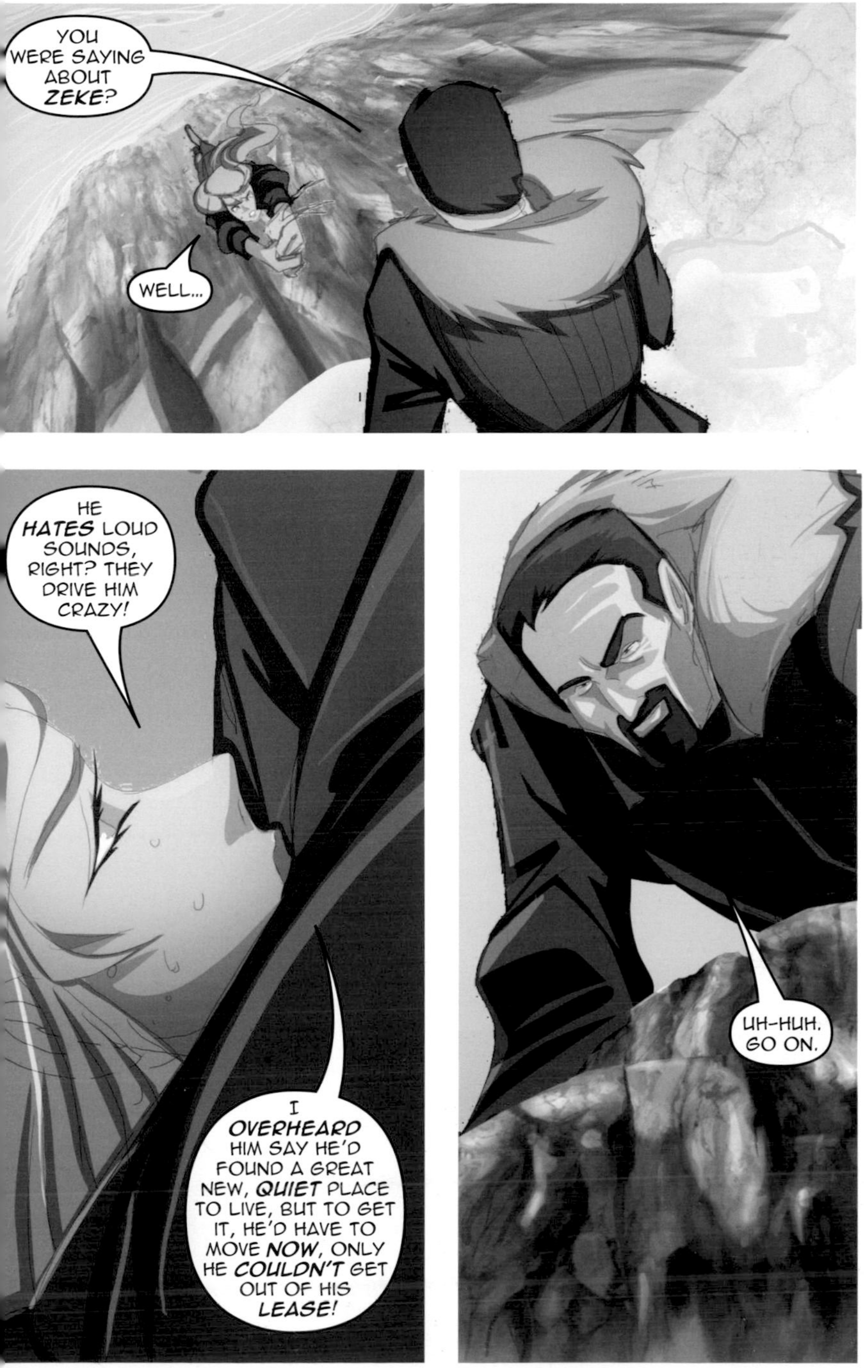
YOU WERE SAYING ABOUT ZEKE?
WELL...
HE HATES LOUD SOUNDS, RIGHT? THEY DRIVE HIM CRAZY!
I OVERHEARD HIM SAY HE'D FOUND A GREAT NEW, QUIET PLACE TO LIVE, BUT TO GET IT, HE'D HAVE TO MOVE NOW, ONLY HE COULDN'T GET OUT OF HIS LEASE!
UH-HUH. GO ON.

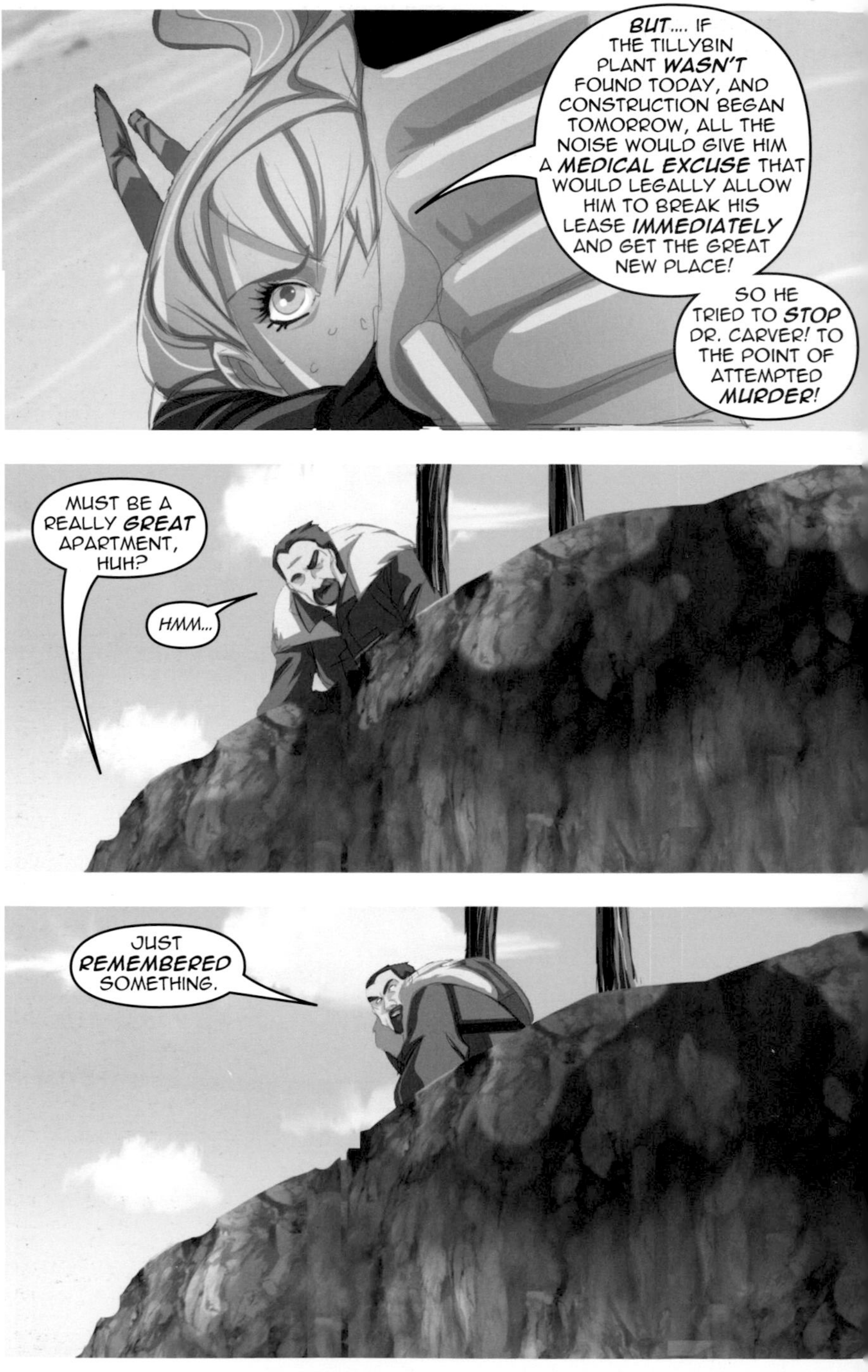
BUT.... IF THE TILLYBIN PLANT WASN'T FOUND TODAY, AND CONSTRUCTION BEGAN TOMORROW, ALL THE NOISE WOULD GIVE HIM A MEDICAL EXCUSE THAT WOULD LEGALLY ALLOW HIM TO BREAK HIS LEASE IMMEDIATELY AND GET THE GREAT NEW PLACE!
SO HE TRIED TO STOP DR. CARVER! TO THE POINT OF ATTEMPTED MURDER!
MUST BE A REALLY GREAT APARTMENT, HUH?
HMM...
JUST REMEMBERED SOMETHING.

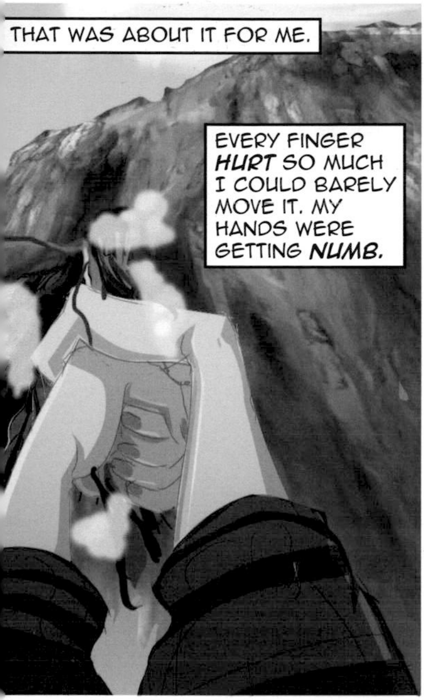
THAT WAS ABOUT IT FOR ME.
EVERY FINGER *HURT* SO MUCH I COULD BARELY MOVE IT. MY HANDS WERE GETTING *NUMB.*

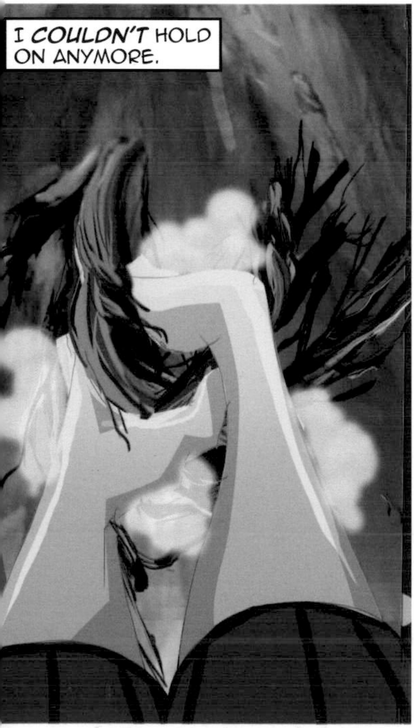
I *COULDN'T* HOLD ON ANYMORE.

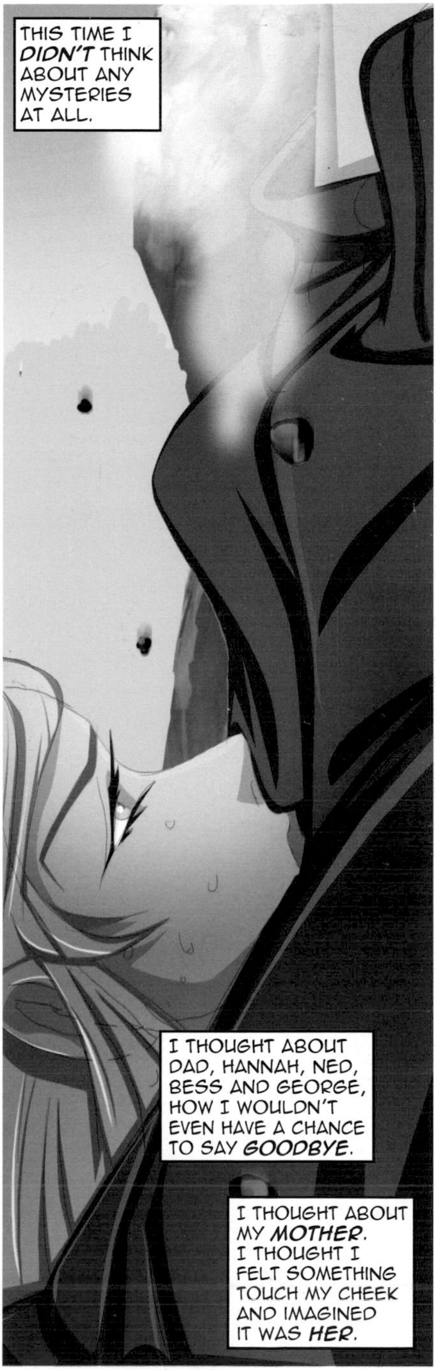
THIS TIME I *DIDN'T* THINK ABOUT ANY MYSTERIES AT ALL.
I THOUGHT ABOUT DAD, HANNAH, NED, BESS AND GEORGE, HOW I WOULDN'T EVEN HAVE A CHANCE TO SAY *GOODBYE*.
I THOUGHT ABOUT MY *MOTHER*. I THOUGHT I FELT SOMETHING TOUCH MY CHEEK AND IMAGINED IT WAS *HER*.

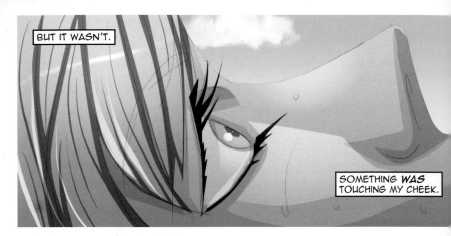

BUT IT WASN'T.

SOMETHING *WAS* TOUCHING MY CHEEK.

A *ROPE.*

I JUST REMEMBERED I HAD SOME CLIMBING EQUIPMENT IN THE CAR.

I TIED THE OTHER END TO A BOULDER. HOOK THAT INTO YOUR BELT.

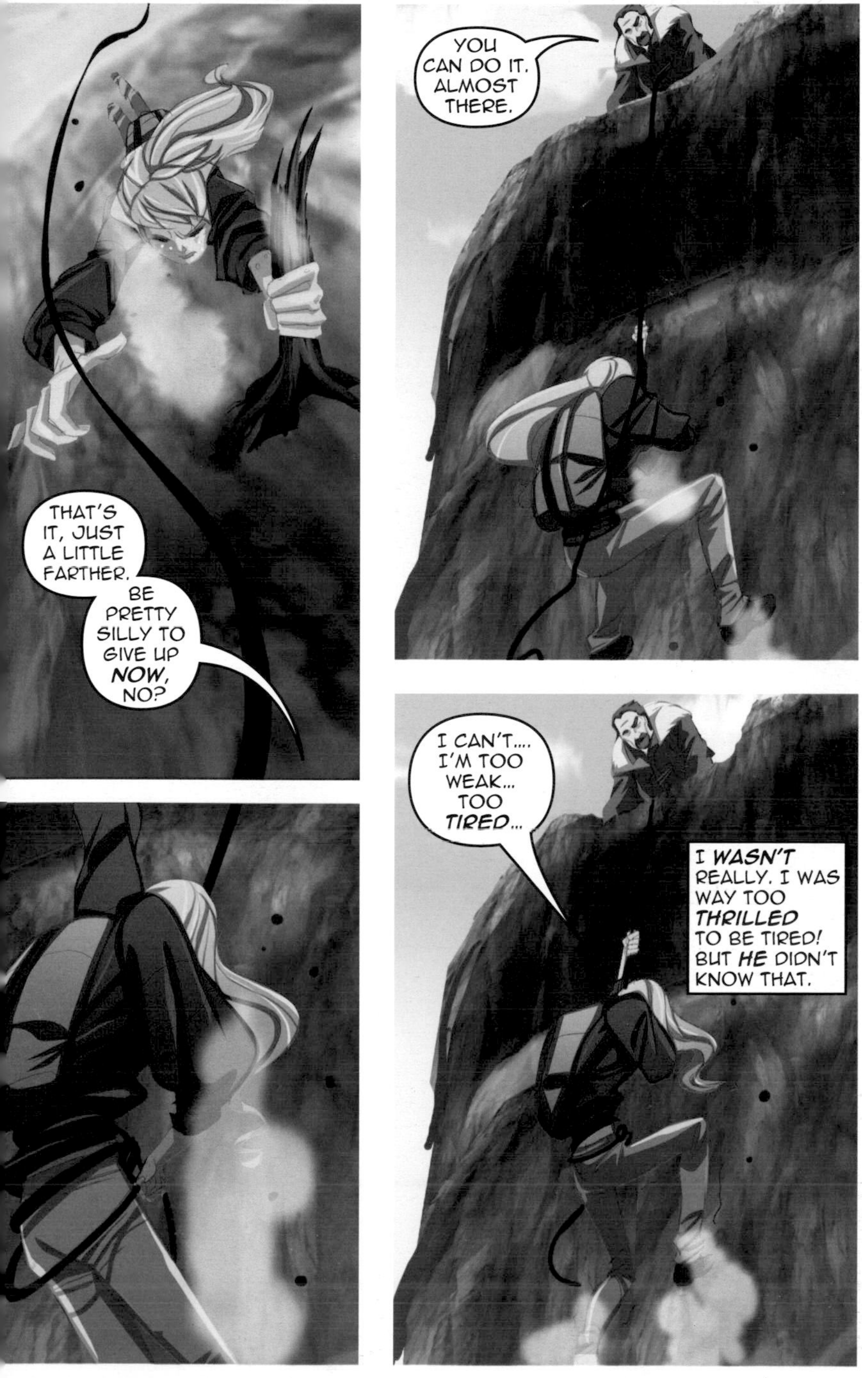
THAT'S IT, JUST A LITTLE FARTHER.
BE PRETTY SILLY TO GIVE UP NOW, NO?
YOU CAN DO IT. ALMOST THERE.
I CAN'T.... I'M TOO WEAK... TOO TIRED...
I WASN'T REALLY. I WAS WAY TOO THRILLED TO BE TIRED! BUT HE DIDN'T KNOW THAT.

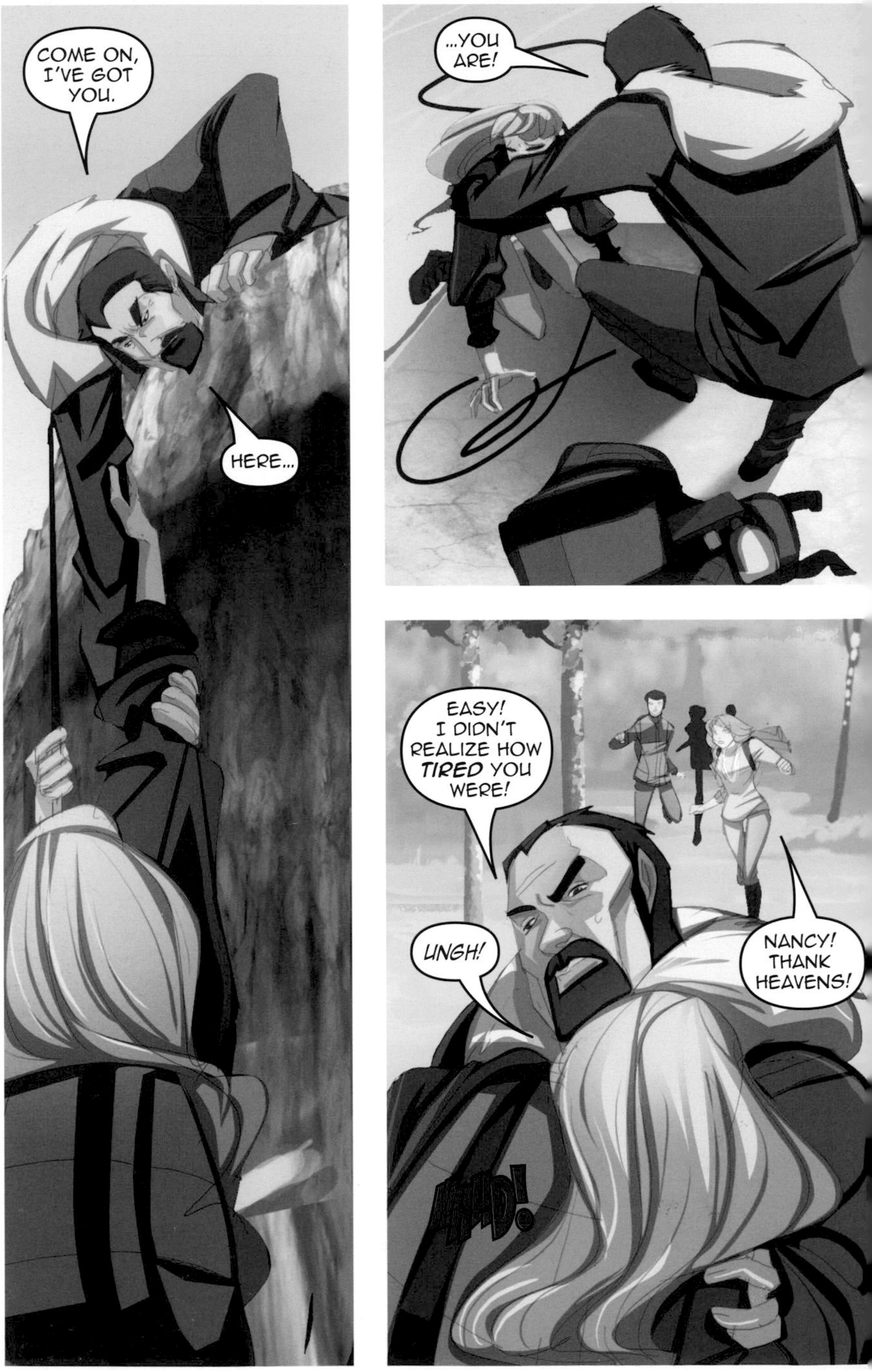
COME ON, I'VE GOT YOU.
HERE...
...YOU ARE!
EASY! I DIDN'T REALIZE HOW TIRED YOU WERE!
UNGH!
NANCY! THANK HEAVENS!

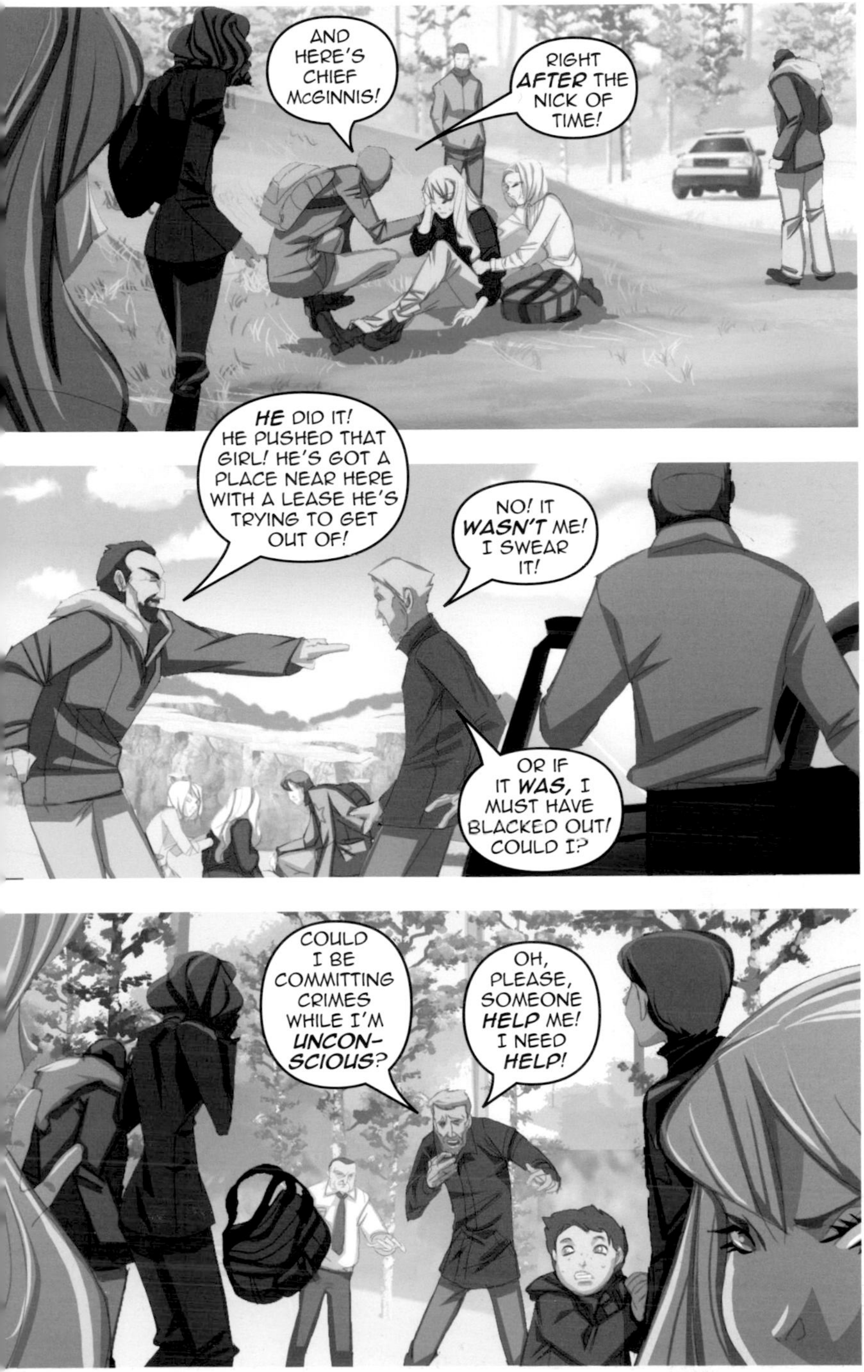
AND HERE'S CHIEF McGINNIS!
RIGHT AFTER THE NICK OF TIME!
HE DID IT! HE PUSHED THAT GIRL! HE'S GOT A PLACE NEAR HERE WITH A LEASE HE'S TRYING TO GET OUT OF!
NO! IT WASN'T ME! I SWEAR IT!
OR IF IT WAS, I MUST HAVE BLACKED OUT! COULD I?
COULD I BE COMMITTING CRIMES WHILE I'M UNCON-SCIOUS?
OH, PLEASE, SOMEONE HELP ME! I NEED HELP!

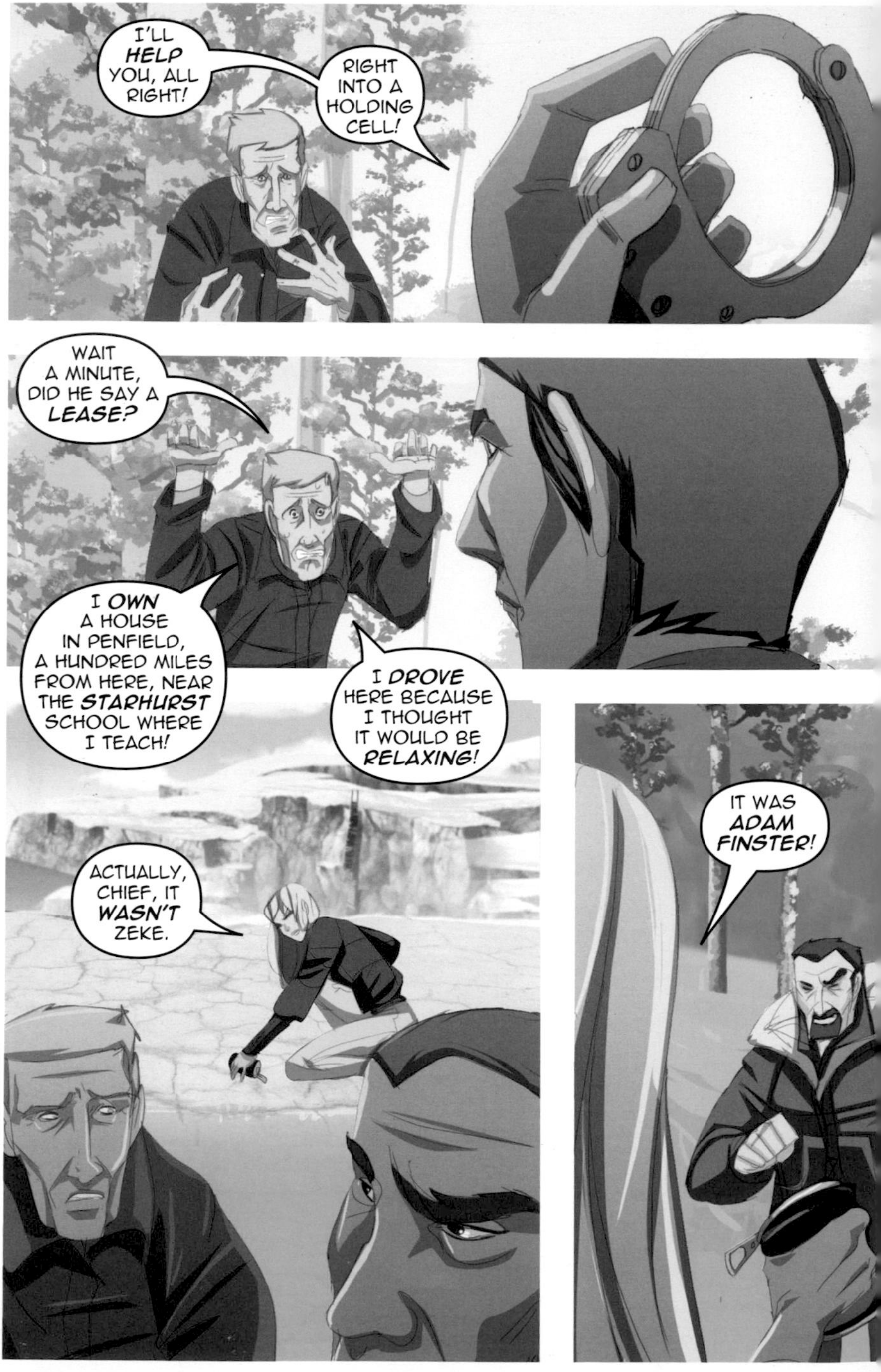
I'LL **HELP** YOU, ALL RIGHT!
RIGHT INTO A HOLDING CELL!
WAIT A MINUTE, DID HE SAY A **LEASE?**
I **OWN** A HOUSE IN PENFIELD, A HUNDRED MILES FROM HERE, NEAR THE **STARHURST** SCHOOL WHERE I TEACH!
I **DROVE** HERE BECAUSE I THOUGHT IT WOULD BE **RELAXING**!
ACTUALLY, CHIEF, IT **WASN'T** ZEKE.
IT WAS **ADAM FINSTER!**

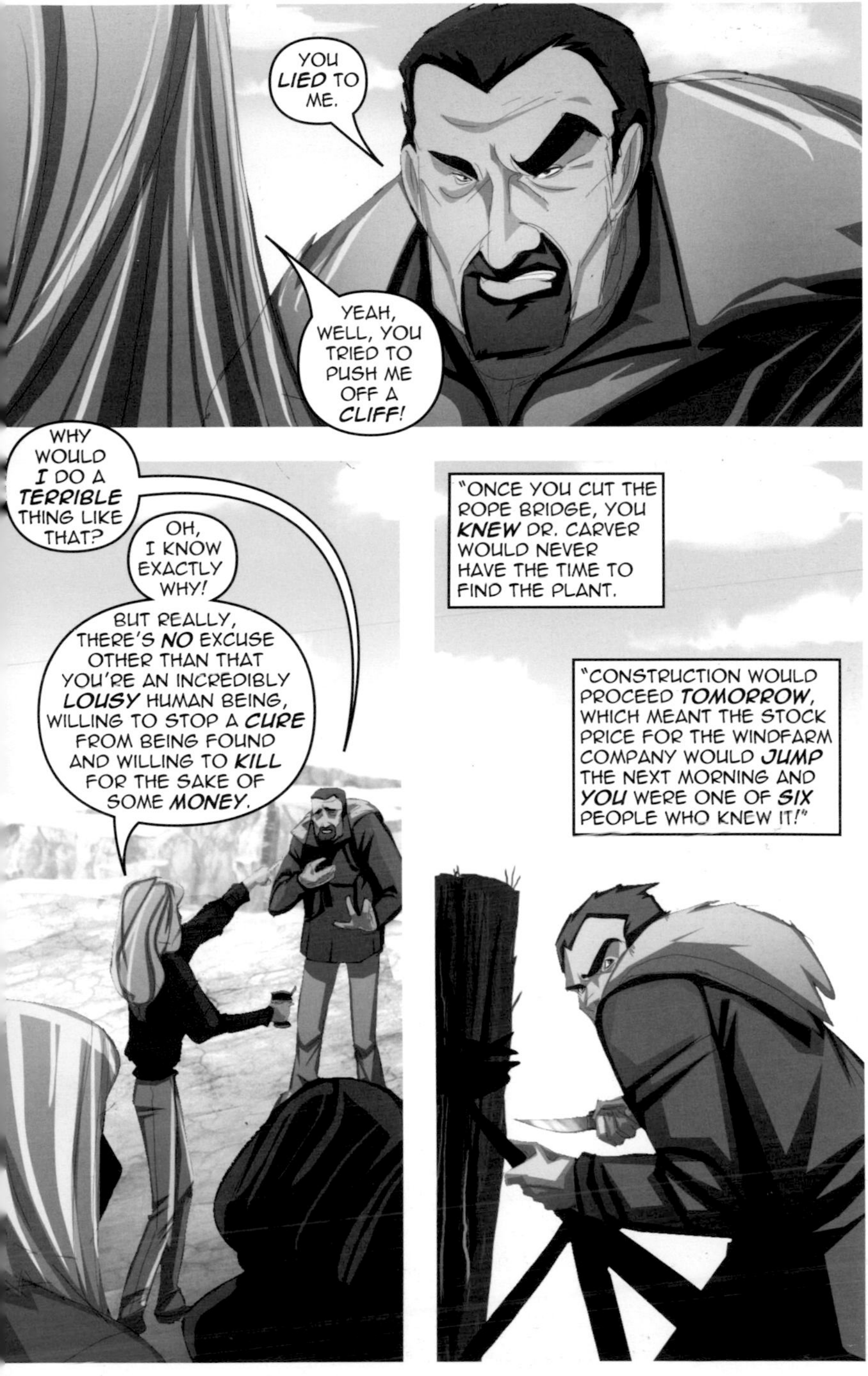
YOU LIED TO ME.
YEAH, WELL, YOU TRIED TO PUSH ME OFF A CLIFF!
WHY WOULD I DO A TERRIBLE THING LIKE THAT?
OH, I KNOW EXACTLY WHY!
BUT REALLY, THERE'S NO EXCUSE OTHER THAN THAT YOU'RE AN INCREDIBLY LOUSY HUMAN BEING, WILLING TO STOP A CURE FROM BEING FOUND AND WILLING TO KILL FOR THE SAKE OF SOME MONEY.
"ONCE YOU CUT THE ROPE BRIDGE, YOU KNEW DR. CARVER WOULD NEVER HAVE THE TIME TO FIND THE PLANT.
"CONSTRUCTION WOULD PROCEED TOMORROW, WHICH MEANT THE STOCK PRICE FOR THE WINDFARM COMPANY WOULD JUMP THE NEXT MORNING AND YOU WERE ONE OF SIX PEOPLE WHO KNEW IT!"

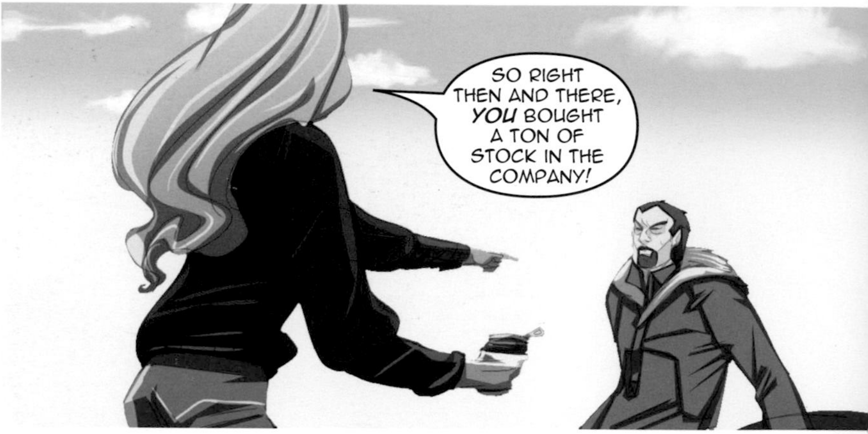
SO RIGHT THEN AND THERE, YOU BOUGHT A TON OF STOCK IN THE COMPANY!

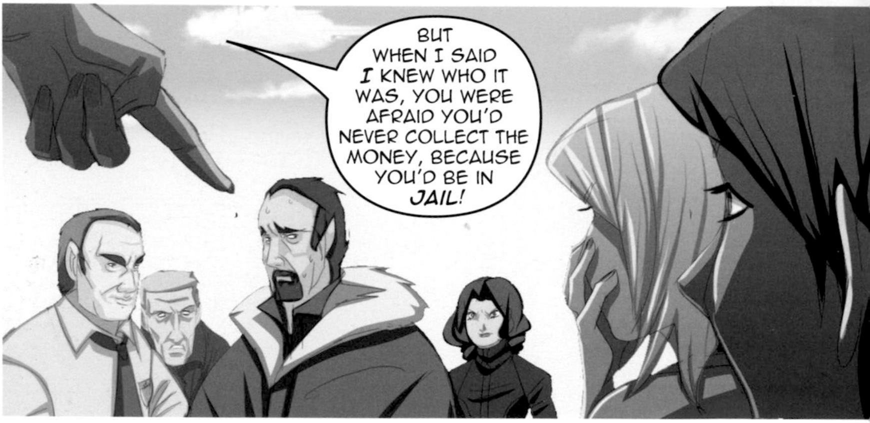
BUT WHEN I SAID I KNEW WHO IT WAS, YOU WERE AFRAID YOU'D NEVER COLLECT THE MONEY, BECAUSE YOU'D BE IN JAIL!

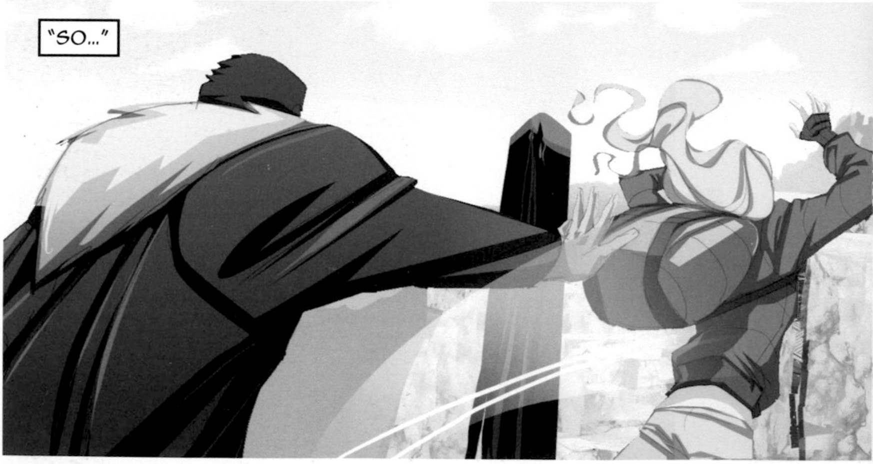
"SO..."

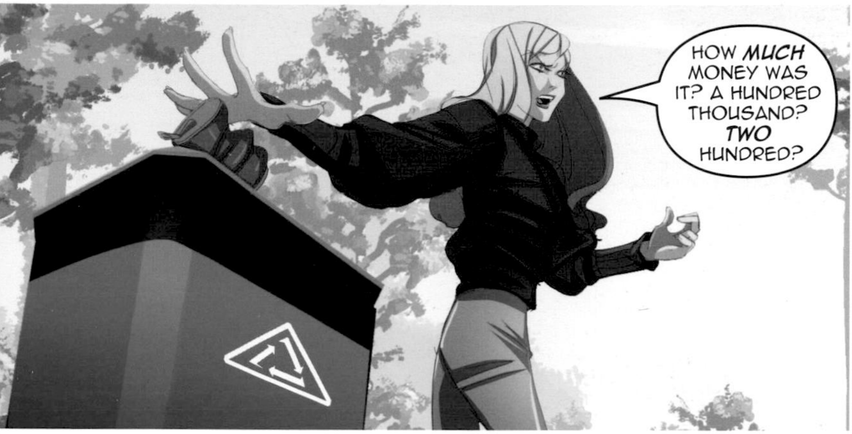
HOW MUCH MONEY WAS IT? A HUNDRED THOUSAND? TWO HUNDRED?

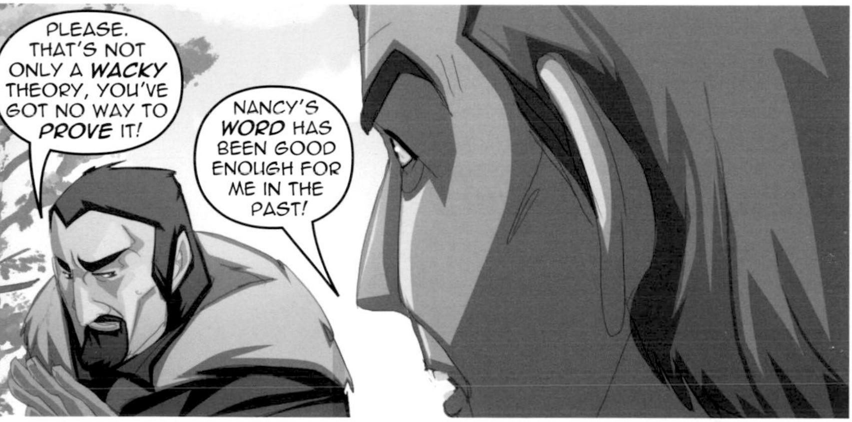
PLEASE. THAT'S NOT ONLY A WACKY THEORY, YOU'VE GOT NO WAY TO PROVE IT!
NANCY'S WORD HAS BEEN GOOD ENOUGH FOR ME IN THE PAST!

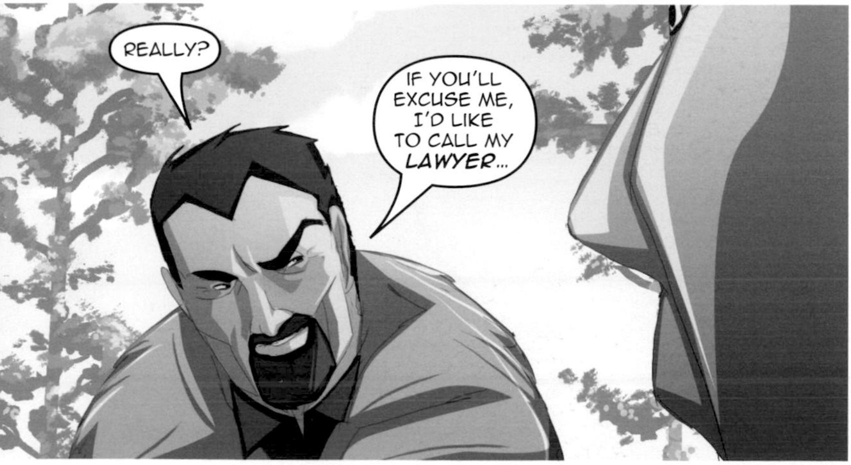
REALLY?
IF YOU'LL EXCUSE ME, I'D LIKE TO CALL MY LAWYER...

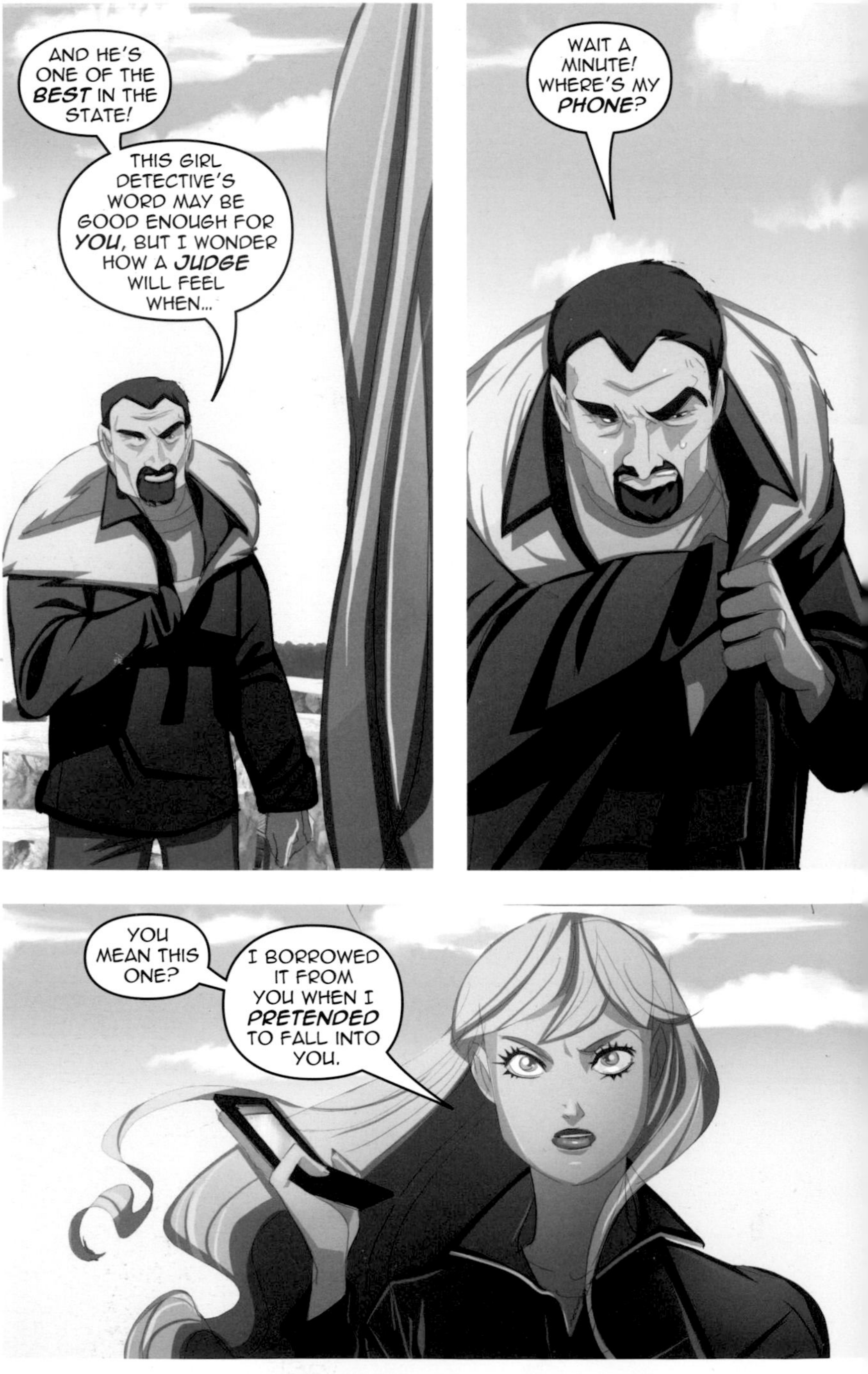
AND HE'S ONE OF THE BEST IN THE STATE!
THIS GIRL DETECTIVE'S WORD MAY BE GOOD ENOUGH FOR YOU, BUT I WONDER HOW A JUDGE WILL FEEL WHEN...
WAIT A MINUTE! WHERE'S MY PHONE?
YOU MEAN THIS ONE?
I BORROWED IT FROM YOU WHEN I PRETENDED TO FALL INTO YOU.

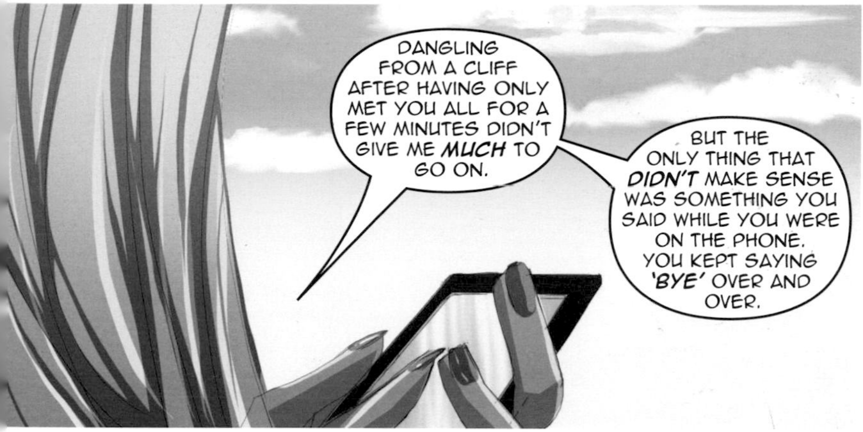
DANGLING FROM A CLIFF AFTER HAVING ONLY MET YOU ALL FOR A FEW MINUTES DIDN'T GIVE ME *MUCH* TO GO ON.
BUT THE ONLY THING THAT *DIDN'T* MAKE SENSE WAS SOMETHING YOU SAID WHILE YOU WERE ON THE PHONE. YOU KEPT SAYING *'BYE'* OVER AND OVER.

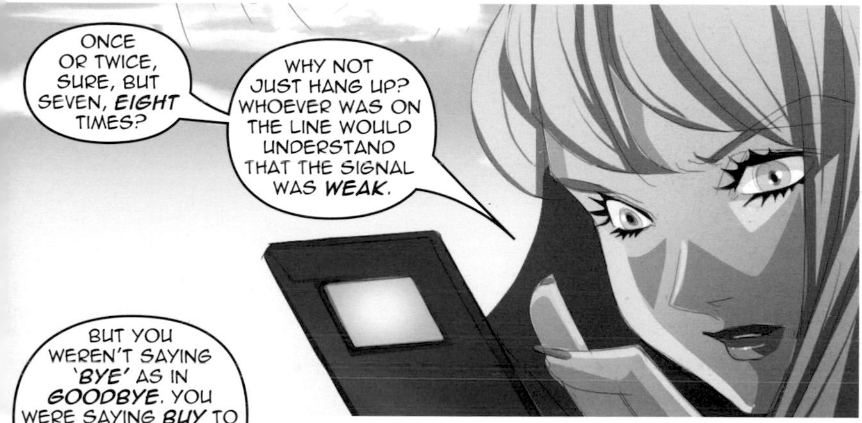
ONCE OR TWICE, SURE, BUT SEVEN, *EIGHT* TIMES?
WHY NOT JUST HANG UP? WHOEVER WAS ON THE LINE WOULD UNDERSTAND THAT THE SIGNAL WAS *WEAK*.

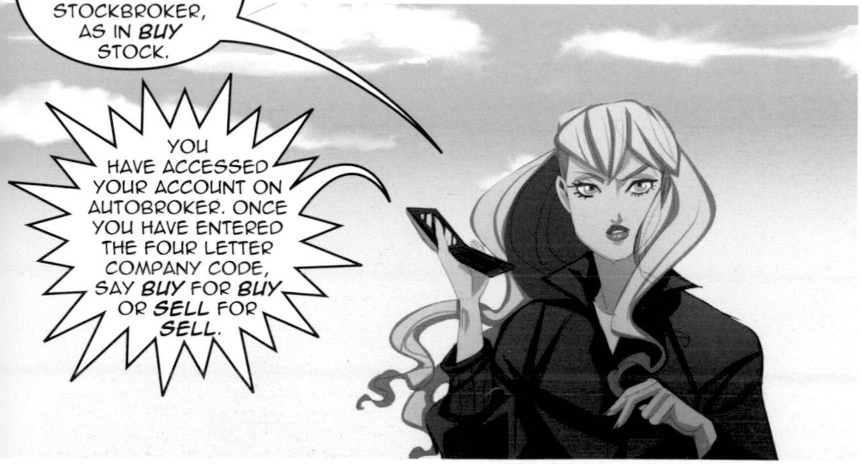
BUT YOU WEREN'T SAYING *'BYE'* AS IN *GOODBYE*. YOU WERE SAYING *BUY* TO YOUR AUTOMATED STOCKBROKER, AS IN *BUY* STOCK.
YOU HAVE ACCESSED YOUR ACCOUNT ON AUTOBROKER. ONCE YOU HAVE ENTERED THE FOUR LETTER COMPANY CODE, SAY *BUY* FOR *BUY* OR *SELL* FOR *SELL*.

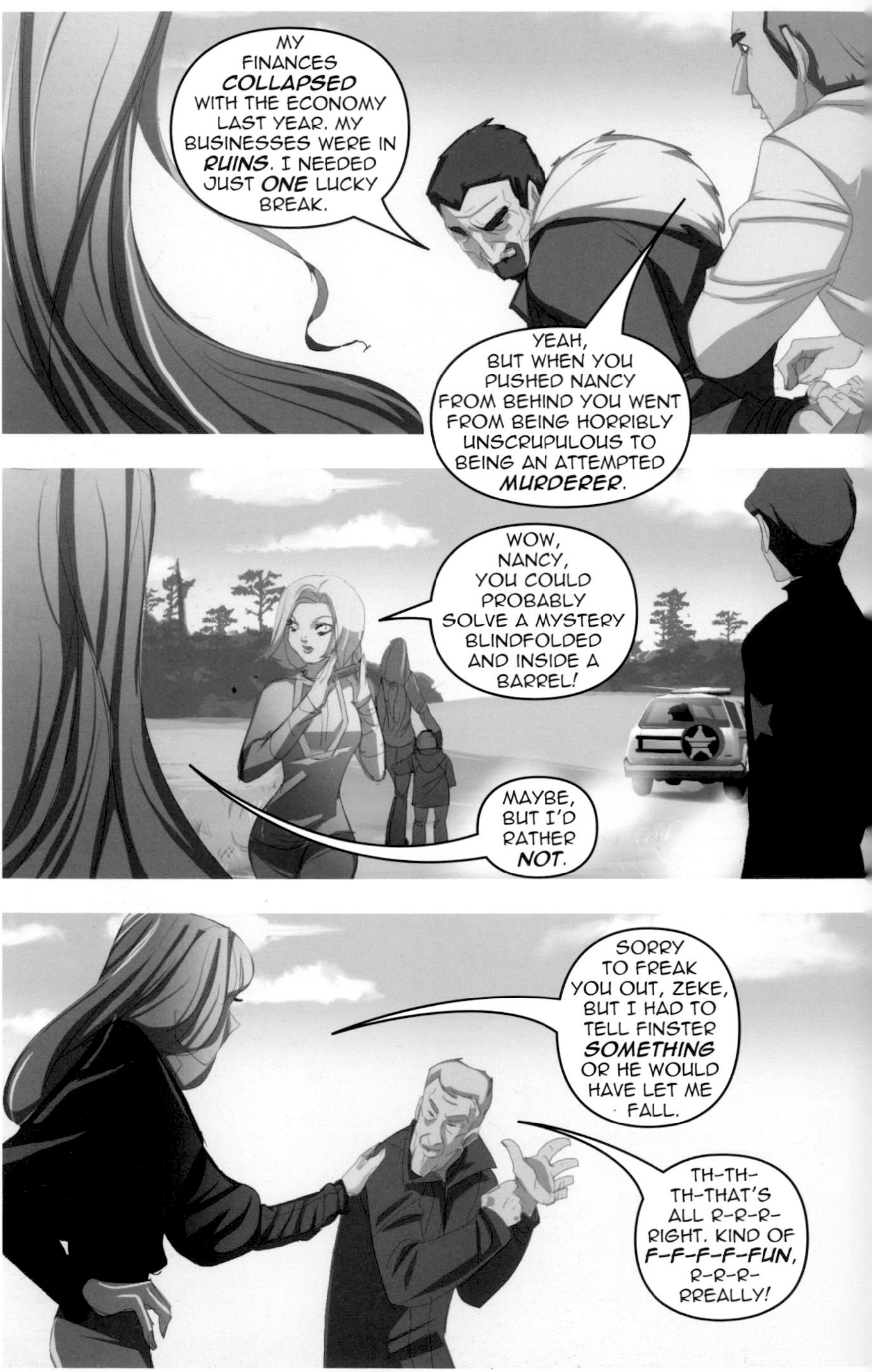
MY FINANCES COLLAPSED WITH THE ECONOMY LAST YEAR. MY BUSINESSES WERE IN RUINS. I NEEDED JUST ONE LUCKY BREAK.
YEAH, BUT WHEN YOU PUSHED NANCY FROM BEHIND YOU WENT FROM BEING HORRIBLY UNSCRUPULOUS TO BEING AN ATTEMPTED MURDERER.
WOW, NANCY, YOU COULD PROBABLY SOLVE A MYSTERY BLINDFOLDED AND INSIDE A BARREL!
MAYBE, BUT I'D RATHER NOT.
SORRY TO FREAK YOU OUT, ZEKE, BUT I HAD TO TELL FINSTER SOMETHING OR HE WOULD HAVE LET ME FALL.
TH-TH-TH-THAT'S ALL R-R-R-RIGHT. KIND OF F-F-F-F-FUN, R-R-R-RREALLY!

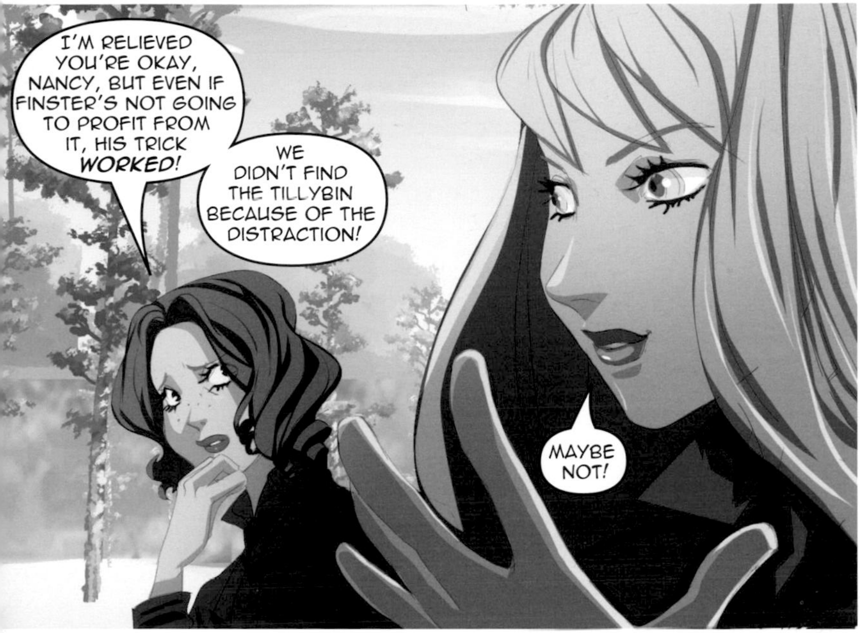
I'M RELIEVED YOU'RE OKAY, NANCY, BUT EVEN IF FINSTER'S NOT GOING TO PROFIT FROM IT, HIS TRICK *WORKED!*
WE DIDN'T FIND THE TILLYBIN BECAUSE OF THE DISTRACTION!
MAYBE NOT!

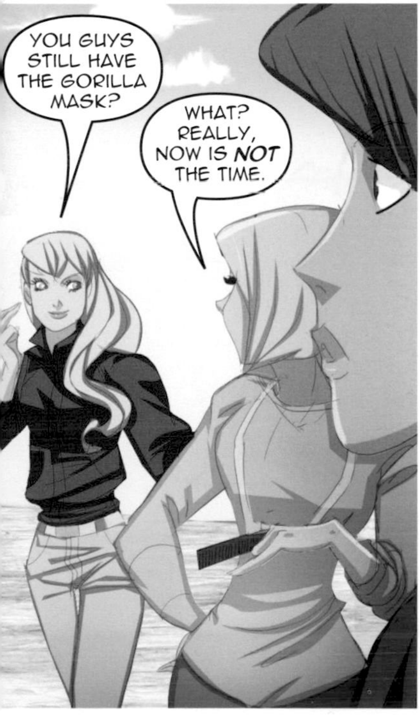
YOU GUYS STILL HAVE THE GORILLA MASK?
WHAT? REALLY, NOW IS *NOT* THE TIME.

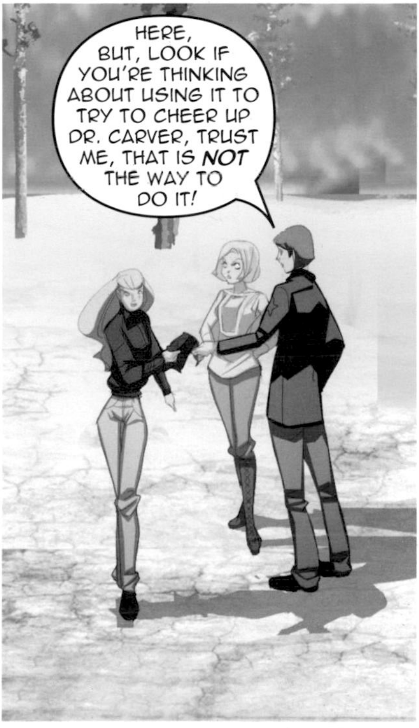
HERE, BUT, LOOK IF YOU'RE THINKING ABOUT USING IT TO TRY TO CHEER UP DR. CARVER, TRUST ME, THAT IS *NOT* THE WAY TO DO IT!

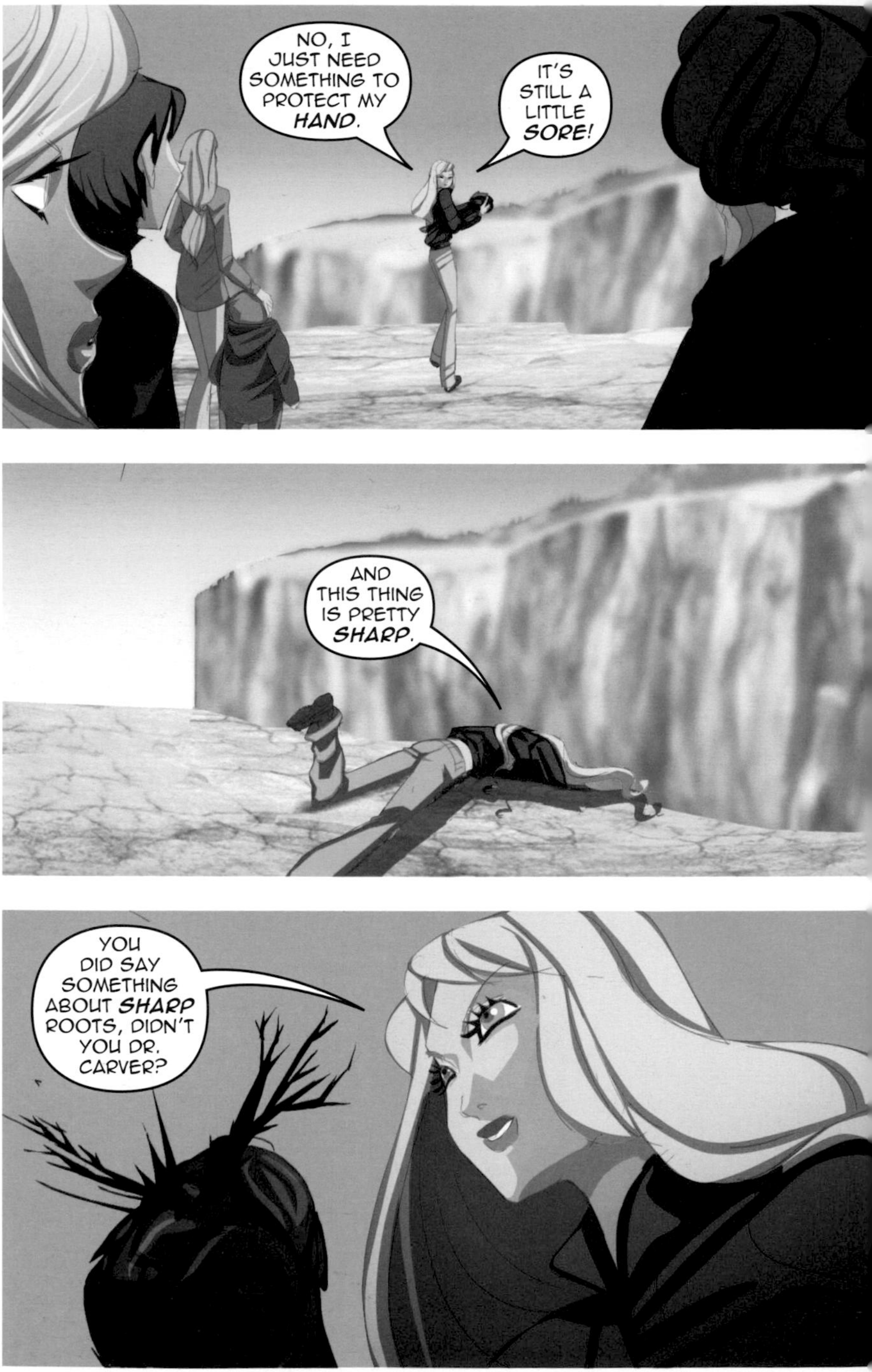
NO, I JUST NEED SOMETHING TO PROTECT MY HAND.
IT'S STILL A LITTLE SORE!
AND THIS THING IS PRETTY SHARP.
YOU DID SAY SOMETHING ABOUT SHARP ROOTS, DIDN'T YOU DR. CARVER?

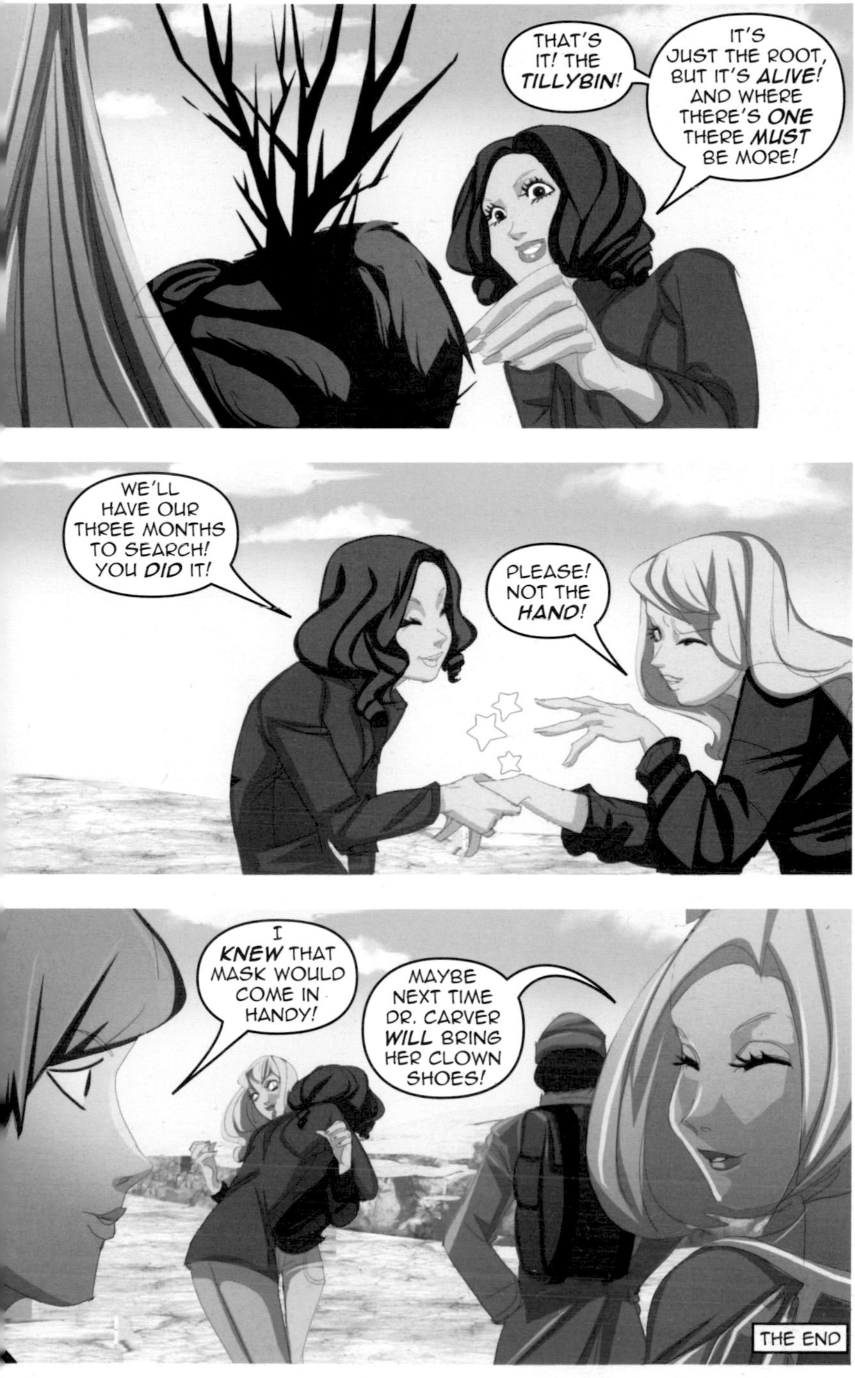
THAT'S IT! THE TILLYBIN!
IT'S JUST THE ROOT, BUT IT'S ALIVE! AND WHERE THERE'S ONE THERE MUST BE MORE!
WE'LL HAVE OUR THREE MONTHS TO SEARCH! YOU DID IT!
PLEASE! NOT THE HAND!
I KNEW THAT MASK WOULD COME IN HANDY!
MAYBE NEXT TIME DR. CARVER WILL BRING HER CLOWN SHOES!
THE END

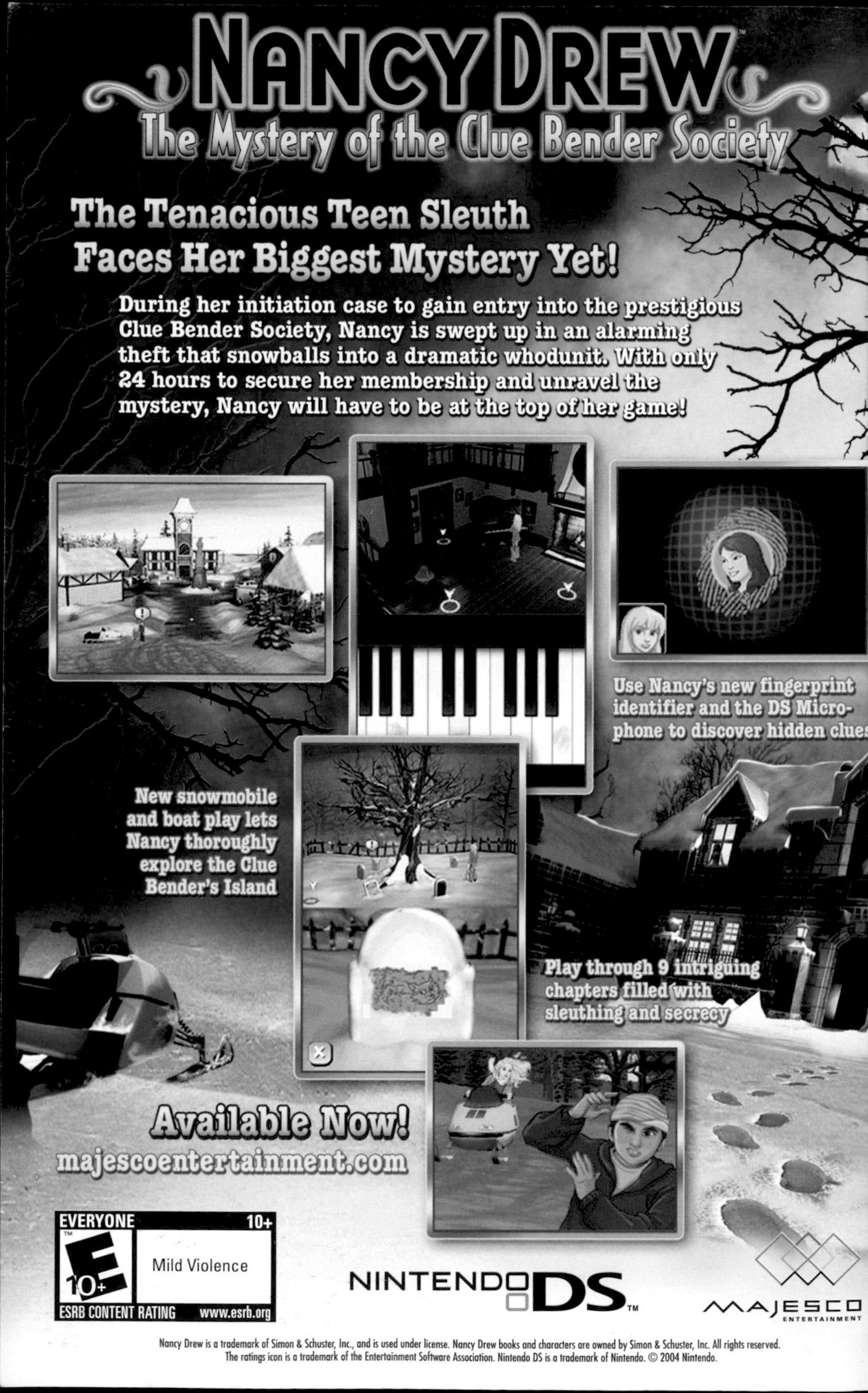
NANCY DREW™
The Mystery of the Clue Bender Society
The Tenacious Teen Sleuth Faces Her Biggest Mystery Yet!
During her initiation case to gain entry into the prestigious Clue Bender Society, Nancy is swept up in an alarming theft that snowballs into a dramatic whodunit. With only 24 hours to secure her membership and unravel the mystery, Nancy will have to be at the top of her game!
Use Nancy's new fingerprint identifier and the DS Microphone to discover hidden clues
New snowmobile and boat play lets Nancy thoroughly explore the Clue Bender's Island
Play through 9 intriguing chapters filled with sleuthing and secrecy
Available Now!
majescoentertainment.com
EVERYONE 10+
E 10+
Mild Violence
ESRB CONTENT RATING www.esrb.org
NINTENDO DS™
MAJESCO ENTERTAINMENT
Nancy Drew is a trademark of Simon & Schuster, Inc., and is used under license. Nancy Drew books and characters are owned by Simon & Schuster, Inc. All rights reserved.
The ratings icon is a trademark of the Entertainment Software Association. Nintendo DS is a trademark of Nintendo. © 2004 Nintendo.

NANCY DREW GIRL DETECTIVE HERE, BUT THE ONLY MYSTERY TO SOLVE SO FAR IS HOW MY TOTALLY CAREFUL DRIVING MADE MY PASSENGER ZEKE DEFNER SO SICK!
GET A LOAD OF THIS PLACE!
THE STARHURST SCHOOL FOR GIRLS MAKES HOGWARTS LOOK LIKE A SLUM!
SURE, IF YOU LIKE RITZY TOP-NOTCH PRIVATE BOARDING SCHOOLS! AND I KNOW I DO! LET'S CHECK IT OUT!
MS. DREW... I APPRECIATE THE LIFT TO MY JOB AFTER ALL THE EXCITEMENT, BUT DID YOU HAVE TO GO SO FAST?
BUT I NEVER WENT OVER THE SPEED LIMIT!
CHAPTER ONE: MY FRIENDS' ENEMY IS ALSO MY FRIEND!

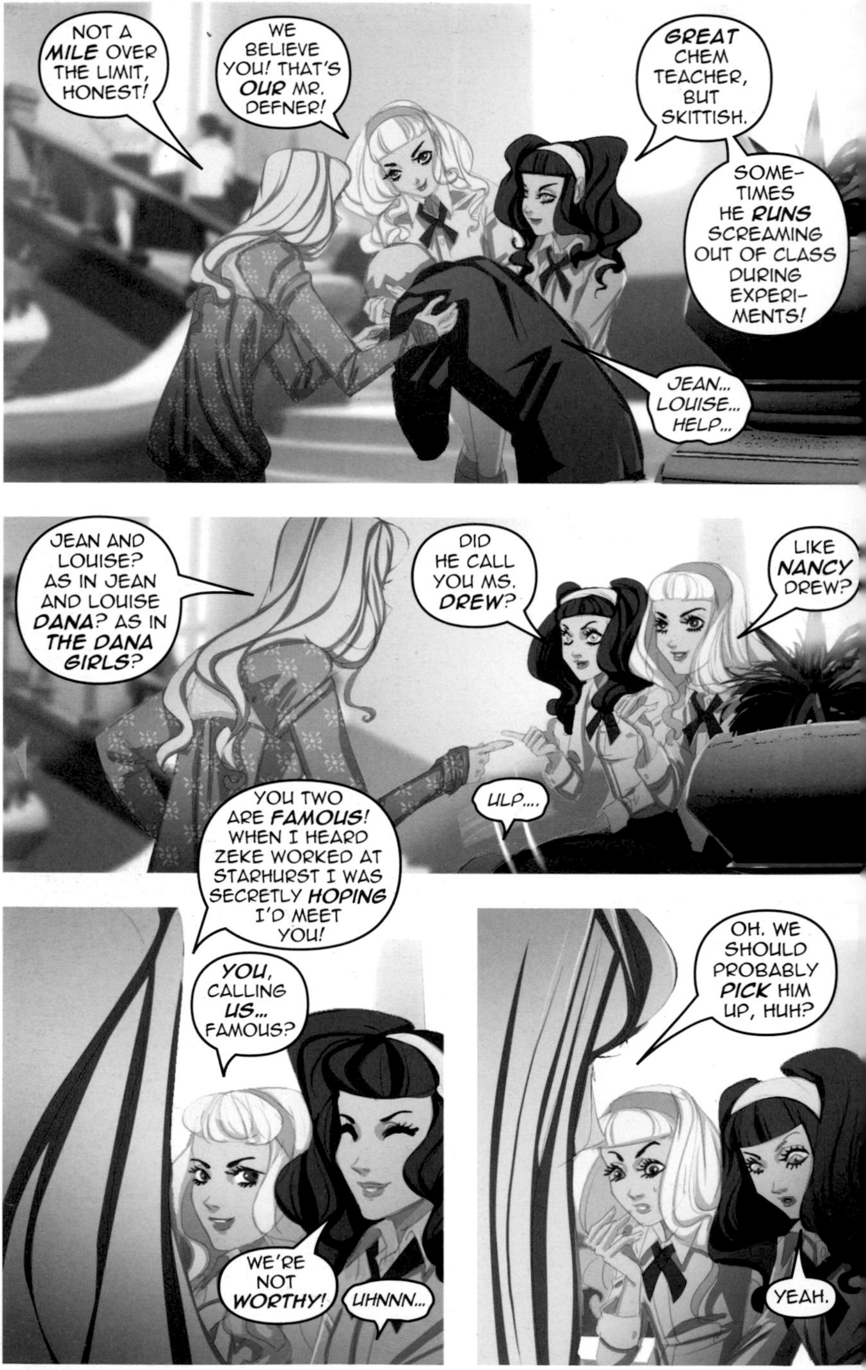
NOT A MILE OVER THE LIMIT, HONEST!
WE BELIEVE YOU! THAT'S OUR MR. DEFNER!
GREAT CHEM TEACHER, BUT SKITTISH.
SOME-TIMES HE RUNS SCREAMING OUT OF CLASS DURING EXPERI-MENTS!
JEAN... LOUISE... HELP...
JEAN AND LOUISE? AS IN JEAN AND LOUISE DANA? AS IN THE DANA GIRLS?
DID HE CALL YOU MS. DREW?
LIKE NANCY DREW?
YOU TWO ARE FAMOUS! WHEN I HEARD ZEKE WORKED AT STARHURST I WAS SECRETLY HOPING I'D MEET YOU!
ULP....
YOU, CALLING US... FAMOUS?
WE'RE NOT WORTHY!
UHNNN...
OH. WE SHOULD PROBABLY PICK HIM UP, HUH?
YEAH.

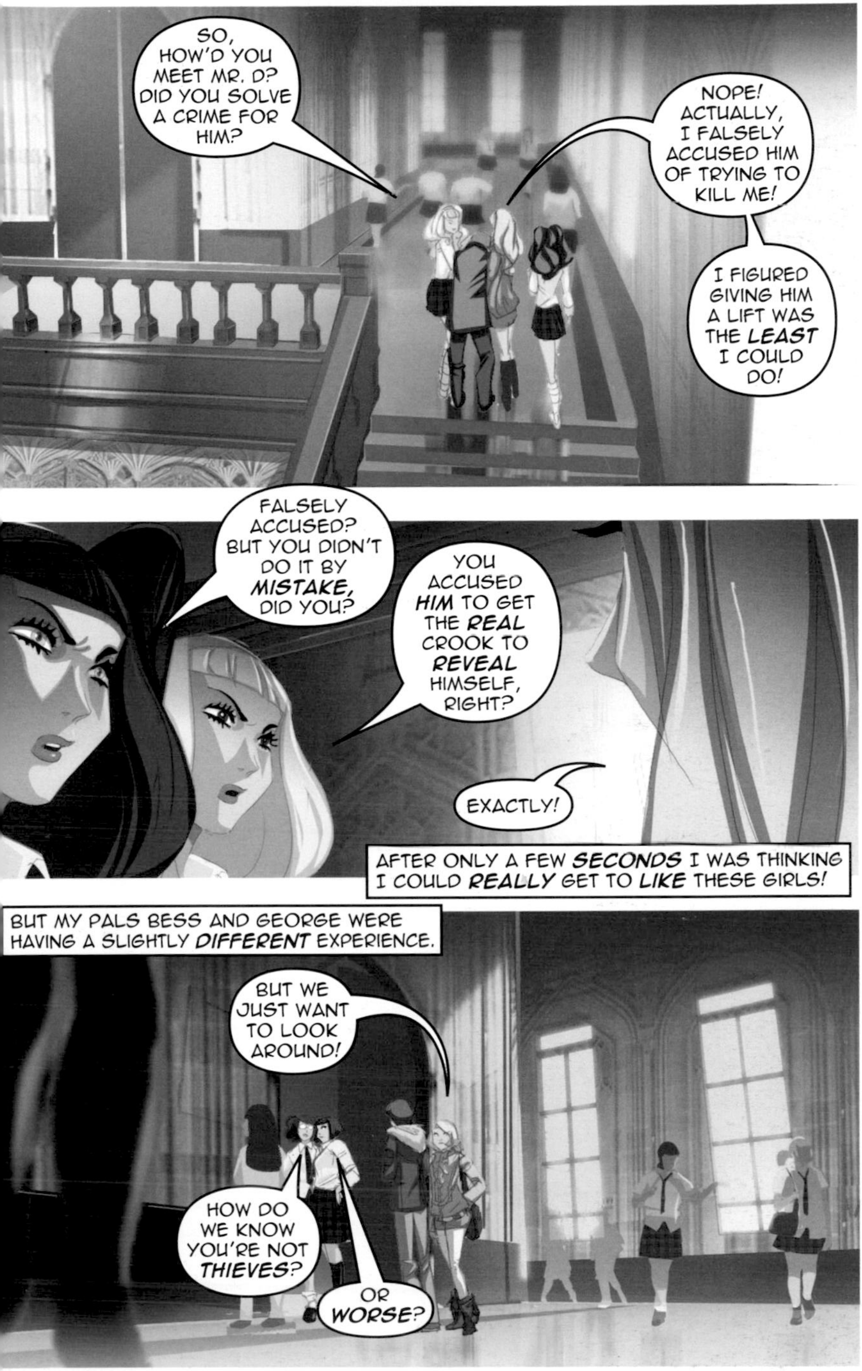
SO, HOW'D YOU MEET MR. D? DID YOU SOLVE A CRIME FOR HIM?
NOPE! ACTUALLY, I FALSELY ACCUSED HIM OF TRYING TO KILL ME!
I FIGURED GIVING HIM A LIFT WAS THE LEAST I COULD DO!
FALSELY ACCUSED? BUT YOU DIDN'T DO IT BY MISTAKE, DID YOU?
YOU ACCUSED HIM TO GET THE REAL CROOK TO REVEAL HIMSELF, RIGHT?
EXACTLY!
AFTER ONLY A FEW SECONDS I WAS THINKING I COULD REALLY GET TO LIKE THESE GIRLS!
BUT MY PALS BESS AND GEORGE WERE HAVING A SLIGHTLY DIFFERENT EXPERIENCE.
BUT WE JUST WANT TO LOOK AROUND!
HOW DO WE KNOW YOU'RE NOT THIEVES?
OR WORSE?

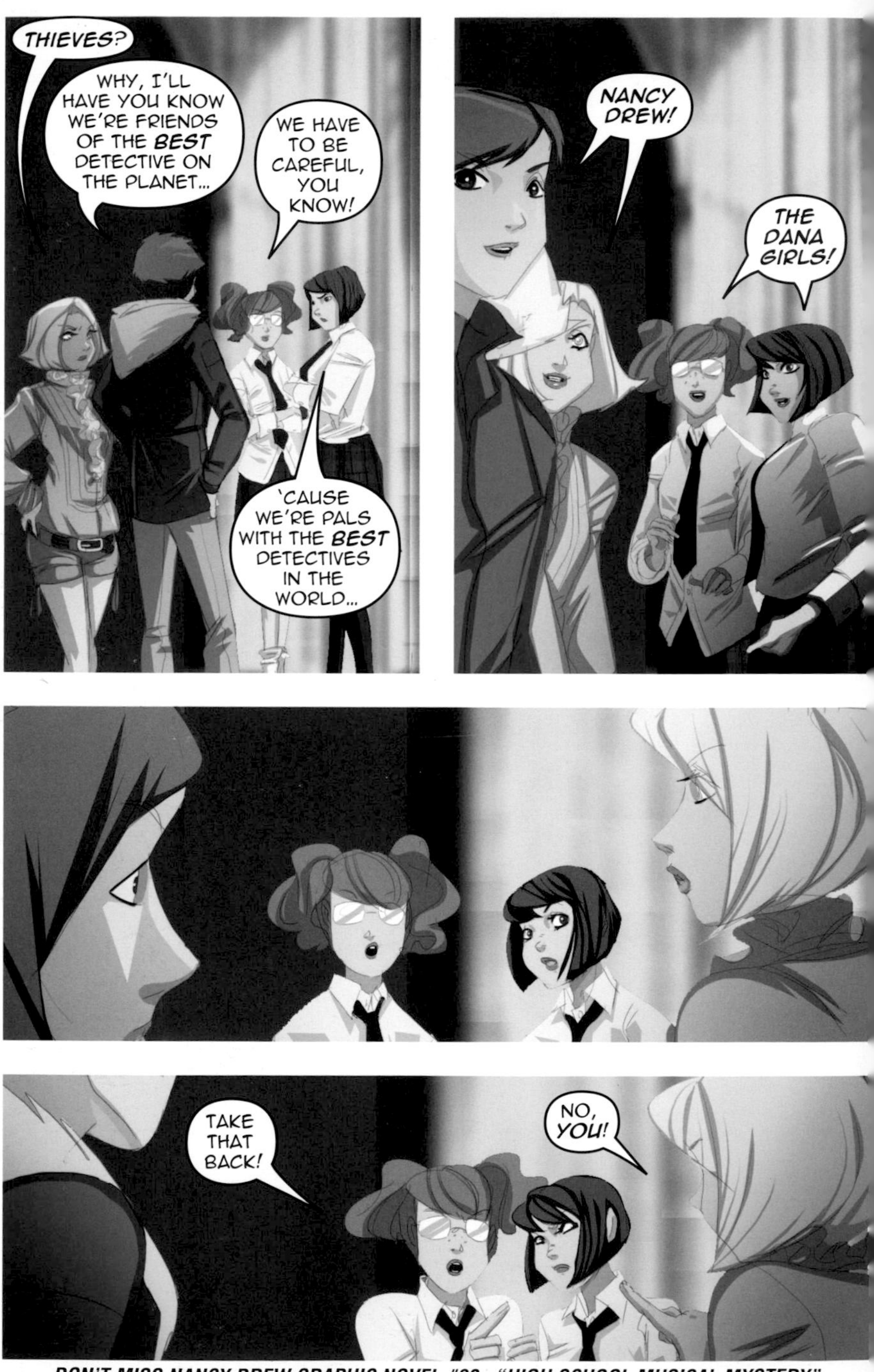
THIEVES?
WHY, I'LL HAVE YOU KNOW WE'RE FRIENDS OF THE *BEST* DETECTIVE ON THE PLANET...
WE HAVE TO BE CAREFUL, YOU KNOW!
'CAUSE WE'RE PALS WITH THE *BEST* DETECTIVES IN THE WORLD...
NANCY DREW!
THE DANA GIRLS!
TAKE THAT BACK!
NO, *YOU!*

***DON'T MISS NANCY DREW GRAPHIC NOVEL #20– "HIGH SCHOOL MUSICAL MYSTERY"***

# THE HARDY BOYS

## A NEW GRAPHIC NOVEL EVERY 3 MONTHS!

NEW!

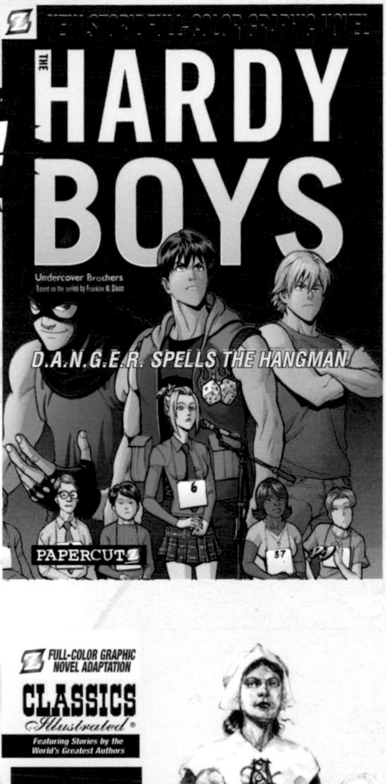

THE HARDY BOYS
Undercover Brothers
D.A.N.G.E.R. SPELLS THE HANGMAN
PAPERCUTZ


#14 "Haley Danielle's Top Eight!"
ISBN – 978-1-59707-113-0
#15 "Live Free, Die Hardy!"
ISBN – 978-1-59707-123-9
#16 "SHHHHHH!"
ISBN – 978-1-59707-138-3
#17 "Word Up!"
ISBN – 978-1-59707-147-5
NEW! #18 "D.A.N.G.E.R. Spells The Hangman!"
ISBN – 978-1-59707-160-4
Also available – Hardy Boys #1-13
All: Pocket sized, 96-112 pp., full-color, $7.95
Also available in hardcover! $12.95

THE HARDY BOYS BOXED SETS

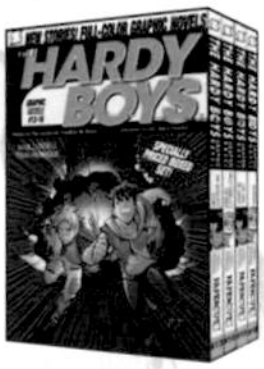

HARDY BOYS


#1-4 ISBN – 978-1-59707-040-9
#5-8 ISBN – 978-1-59707-075-1
#9-12 ISBN – 978-1-59707-125-3
#13-16 ISBN – 978-1-59707-173-4
All: Full-color, $29.95

## CLASSICS *Illustrated*

**Featuring Stories by the World's Greatest Authors**

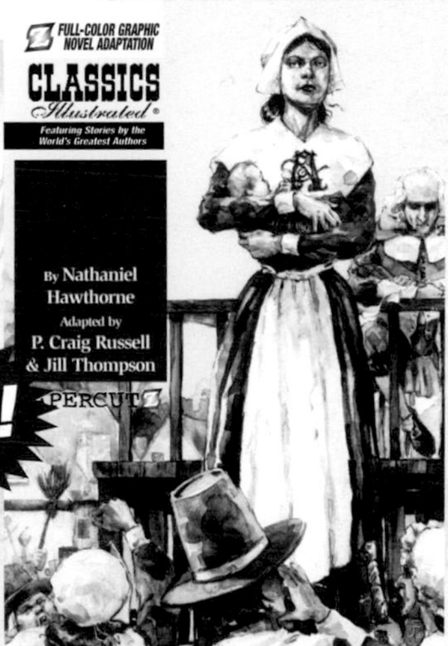

FULL-COLOR GRAPHIC NOVEL ADAPTATION
CLASSICS Illustrated
Featuring Stories by the World's Greatest Authors
By Nathaniel Hawthorne
Adapted by
P. Craig Russell
& Jill Thompson


NEW!

#1 "Great Expectations"
ISBN - 978-1-59707-097-3
#2 "The Invisible Man"
ISBN - 978-1-59707-106-2
#3 "Through the Looking-Glass"
ISBN - 978-1-59707-115-4
#4 "The Raven and Other Poems"
ISBN - 978-1-59707-140-6
#5 "Hamlet"
ISBN - 978-1-59707-149-9
NEW! #6 "The Scarlet Letter"
ISBN - 978-1-59707-162-8
All: 6 1/2 x 9, 56 pp., full-color, $9.95, hardcover

ON SALE AT BOOKSTORES EVERYWHERE!

Please add $4.00 postage and handling. Add $1.00 for each additional item.
Make check payable to NBM publishing. Send To:
Papercutz, 40 Exchange Place, Suite 1308,
New York, New York 10005, 1-800-886-1223
www.papercutz.com

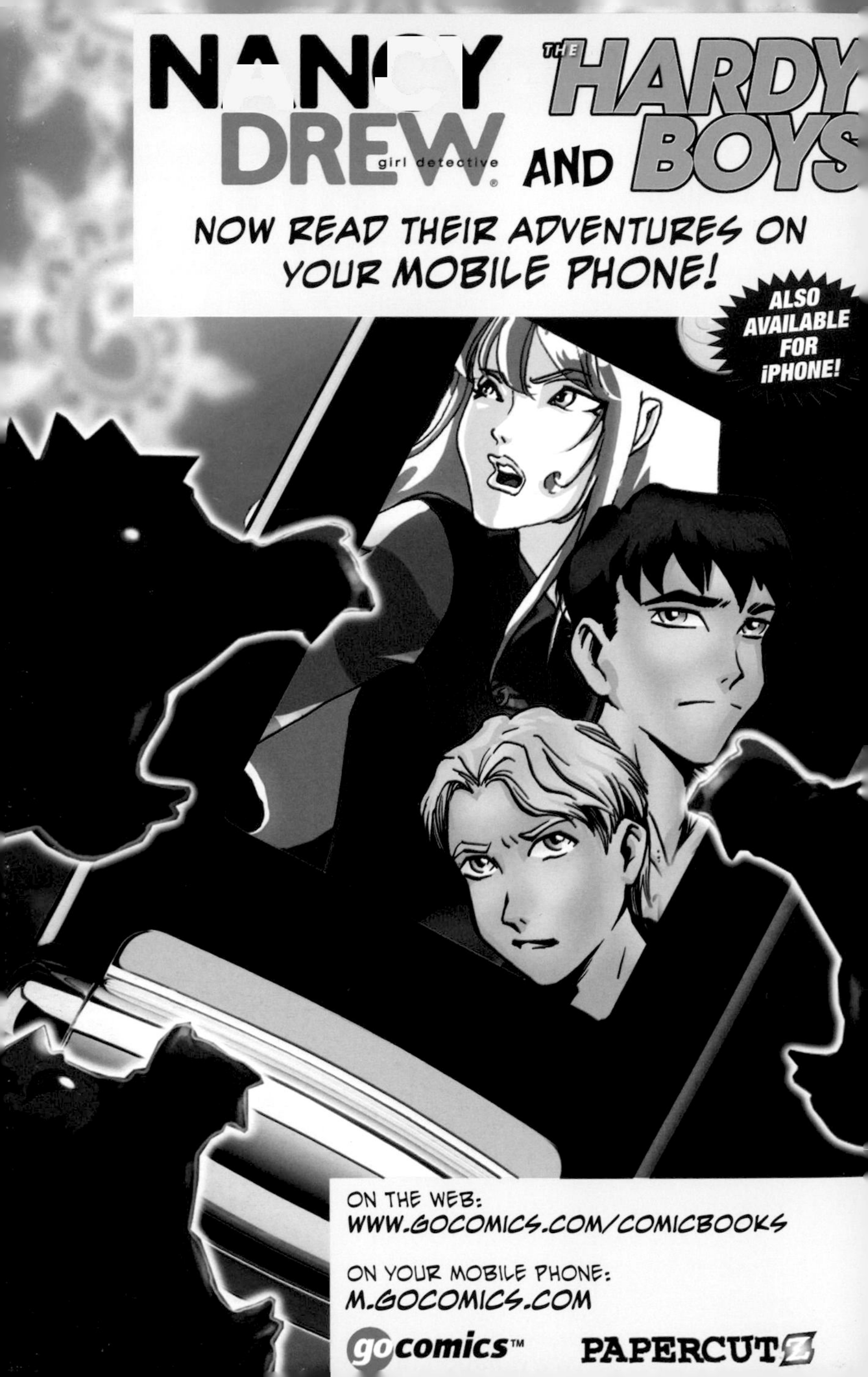
NANCY DREW girl detective
AND
THE HARDY BOYS
NOW READ THEIR ADVENTURES ON YOUR MOBILE PHONE!
ALSO AVAILABLE FOR iPHONE!
ON THE WEB:
WWW.GOCOMICS.COM/COMICBOOKS
ON YOUR MOBILE PHONE:
M.GOCOMICS.COM
gocomics™
PAPERCUTZ

# WATCH OUT FOR PAPERCUTZ ™

Welcome to the Backpages of NANCY DREW Graphic Novel #19 "Cliffhanger." I'm Jim Salicrup, Editor-in-Chief of Papercutz, the publisher of graphic novels such as BIONICLE, CLASSICS ILLUSTRATED, GERONIMO STILTON, HARDY BOYS, TALES FROM THE CRYPT, and coming soon – DISNEY FAIRIES, featuring Tinker Bell and her magical friends! In these Papercutz Backpages, we like to let you know about all the exciting things going on at Papercutz, but we're doing so much lately, we're running out of room.

That's why it's always a good idea to visit papercutz.com to find out the very latest news and information about your favorite graphic novel publisher. Be sure to check out the Papercutz Blog while you're there! It's a great opportunity to communicate directly with NANCY DREW writers Stefan Petrucha and Sarah Kinney and artist Sho Murase!

As we're sure you've noticed, the cover of this NANCY DREW graphic novel features the new NANCY DREW logo as seen on the all-new NANCY DREW novels from Aladdin! We love the bold new look and hope you do too. Also, what do you think of the mystery in "Cliffhanger"? Were you able to figure out who pushed Nancy off the cliff before she figured it out? If so, you've just outwitted the world-famous Girl Detective! So, are you ready to solve another mystery? Check out the preview of NANCY DREW #20 "High School Musical Mystery" and tell us what's so special about two of the girls you meet – and what else do they have in common with Nancy Drew that's NOT mentioned in the preview? Need a clue? Well, let's just say it's all part of a special celebration that starts in 2010!

We better end this edition of Watch Out For Papercutz right now, before we blurt out the answers! But we promise all will be revealed in NANCY DREW #20 "High School Musical Mystery"! Don't miss it!

Thanks,

Jim

# New from Papercutz

Geronimo Stilton

## Graphic Novels

6 1/2 x 9, 56 pages full-color
Hardcover only: $9.95/$12.75 Canada

All-new, full-color Graphic Novel
Geronimo Stilton
THE DISCOVERY OF AMERICA
PAPERCUTZ

#1 "The Discovery of America"
ISBN - 978-1-59707-158-1

All-new, full-color Graphic Novel
Geronimo Stilton
THE SECRET OF THE SPHINX
PAPERCUTZ

#2 "The Secret of the Sphinx"
ISBN - 978-1-59707-159-8

All-new, full-color Graphic Novel
Geronimo Stilton
THE COLISEUM CON
PAPERCUTZ

#3 "The Coliseum Con"
ISBN - 978-1-59707-172-7

All-new, full-color Graphic Novel
Geronimo Stilton
FOLLOWING THE TRAIL OF MARCO POLO
PAPERCUTZ

Coming in April: #4
"Following the Trail of Marco Polo"
ISBN - 978-1-59707-188-8

## Saving the future, by protecting the past!

GERONIMO STILTON IS THE EDITOR OF THE RODENT'S GAZETTE, THE MOST FAMOUS PAPER ON MOUSE ISLAND. IN HIS FREE TIME HE LOVES TO TELL FUN, HAPPY STORIES. IN THESE ADVENTURES, GERONIMO HAS TO FACE HIS WORST ENEMIES, THE PIRATE CATS, WHO HAVE DISCOVERED A WAY TO TRAVEL BACK IN TIME AND CHANGE HISTORY...

Available Now at Booksellers Everywhere. Or order from Papercutz:
Please add $4.00 postage and handling, $1.00 for each additional item. Make check payable to NBM publishing.
Send To: Papercutz, 40 Exchange Place, Suite 1308, New York, New York 10005

Or call 1-800-886-1223. MC, VISA, and AMEX accepted

www.papercutz.com

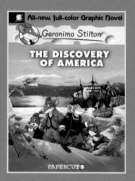

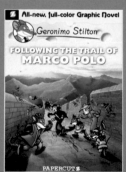

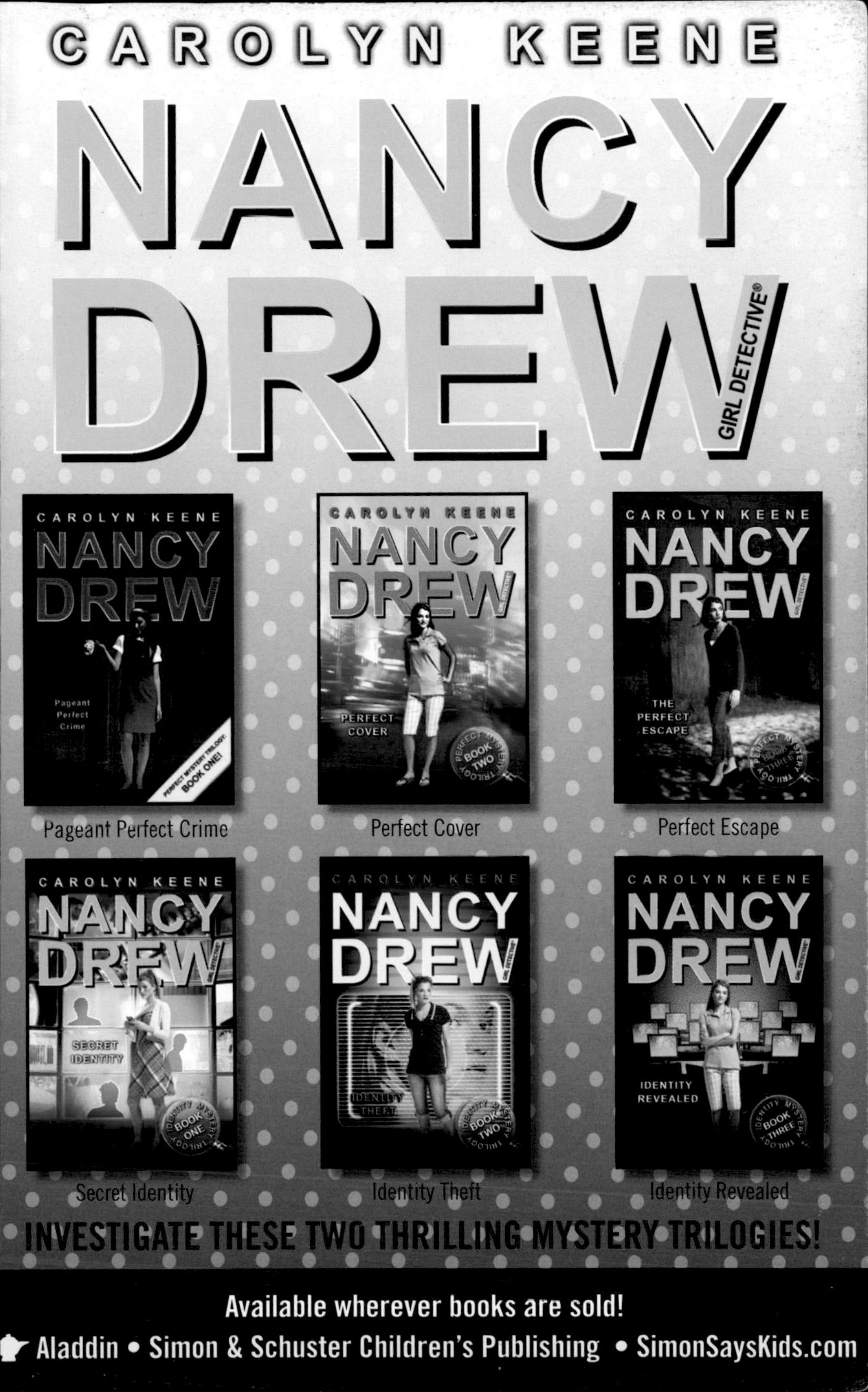

CAROLYN KEENE
NANCY DREW
GIRL DETECTIVE®
Pageant Perfect Crime
Perfect Cover
Perfect Escape
Secret Identity
Identity Theft
Identity Revealed
INVESTIGATE THESE TWO THRILLING MYSTERY TRILOGIES!
Available wherever books are sold!
Aladdin • Simon & Schuster Children's Publishing • SimonSaysKids.com

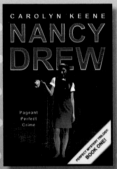

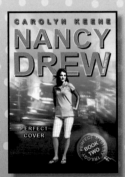

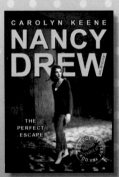

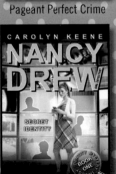

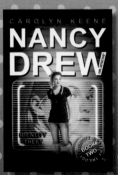

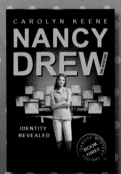

# MEET HARDY BOYS GRAPHIC NOVELS ARTIST "PH"-
# PAULO HENRIQUE!

A **PAPERCUTZ**™ PROFILE

Hi there, my name is Paulo Henrique and most of you know me as the artist of THE HARDY BOYS Graphic Novels for Papercutz. One thing you might not know is that I prefer to go by "PH" instead of "Paulo Henrique." I'd like to share a bit about myself and let you all ask any questions you may have for me over on the Papercutz Blog (go to www.papercutz.com). I always like to hear from fans.

I was born in Sao Paulo, Brazil where I started drawing at a very young age. The first thing I remember drawing was from when I was 6 years old. I was in art class and I drew a picture of Darth Vader – the villain from STAR WARS. The teacher said she thought that I had drawn a bride in a black wedding dress! I always liked bad guys the best, but I knew that Vader was a good guy under that mask. That's why I liked him so much as a kid.

After that, I just kept on drawing and drawing. I really like "larger than life" characters, and when I was growing up I was drawn to Manga-style art before I even knew that's what it was called. Manga is actually the Japanese word for comics, but there are many unique elements of this Japanese art style that we use in THE HARDY BOYS a lot. An easy way to identify the style is characters with cartoonishly exaggerated faces and bodies. If you want a good example of some Manga-esque HARDY BOYS, look at the fourth page of comics in THE HARDY BOYS Graphic Novel #14

"Haley Danielle's Top Eight!":

Some of the best-known artists who shaped what we know as Manga today are Machiko Hasegawa and Osamu Tezuka. You have probably seen Tezuka's "Astro Boy" at some point in your life. Google it! The history of Manga goes all the way back to the 1800's and there's a lot of info on the Internet if you do some searching.

Back to my art! Some of you may want to know who my favorite comics characters are and how I got started. Well, I love that Blue Bomber! I'm talking about Megaman. I started drawing him when I was a teenager and I've beaten all of the original Nintendo games. Megaman is a Manga character and he jump-started my career. In 1997, I was hired to draw the MEGAMAN comicbook for Brazilian publisher Magnum and ended up working with Sidney Lima, who would work on ZORRO and THE HARDY BOYS at Papercutz years later. At that time, a lot of publishers got interested in Manga, so I met with Magnum and did a test for Megaman. Both Sidney Lima and I ended up getting the job, and we became friends.

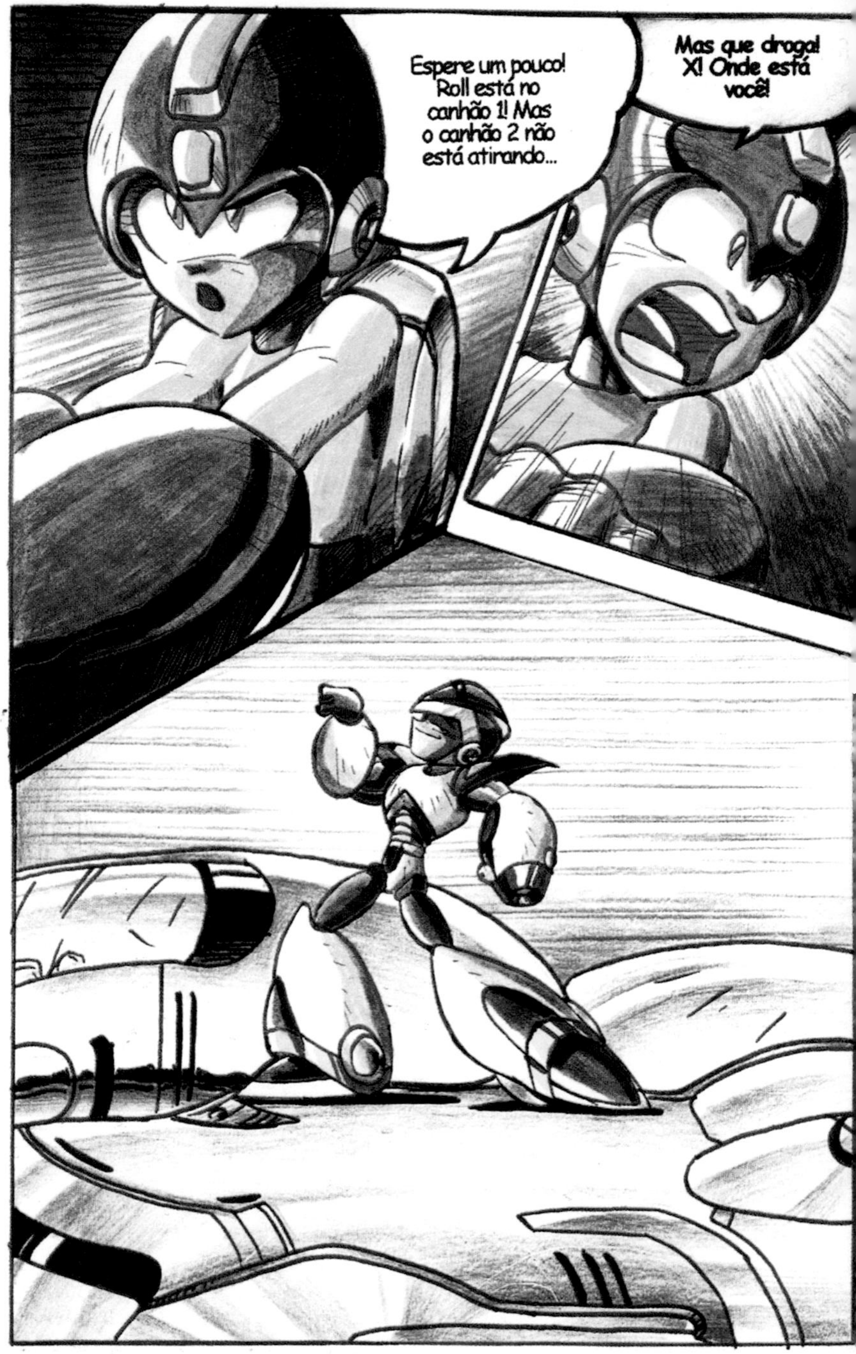
Espere um pouco! Roll está no canhão 1! Mas o canhão 2 não está atirando...
Mas que droga! X! Onde está você!

Years later I started to work for Yabu Media and was doing an electronic graphic novel called COMBO RANGERS, so I called him to work with me. This led to us collaborating on THE HARDY BOYS. He is a good friend and a great artist. I have to thank him for introducing me to Papercutz and THE HARDY BOYS. The MEGAMAN series took off, and I ended up teaching Manga-style drawing to young artists at a place called Impacto Studios in Brazil.

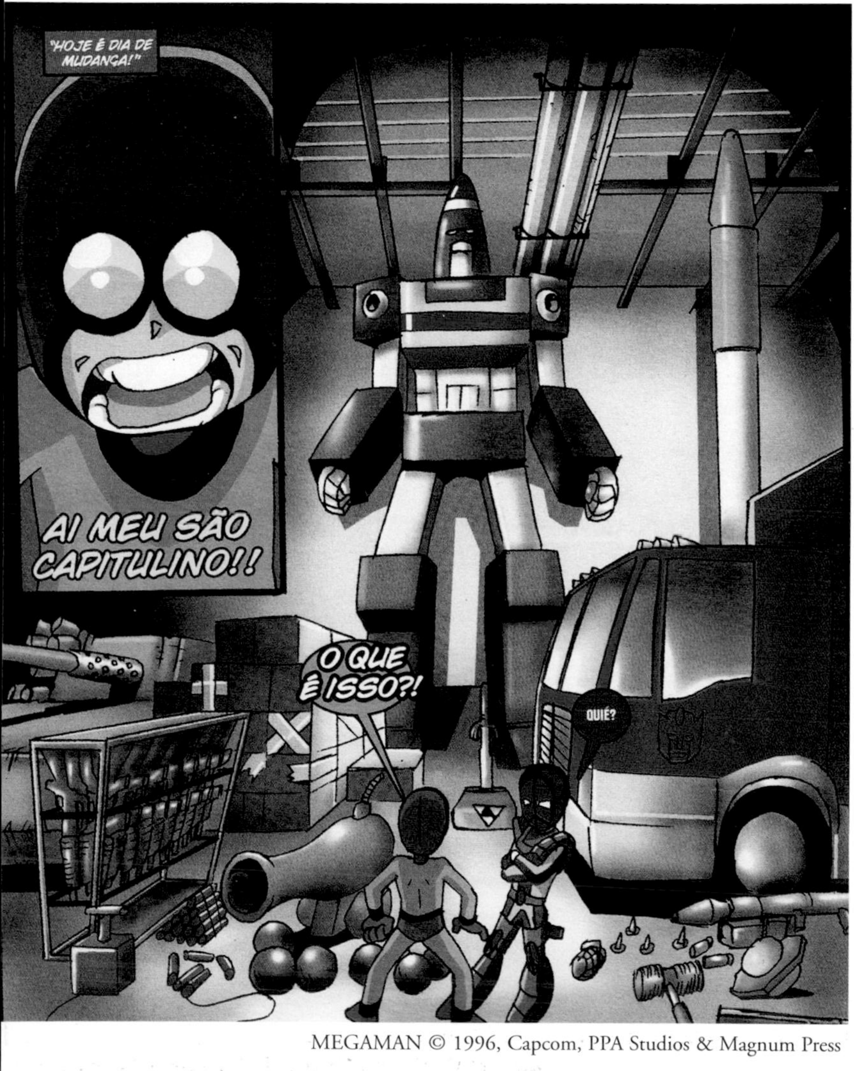
"HOJE É DIA DE MUDANÇA!"
AI MEU SÃO CAPITULINO!!
O QUE É ISSO?!
QUIÉ?

MEGAMAN © 1996, Capcom, PPA Studios & Magnum Press

Impacto Studios is a place where young artists can come to learn and improve their art, while more established artists teach classes to students and are introduced to companies that may want to hire them. At Impacto, I became friends with Klebs Junior, the founder of the studio and a comicbook artist himself. Klebs is well-known in comics. Aside from founding Impacto he also illustrated SNAKES ON A PLANE (DC), EXCALIBUR (Marvel Comics), HARBINGER and a bunch of other titles. Klebs became my agent and helped get my work to America. When he heard that Top Cow Productions at Image Comics was looking for an artist for their MYTH WARRIORS series, he set up a test for me. Top Cow hired me and my work ended up getting distributed to a much larger audience in the US.

I worked for a lot of different magazines and publications in Brazil, but it wasn't until THE HARDY BOYS #6 "Hyde and Shriek" that I started working on that series. My friend Sidney needed some help. He asked me to help draw THE HARDY BOYS #6 and then I started drawing it full-time and have no plans to stop! I just finished my 12th volume of the series.

Aside from comics, I really love music. I have remixed a lot of Megaman songs from the

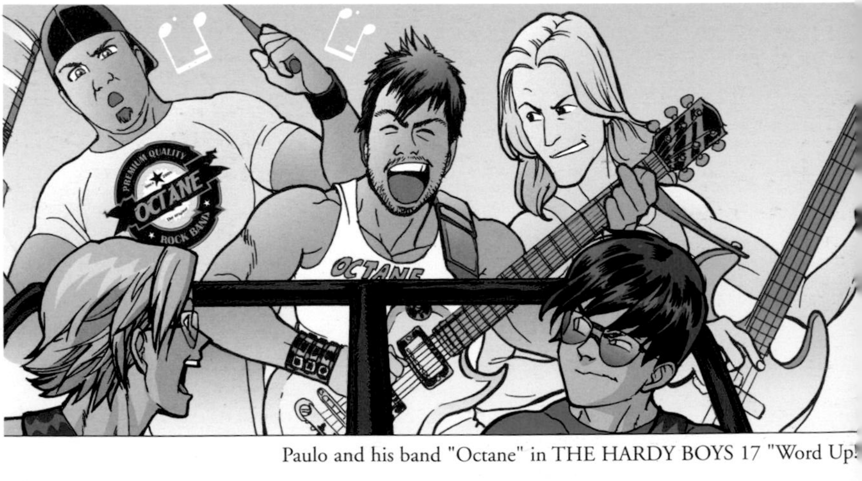
PREMIUM QUALITY
OCTANE
ROCK BAND
OCTANE

Paulo and his band "Octane" in THE HARDY BOYS 17 "Word Up!

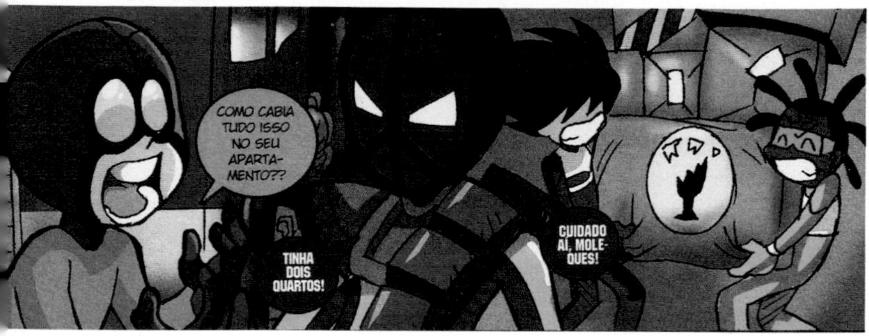
COMO CABIA TUDO ISSO NO SEU APARTA-MENTO??
TINHA DOIS QUARTOS!
CUIDADO AÍ, MOLE-QUES!

More art from Paulo's work on COMBO RANGERS

video games and I play guitar and sing in a hard rock trio called "Octane" in Brazil. You can find us on MySpace and YouTube. As far as my favorite groups go, I like Avenged Sevenfold, Story of the Year, and System of a Down. From the "Old School" I love Iron Maiden and Metallica. I also like pop and classical music. I love Beethoven, Bach, and Mozart. I don't understand classical music, but I appreciate it so much. I like some Brazilian pop music but I really dislike, (I don't want to say hate, it's a strong word)…SAMBA! Samba's the national music of Brazil. It's upbeat and encourages listeners to dance. It's not for me, though.

So all of you who may have questions for me, please post them on the Papercutz Blog and I'll try to answer as quickly as possible! My favorite titles from THE HARDY BOYS so far are #8: "A Hardy Day's Night" (just a beautiful father and son story) and #15: "Live Free, Die Hardy!" which was action-packed. I've got to thank Jim Salicrup, Terry Nantier, Scott Lobdell, Laurie E. Smith, and Mark Lerer for all of their hard work and support. Perhaps most importantly: thanks to THE HARDY BOYS fans! Without you we wouldn't be able to put these great graphic novels together. Thanks and be sure to ask me questions!

– PH